Watch for other titles from
Dagger Books and
J.B. Kohl and Eric Beetner at
www.secondwindpublishing.com

# One Too Many Blows to the Head

By

J.B. Kohl
and
Eric Beetner

Dagger Books
Published by Second Wind Publishing, LLC.
Kernersville

Dagger Books
Second Wind Publishing, LLC
931-B South Main Street, Box 145
Kernersville, NC 27284

This book is a work of fiction. Names, characters, locations and events are either a product of the author's imagination, fictitious or used fictitiously. Any resemblance to any event, locale or person, living or dead, is purely coincidental.

Copyright © 2009 by J.B. Kohl and Eric Beetner

All rights reserved, including the right of reproduction in whole or part in any format.

First Dagger Books edition published September 2009. Dagger Books, Running Angel, and all production design are trademarks of Second Wind Publishing, used under license.

For information regarding bulk purchases of this book, digital purchase and special discounts, please contact the publisher at www.secondwindpublishing.com

Cover painting by Marc Sasso.

Manufactured in the United States of America

ISBN 978-1-935171-32-4

# Dedication

From J.B. - For my parents, Jim and Connie. Thanks for always believing in me.

From Eric - To my M girls, the loves of my life, and to my little G, in my heart if not yet in my arms.

# 1

*Ray Ward*
*Excelsior Fight Hall*
*Kansas City, Spring 1940*

The bell rang and round two started just like the first. The young black kid came out with his arms swinging and his feet moving a mile a minute, like one of the Nicholas brothers doing a tap dance. I wondered if maybe they were related.

He busted jabs through the white kid's defenses, what there was of them anyway, and he knew just when to hook up and catch his dazed opponent right on the chin.

Not that anyone but me was noticing. This was the walkout fight; the undercard that goes on after the main event. It was late, almost eleven thirty. The main went the full twelve rounds and ended in a draw. The crowd was pissed about that so when it was done they started filing out, throwing their ticket stubs down in anger.

I sat in the shadows against the back wall; kind of how I'd lived the past year. I didn't know if I was looking for a new boxer to manage but if I was, this kid had the goods. I figured I could mold him into something at least a little bit like Rex.

My brother, Rex. Dead a year now.

I'm Ray. Rex was six years younger. He was a boxer and a damn good one. Our Pop was a fighter. Welterweight. Skinny little bastard but could punch like a south bound freight train. He taught Rex and me. I was no good at it.

I can hit all right. I know how to run the defense too, which is just as important. My right is good enough to lay out a drunk in one punch. That comes in handy in bar fights let me tell you, but my muscles don't coil up tight enough to slug it out with a real fighter. Rex was different. He studied under the old man and when Rex hit you, boy, you knew you'd been hit.

I knew I was going to stop punching and start managing him when he was fifteen and he shut my lights out at twenty-one.

He came at me like an angry hornet and stung just as bad—gave me a chipped tooth and a cut over my left eye as a souvenir. And that was just from sparring.

By eighteen he was making the rounds and working up a fifteen and zero record with twelve knockouts. We worked a legit fight ring in Moline, Illinois then a basement six-rounder in Davenport that only went three rounds. The promoter got good and drunk that night on all the money he made. No one ever bet on a kid as young as Rex unless they'd seen him fight before. He'd throw down with guys twice his age and twenty pounds heavier and still give them a drubbing.

All the while I stayed in his corner. I was manager, cut man, spit bucket boy—the whole nine. We were making traveling money, but not enough to hire a whole crew. Besides, we didn't need anybody else, us being brothers and all. Most of our coaching went unspoken. He knew when he screwed up and I sure as hell didn't have to tell him.

One night in Lawrence he came back to the corner after the seventh and our entire exchange went like this:

Me: "You see it?"

Him: "I see it."

Me: "Then go get it."

He went out and beat the tar out of a guy who looked like he could bend a crowbar and then pick his teeth with it—what teeth he had left after Rex was done with him.

Yeah, we were going places.

This was our way of living down the trouble we had with Pop. You see, most fighters get into the ring because they think it's easy money and then get out of the game because they get punched out or realize they're no good. The consequences of being no good are a headache every Sunday after fight night and then, eventually, a splitting headache every day of your life that don't go away. And that just ain't worth the twenty-five bucks in the purse.

Then there are career guys—fellas with thick heads on thick necks who are too dumb to know any other way to make a buck besides punching smaller guys for money. This was Pop. Even when I was a kid I knew he was as dumb as a bag of rocks but what can you do? He's my Pop so I got to love him. He didn't get an education so I figured he had an excuse for being dim but he wasn't so stupid he couldn't earn a living. He figured out ways to make do. He just had to find ways that didn't use the smallest muscle in his body—his brain.

During the Depression he started riding the rails looking for work. The hobo camps in those days were rough spots. Guys would slit your throat for a can of beans. Men learned to fight in those camps and if they wanted to make it out, they had to be good. The fights were bare-knuckle brawls with no referee. Two men making fist music by a campfire with twelve angry drunks hooting and hollering for blood and hoping to be first in line when someone got k.o.'d so they could swoop in and steal his shoes.

Pop got in with a promoter who trolled the camps looking for sluggers he could prop up and use for target practice with his real Joes. He'd line 'em up, pay 'em fifty cents to go in the ring and get the snot beat out of them and then send them right back to the camps with a broken nose or a shattered hand. In those times the fights were a sure bet for promoters looking to fill a venue. When the whole country is depressed what better entertainment is there than to go watch some sucker get his clock cleaned?

Crowds back then were out for blood too, so said Pop. The fans didn't feel they got their dime's worth unless the canvas was painted red by the end of the night.

When you make a life out of fighting, fighting becomes your life. Pop started in on me and Rex when we were kids. I first got wind of how good his jab was at the dinner table back home. If I was horsing around I'd get a sock in the ear that stung outside and rang inside and I never would have seen him move his arm. He'd reach out and pop me a good one and then be back with a fork full of mashed potatoes before I knew what hit me.

It was when he started in on Mom that we had trouble. There wasn't much we could do at first, being so young. By the time we got old enough to do any fighting back we didn't know any better; it was just how it was around the house. Mom never complained and we just grew up thinking that was the way things went. Guess we weren't much smarter than the old man.

Then the bastard beat her face in so bad she went into a coma for three days. When she came out of it she wasn't the same. She had a far away look most of the time and she was jittery like a mouse stealing cheese off a trap. Loud noises made her shriek and we couldn't come up on her from behind.

Pop didn't stay around much longer after that. I think because of the way Rex and I started looking at him. It was that summer when Rex turned from fifteen to sixteen and I first saw how he could really fight. Pop did too. He saw how Rex punched better than he ever could and I think he got scared that when we finally decided to fight back that he would lose, and lose permanently. So he took a powder.

That was five years ago. Pop always talked about heading for the coast and I'm sure he did just that. He used to talk about Mexico too but I doubt he had the guts. He could make enough dough to keep in booze and a steak every Saturday if he kept on punching. Eventually I figured he'd punch himself out and die in a motel of a cerebral hemorrhage. I only hoped that someone would do the homework enough to let me know so I could dance a jig.

Mom lasted a few more years. Most of the money Rex and I made when he first started punching for dollars went back to her. When she passed we stayed in the house but we were on the road so much it looked exactly the same way as the day she died.

So that's the history lesson.

The bell rang in the fourth round and the place was

nearly empty. The black kid, Lewis he was called, came out fast and nimble like it was round one and he hadn't already been punching himself silly through three.

I started thinking maybe I should take a closer look at young Lewis. Maybe it was time to get back in the game. It felt like more than a year since...since all that happened.

It happened here. In the Excelsior. I don't know why I come back time and again, but I do about once a week. Self torture. Guilt. All of the above.

I never sat too close for fear that someone might recognize me and I'd have to rehash the whole thing out loud. I played the film back in my head plenty, thanks anyway—Rex's death in that ring and then all the killing that went on after.

I never saw much of Pop in me until after that first killing. I looked in the mirror when I washed my hands and it was like looking at a picture of him. Scared me senseless but also made me feel like the hands that committed the crime weren't really mine. That's what I wanted to believe.

I didn't start the whole mess. But I got angry and it built. Once that cork popped, there wasn't much I could do to stop it. I'd never killed anybody before Rex died but after it was all said and done I'd left enough bodies in my wake to start a baseball team.

A guy sees his brother killed in front of him and he damn well wants to do something about it. Only Bible verse I know in the whole wide world is "an eye for an eye."

Just as I figured he would, the ref called the fight after the white kid's eye opened up. Maybe he got the high sign from the owner to shut it down since no one was left in the joint anyway. I got up and walked down the tunnel after Lewis. He headed back to the locker room carrying his own stool. I wondered if anyone had ever given him a lesson before in his life or if he just grew up fighting like so many of the black boys I knew when I was a kid.

It wouldn't be normal practice for a white man to manage a black fighter, but I didn't give a shit and besides, a little publicity was a good thing in this racket. If half the people in the audience were there to see your boy get the tar beat out of him, so be it; as long as their money was green.

No one stopped me as I headed deeper into the tunnel toward the locker rooms. The staff had checked out as soon as the bell rang. Smokes were already lit and bottles already opened.

I hadn't been to the locker rooms since that night. As many times as I'd been in the building, I never went back to the last place I saw my brother.

I stopped walking. Lewis was good, damn good, but I'd have to catch up with him another night. I wasn't ready yet.

A hell of a lot happened in the days after Rex was killed. A hell of a lot to forget. Sometimes I feel like I've forgotten part of it, but I know it's there just under the surface. Scratch a tiny bit and I can tell you the whole story from first bell to the final round.

# 2

*Detective Dean Fokoli*
*Kansas City, Spring 1939*

In my sleep, I reached out for Laura. Her side of the bed was cold. I opened my eyes and listened to the sounds of her moving around in the kitchen. There was the clink of ice in a glass followed by the shuffling of her feet to the table. I could tell by the way she fell into the chair she'd been at the bottle for a couple of hours already—and I was in bed, sleeping through it all. I showered and shaved and started the coffee. Then I poured Laura a cup. She swiped at it with a clumsy hand and sent it sailing across the kitchen. "Bastard," she mumbled.

There wasn't much I could say to that, so I helped her stand up while I ducked the swings she aimed at my face. She didn't smell right anymore. The whites of her eyes were turning brown—just a little, but I could see it.

I undressed her and put her in the shower. She bit me. It wasn't a hard bite, but it smarted a little. "I hate you," she said, but she was barely conscious by then. I washed her hair, washed her body, toweled her off, and put her on the bed. Then I dressed—and poured out every bottle I could find, knowing it wasn't all of them. When I carried them out to the trash I stood over the can and pulled out my wallet. I'd kept the picture of Sylvia, thinking maybe Laura would agree to the divorce, thinking maybe me and Sylvia would leave Kansas City and make a fresh start someplace else—someplace better.

It was water under the bridge. I pulled the photo out and dropped it on top of Laura's bottles.

I didn't look back as I climbed in the car and left for work. There really wasn't any point. I pulled away from the curb and tried to whistle. Spring in Kansas City is a crap shoot. It can be rainy or sunny, warm or cold. Today was sunny and warm and reminded me of baseball games and cut grass. Good things. The drive to work was nice.

Captain Tolene was standing at my desk sifting through case files—ones I'd been working on for awhile. "Morning, Dean," he said when he saw me, like snooping through my stuff was just an ordinary thing to be doing on an ordinary day.

"Help you?" I asked.

Most everyone in the homicide division was already in, typing reports, reviewing new cases. They tried to ignore what Tolene was doing. It wasn't easy, so they ignored me too. I shook my head and waited.

"Just looking a few things over," Tolene said. He smiled when he said it, but it was tight, and it didn't quite reach his eyes. Seemed like he had that problem a lot lately.

He was leaning against my chair a little, making it impossible for me to sit down without asking him to move. I wasn't about to ask him to do anything of the sort, so I stood there, hat in hand, and shuffled my feet. He moved the file up a bit, enough so I could see the name on the label. Mark Pollard. My old partner. Dead now. My fault. No proof of that, you understand, but Tolene still sniffed around as much as he could, hoping something would break so he could nail me.

He snapped the folder shut. "Mind if I hold onto this for awhile?"

"Sure," I said. "Knock yourself out."

He gave another one of those tight smiles and disappeared into his office with the file.

I looked around the squad room. Heads stayed bent over desks, phones rang here and there, and the room seemed to be working at full speed. But quietness lingered, like when a hunter in the field is too loud and all the birds and bugs grow still. Right then it felt a little like I was in the crosshairs.

My new partner wasn't in yet. Just as well. Hard to train a guy who can't respect you. Matter of time, I told myself. It's all just a matter of time. Didn't know what I meant by that then. Felt like things were shutting down, closing up—for me, for Laura, for the job. Maybe that's what I meant.

My phone rang and I sat down to answer it. It was Ted, wanting my bet for the fight Saturday night. Rex Ward vs. Kid Delancey.

I told him who I liked for the fight. Then I got to work.

Matter of time, I said to myself again. Matter of time.

# 3

*Ray*

It was the Friday before the fight and Rex wasn't home yet. He'd been out to see his girl, Glenda. He saw her once a week when we weren't on the road. Sometimes more. I didn't know if they were sleeping together and if they were he'd never tell me so I let it go. There were times he didn't come home at night so I hoped for his sake he wasn't sleeping on her couch with a case of blue balls. That could ruin his concentration in the ring.

We had more rooms than we needed in Mom's old house and some, like the parlor with the sewing machine still set up, just went to waste and filled with growing piles of dust. The place needed new paint, a few repairs in the plaster, some nails in the floorboards, but otherwise our childhood home was solid and whichever one of us got married first would get to raise a family there. Not that I had any prospects. I hadn't dated regular in four or five years, since I took over managing Rex full time. I had a gal over in Lawrence I saw whenever we passed through for a fight but that wasn't more than every few months and I knew damn well there were other men who came calling during the in-between times.

I fixed the standard day-before-a-fight breakfast of five eggs, small steak, tomatoes, and buttermilk to drink. The morning of the bout was just one egg and toast, no butter.

By the time I had the plate piled high with food Rex walked in the door like he'd smelled it all the way across town.

We barely spoke in the way that brothers don't have to. I didn't want to pry into his personal life and we didn't need to say stuff like, "Pass the salt." We spent so much time together I knew we both needed some sort of life that we could call all our own. Glenda for him and . . . well, nothing for me, but he didn't need to know that. Fielding phone calls to schedule fights was a full time job and keeping Rex in top shape was another one. We had the basement converted into a training gym and I preferred to have Rex work out there rather than any of the places I'd visited in the city. We could train away from prying eyes and away from distractions like hot shot kids who wanted to spar with a known fighter like Rex. Whenever anyone did talk Rex into the ring to spar around they ended up putting on a show trying to act tough which Rex had no patience for.

Pop taught us that the worst thing to be in the ring was a show boater. Rex would let the kids make their point and then stop taking it easy on them. In no time the fight was over and the kid knew he had just learned a lesson.

After breakfast we worked out lightly. Rex told me about a movie he saw the night before with Glenda. *Ellery Queen, Master Detective* which he said was fine, but he questioned the title since Queen was obviously no master at detecting. Rex solved the mystery from the comfort of his seat long before Ralph Bellamy did on screen. The second feature was one called *Rebecca* which he and Glenda didn't stay for because he said it was a bunch of people talking about a bunch of nothing that was supposed to be thrilling but wasn't in the least.

We had a good thing going. Rex was getting noticed and the calls were coming in from farther and farther away. We fought once in Chicago two months prior on an undercard and I felt sure that a decent bout, one that would make Rex a real contender, would come our way soon. One good fight up in Chicago meant we could come back to Kansas and make a run at a state championship.

First things first. We needed to win the fight we had scheduled for tomorrow night. Another up-and-comer. A simple payday fight.

The night of the fight was typical. It was in Kansas City and it felt good not to travel. I didn't know anything about our opponent other than he had twenty-two pounds on Rex and was supposed to be a hot prospect.

Kid Delancey. Why is it managers always talk their boys into taking on "Kid" in front of their names? Kid this and Kid that. Why would you want people to think you're a kid? Rex and I never went in for the fancy names or star-spangled silk trunks. Rex was there to work and he dressed for the job at hand. Nothing looked sillier than a brand new pair of trunks on a guy when the ref is standing over him counting to ten.

We arrived at the Excelsior about an hour and a half before the fight, as usual. Rex started prepping himself and I went straight to the box office to ask after our payment. I liked to put in at least three appearances at the door to let them know that I had my eye on them. I made a point of counting heads as the people arrived and made sure they saw me do it so they wouldn't try to gyp us from the door receipts at the end of the night.

I found the owner of the place, Drake, and let him know we were there. Rex had fought there a few times before so I knew we'd get paid. Drake was an older guy, worn out by the fight game. He stayed in business through the Depression but keeping the place filled week after week was wearing on him and you could see that. Last year when we fought here he told me New Year's Eve 1938 was going to be a big blowout night for him. The place would sell out and he'd have one hell of a party and then cash in and retire. That was five months ago and here he was sipping from a flask and scratching at his crotch like an old dog.

"You know this Kid Delancey?" I asked him.

"He's new. Real jackhammer they say. Six knockouts in six fights."

"Right handed?"

"Yeah. Handsome kid too. For now. That's how they're selling him. I seen his picture in the society pages last month. He was taking out some lady with more class than he's got brains, I can tell you that."

That was a clue. I should have added two and two with the other stuff I'd been ignoring until then but I didn't.

Young fighter, plucked from obscurity and given top tier fights and also making the scene with society girls? Could only be hooked in with the boys from Chicago.

I never had much run-in with the chiselers who controlled the fights in K.C. but you couldn't be in the game and not smell their stink…and it ran all the way up the river to Chicago where the real decisions were made. We'd had offers to take dives and we'd had offers to put on some fancy silk trunks and punch under a different name; as long as we split the purse with them sixty/forty. They could get us better fights in better venues and work toward a championship but Rex and I made more on our own than we could with that kind of help.

When the offer came in to fight Delancey I didn't think twice. As young as Rex was we had to take on newbies all the time. Most fighters met for the first time in the ring and then never saw each other again. A few guys never fought again after a couple of rounds with Rex. I once had the mother of a black boy we fought come and find me in the locker room after the fight. I was ready to have her chew my ear off for the beating her son took but she just wanted to thank me and Rex for making her boy quit the fight game. She said he looked her in the eyes between two puffed up lids barely open enough to see through and told her he was all done in. She thanked me and Rex and Jesus all in the same breath.

I came back to the locker room after my talk with Drake and set back to work on Rex. We were the third fight up that night, just before the main event. Heavyweights. Why do they always like to watch the heavyweights? Those fat S.O.B.s lumbered around the ring like their feet were stuck in tar. The lighter the fighter the better the fight, I say.

I saw a bout one time between two guys who couldn't have been more than 200 pounds between them. Watching them was like watching two alley cats fight over a pot roast. The punches were short and sharp, feet never stopped moving, and between rounds they weren't heaving and gasping for air like those heavyweights looking like fish out of water. I'd never seen a lightweight lean over between rounds and use his spit bucket to throw up into but I'd seen it happen too many times to mention with heavyweights.

From the sounds drifting down the hall it sounded like a pretty full house. Rex didn't say much for about a half hour before a fight and I didn't push him. We both knew what to do. I rubbed him down, laced up his shoes tight, taped his hands, and slid on his gloves. I pulled the laces taught and began crisscrossing them down his wrist in a practiced and measured way, as if the whole fight depended on getting it right. In some ways, it did.

A stubby little guy in a pork pie hat knocked once on the door and then stuck his head in to say, "You're up next. I don't think this one is going the distance so I'd get ready if I was you."

We stepped out into the hall and I could see that the door to the other locker room was open. Delancey was talking and laughing and getting glad-handed by a guy in a cheap suit with a cheaper cigar. Mr. Cheap Suit was all smiles, but it only revealed little yellowed teeth. Delancey was a good looking kid with slicked back blond hair and a dimple in his chin. I made a note to remember this and compare what his face looked like at the end of the bout and it gave me a smile.

Giving Delancey a rub from behind was his manager, Hobbes. I'd heard about him through the grapevine, but had never met the man and I doubt that I'd forget him if I had. His nose was round and took up most of his face and it stood out like Rudolph with a busted blinker, what with all the burst blood vessels and blackheads. His belly was bulbous and his pea green cardigan didn't quite button over it. If suspenders had never been invented he'd have gone without pants for his whole life. He was smiling at whatever the cheap suit was saying and he jerked his head over his shoulder to bark orders at two lackeys that rushed around gathering the spit bucket, a stack of towels, and the stool. Rex didn't look. He was in his own head and thinking of nothing but the fight. I stood in the hallway and started thinking about next week already. Cocky. Bad luck, too. More clues.

We stepped into the main hall. The Excelsior really crams them in. The seats are set in steep rows stacked right on top of each other so, even when it's not, it feels crowded. On that night, it was little more than half full, but the beer had been flowing through the first two bouts so the volume made it sound like the joint was sold out. We went to our corner and got set up. I laid out the bucket and towels and Rex started dancing about on his feet, shifting side to side and up and down on the tips of his toes and then from ball to heel. I checked my pocket and made sure I had my razor. I'd never had to cut Rex, but I knew how. Most guys will just carry a safety razor taken out of its holder, but I carried a straight razor I got from Pop when he showed me how to make a cut. It's the only thing I kept of his after he left. The handle was green with a sparkly inlay and I kept it well-oiled and sharp. If you needed to do the deed between rounds you didn't want to fumble around in your pocket for a loose razor and then worry about pinching it between your fingers and keeping it steady. I just needed to reach in, grab it, then flip it open with my thumb so I could make a nice clean slice to let loose the pooled up blood and keep the swelling down for the time being. But like I said, I never had cause to use it. I chose to teach Rex about defense so he'd never need me to cut him.

Delancey pranced into the arena with his hands over his head, soaking in applause that wasn't there. He had four guys with him who fussed and fretted over him like a June bride. His silk robe was stitched up with his name across the back and he played at slicking back his hair with his gloves. Idiot. All that grease just made them slick enough to slide off Rex if he ever got close enough to lay one on him.

Rex and I still didn't speak. Kind of wish we had now, given what happened.

First round was just for feeling it out. Delancey could punch, I'll give him that. He came out with guns a-blazing, looking to lay on some hurt. Rex danced and floated and got away from most of the jabs. He popped a few of his own in there, but was mostly testing the waters to see what his plan of attack should be. We were scheduled for ten rounds. I figured we'd be out of there in five.

Round two and both men had done their sizing up. At the sound of the bell, Rex raced across the canvas on the attack. Delancey didn't back down. Young and stupid.

Rex connected with a series that sent Delancey back to his own corner. Rex danced in front of him looking for an opening, but he waited it out a little too long because Delancey reared up and swung with that big slab of meat he had on the end of his right arm and caught Rex on the side of the head. It caused more disorientation than real damage, but for a second I thought, "Damn, the kid's gonna end up with a cauliflower ear from that."

Rex caromed off to the left and Delancey was able to spring through the hole and get off the ropes. Once Rex regained his footing we had a real barn burner of a round. The crowd surged forward to the edge of their seats as the punches started landing one after the other. Rex popped a few shots onto Delancey that made his hair come unglued from the top of his head and start to flip-flop around whenever Rex would score. Most of Delancey's blows caught Rex in his defensive pose but there was so much power behind those arms that Delancey's gloves came crashing through to Rex. They weren't scoring shots but they were taking their toll. Maybe we'd be there until the seventh.

Between rounds Hobbes was making a big drama with the ref over phantom fouls and below the belt shots. I'd seen his type before. The bluster is all part of the act. Delancey's team primped and preened between rounds, tying and retying his shoes and gloves, wiping him down with a towel, holding the spit bucket close so he wouldn't have to waste any energy spitting more than ten inches.

Rex took the break to catch his breath like you're supposed to.

Round three was more of the same. The fans were getting what they paid for. They didn't seem to be on one side or the other, just roared a little louder when the punches hit hard. Rex landed more but Delancey had some real power. Hobbes kept up his act, haranguing the ref over made-up violations.

In between three and four Rex and I finally spoke.

"He's flat-footed," I said. "Keep him moving side to side and he can't keep up. Front to back he's a freight train."

"I know. I think his momma was a whore and his dad was an engine car for the Burlington Northern."

I laughed as I slid his mouthpiece back. Those were the last words we said to each other.

As I cleared the stool out of our corner I could see Delancey's team huddled around him like he needed privacy to change into his unmentionables. In between Hobbes' gut and lackey #1 I saw them again retying the laces on his gloves, as if that was going to help him once Rex really got mad. Hobbes was speaking into Delancey's ear but throwing looks across the ring at Rex. Another clue I missed out on.

I figured he could look all he wanted but he wasn't going to crack the code on Rex's style. They finished re-lacing the gloves and Hobbes patted two short slaps on Delancey's back and sent him out into battle.

When I play it back in my head I can see that the gloves he came out with in round three were green leather and the ones he had on before were red. Rex preferred the simple oxblood gloves he used in every bout. Even this one, his last.

Before the bell stopped reverberating, Delancey was across the ring and on the attack. He slammed his fist through Rex's defenses again but this time it went all the way and caught Rex in the nose. He staggered back and Delancey stoked the engine on that freight and came forward again swinging his left. The door in Rex's defense was open a little wider now after that first blow and the left landed right on the button.

I could tell Rex was knocked for a loop. I didn't need to scream out defense instructions; that wasn't our way. He wouldn't have heard me anyway with the way the crowd had risen to their feet, bellowing for more action.

I'd heard tell of it but had never seen it until then. I didn't figure it out until later. Delancey was using weighted gloves. A fist full of buckshot was sewn right over the knuckles so that each of Delancey's already monster punches now crashed into Rex with the added force of a half pound of lead.

Rex fought back. He landed a great sweeping right to Delancey's jaw that backed him off for a beat. The peanut gallery over in Delancey's corner looked momentarily concerned, but when Delancey went right back to work with the heavy gloves they relaxed. Hobbes even threw a look of confidence back across his shoulder to the man in the cheap suit who was chewing the hell out of his unlit cigar in the front row.

Delancey was ignoring Rex's midsection and all attention was on his face as blow after blow came raining down. I'll be honest; the thought of throwing in the towel never crossed my mind. I'd never had to think about it before. It wasn't an option we'd ever discussed.

I could see Rex start to go slack. It was happening in front of me and I was powerless to stop it. I looked to the ref to call the fight. He was watching the action with one eye and checking Delancey's corner with the other. On the take. Paid to stand aside and watch a guy get beat to death.

Rex slumped, but Delancey had him against the ropes and held him up. Rex's nose broke and blood poured down to the canvas below. His gloves hung at his sides now, defenseless. The crowd who had moments before been screaming for the red stuff were now seeing what was happening to Rex and calling for the ref to stop the fight. I thought I was watching someone else. I felt just like I did when I'd see Pop beat on Mom and didn't do a goddamn thing about it.

I don't know how much longer it went on but when the ref stepped in and put his body between Delancey and Rex he smeared blood all over his shirt and slipped a bit on the pool under his feet. Once the clinch was broken Rex slid down the ropes to the canvas and doubled over on his knees so he was kind of squatting there, his head down, arms splayed out to the sides like he was praying or something. To see his back you'd never know anything was wrong.

The bell snapped me out of my own head and I jumped the ropes and went to him. I rolled him over on his back and saw the pulp of his face, the blood mixed with bits of flesh and a few sharp pieces of teeth; white poking through the red.

The noise of the crowd going wild was a nonsensical hum in my ears. When I could finally turn away from what I was seeing I caught a glimpse of Delancey being hustled out of the ring by Hobbes and his other two handlers. They didn't even look back. The man in the cheap suit was gone from the front row, but the rest of the crowd was getting to their feet now; some to get a closer look at the carnage and some to rush out and tell a friend about what they just saw.

Over Rex's shoulder at ringside was a frantically calling radio announcer. He was standing up with his mic in his hand trying to describe Rex's ruined face for those unlucky enough to have missed it firsthand.

I stayed there on my knees hovering over Rex and wondering what to do next. When would it all go back to normal? When would we get saved by the bell?

# 4

*Fokoli*

Fighter Rex Ward took it to the head on Saturday and I ended up with twenty bucks in my pocket. It should have been forty, but when the kid didn't get up again, I didn't feel like bugging Ted for the rest. I don't know, it just seemed like it would have been disrespectful or something. After all the hype about the fight, all the money changing hands, and my friend, Earl's insistence that "His boy, Rex" would tear Delancey apart, and my "Double or nothing Rex doesn't get up again," the whole thing turned sour fast. I took the twenty and kept my trap shut.

We'd been huddled around the radio in the squad room for the fight since six o'clock. There were five of us: Ted Phillips, Bob White, Earl Johnson, Ken Willis, and me. We all work homicide, right? So why do we like fights so much? Well, sometimes it's nice to be in on the action—to hear when the final blow takes place instead of getting there an hour or so after it's all over. Plus, there's the money angle. A cop's life ain't all wine and roses after all, and a run on good bets has been known to get a guy through a tough day or two while waiting for his check to clear.

Chuck Cordes was announcing. He liked Delancey for the win and I guess I was leaning that way too, even before all the betting—not because I thought he had anything special, but because I thought he was hungry enough to take Rex apart.

Chuck talked like Delancey was Prince Charming, all blond hair and dimpled chin and strong arms. I never figured Chuck Cordes for a Nancy, but he sure sounded like one the way he talked about that kid.

Sounded like Delancey had a few guys in his corner. Rex had just his manager—a brother or something. Me and Bob joked that Rex and his brother probably learned how to fight by watching their old man beat up on their mother—and that conversation, with all the laughing and the back-slapping and Ted Phillips collecting the bets and scribbling notes with his stub of a pencil—still leaves a bad taste in my mouth.

"That had to hurt," Bob said when Delancey landed a blow that sent Rex reeling.

Chuck Cordes was screaming about the amount of blood pouring from Rex's face, but we all leaned in closer to the radio anyway. Earl tried to change his bet, but Ted waved him off with a, "Shut the hell up. That guy's going down."

I stood up and walked away from the radio then. I opened the window and lit a cigarette. Bob White came over and asked if I was okay. He was always doing things like that. "What?" I asked. "You wanna hold hands or something?" He wasn't sure if I was joking or not and I let him wonder about that.

Then the fight was over. Rex wasn't getting up. "KNOCK OUT!!!" Chuck screamed.

Me and my cigarette strolled back over to the radio. Ted was checking his notes and passing money around. Earl said, "Hold it. Listen." He turned the volume up.

"Rex is being carried off by the medics. It doesn't look good for the boy from K.C., Ladies and Gentlemen; not good at all."

There were a couple of Goldman's Foot Powder jingles, and a Lucky Strike ad, and then Chuck was back. Rex was dead.

Ted turned the radio off and we all sat there in silence. That's when the thought about the forty bucks tickled at my brain a little, but the twenty in my pocket felt heavy enough and I wondered how quick I could get rid of it.

A heavyweight fight was next, but none of us was too keen on listening. One by one we moved back to our desks. There were reports to finish. There's always a report to finish on a Saturday night when you're a cop. If I ever lost my job, I could be a secretary.

A little while longer and everyone was ready to call it a

day. I could tell Bob White wanted to leave too, but he was new and I was teaching him a thing or two about police work . . . there's always paperwork.

When the phone rang two hours later, I'd managed to put Rex and his pulverized head out of my mind and was trying to figure a way to get that extra twenty bucks due me without sounding like a heel.

# 5

*Ray*

I sat in the locker room with Rex laid out before me on the same table where I gave him a rub down an hour before. I didn't look at his body, but just beyond it, at the wall, where the room's single bare bulb cast the outline of his face. Except the shape on the wall bore no resemblance to Rex. None of the landmarks were there.

Rex was dead. I watched it happen. Sure, Delancey had a good right arm, but no one could have done this with just a fist, let alone one wrapped up in a padded glove. What happened to Rex was a beating usually performed by a baseball bat. Someone had ordered this done. I wanted to know who.

An exposed pipe dripped condensation down the concrete wall in a single, slow rivulet that reflected the harsh sixty-watt light. Moisture trickled to the floor where it pooled in a dinner-plate-sized puddle cloudy with mold. I stared at the line of water and thought to myself: everything leaves a trail.

The man in the pork pie hat knocked quiet as a nun before he stuck his head in. He held his hat in hand and beads of sweat stood on his bald head in neat little rows.

"R-Ray? The man is here."

"What man?" I asked.

Pork Pie swallowed hard, like there was something he didn't want to say.

"The meat wagon," he finally muttered. A guy like him only knew the street term. Probably never heard the word coroner in his life.

"I'm done." I stood up and didn't look back. That hamburger on the table wasn't my brother, not like I knew him, and that wasn't going to be the image I carried around with me from here on out.

"I'll be around for his things," I said grabbing my jacket and gym bag. I pushed past Pork Pie and almost ran into the two guys carrying the stretcher for Rex's body. They avoided my eyes as I passed.

I had so many questions I didn't know where to start. I wasn't about to go home, but I didn't know what I could find out tonight. I wanted to talk to Delancey, but I had no idea where he lived. Best way to a fighter is through the manager though, so I figured I'd start with Hobbes.

On my way out of the arena I stopped by to see Drake and get my money. If I didn't get it now I'd never see it and I might need cash if I had to get out of town quick. I figured the need for escape might become pressing if the temperature in my blood kept rising.

Drake had been drinking. Well, more than normal.

"Jesus, Ray. Jesus God Damn Christ. And Joseph and Mary and all them bastards. Why'd it have to happen?"

"It didn't have to happen."

"And in my place. I'm just sick, Ray. Sick." He took another swig but didn't offer me any. "You know I liked Rex, don't ya Ray?"

"Yeah, I know."

"Just one of them things that makes this a goddamn terrible business to be in."

I held out a hand. "I'd like our share from tonight."

"Oh Christ, Ray, of course. Jesus Christ, of course." Drake set the bottle down and brought out the tin box from his bottom desk drawer. He counted out our share of the door in one dollar bills. I didn't trust his math in the state he was in and it was obvious he didn't either. After he finished counting he took a wad of bills, added them to the top of the stack, in case he counted wrong, and pushed it over to me. I picked it up and separated the cash into four stacks of twenty with six bucks left over. I pushed the stacks of singles back to him and asked to exchange for twenties.

"Oh Jesus, of course Ray. No problem." Drake fumbled back into the drawer and got another, bigger tin box. This one had a combination lock and it contained the big bills.

"So, Drake, where would I find Hobbes?"

"Hobbes? What the hell do you want him for?"

"I want to ask him some questions."

"Jesus Ray, you don't think it was foul play do you?"

I reached over and snatched the twenties out of his hand. "Just tell me where he works out of."

"He's got a gym over on Whitney Street. Jesus Ray, don't go stirring up trouble now."

"Thanks Drake."

I took my money and left.

In all honesty, I went to Hobbes's place to talk, to ask questions. I had no intention of starting any trouble. Like I said, I'm not the fighter in the family. I wasn't sure what I was going to say or do, but my feet just started moving like I wasn't in control of them. I kind of wish that Drake had offered me a drink before I left . . . for courage.

Out in front of the arena people from the fight were still hanging around. A guy in a feathered hat with a real drunk on was telling a cab driver all about the bloodshed.

"I never sheen so mush blood . . ." He was bobbing and weaving more than Rex in the ring.

On any other night the cabbie would have probably shooed him away, but this was real good stuff. The drunk could lay on the usual exaggeration and still not do it justice. I wondered how many fight fans he had already shuttled home, listening to their varied accounts of the carnage.

I decided not to take the car. I figured the walk would do me good in settling my nerves and maybe cooling my head a little. I'd always been good at controlling my anger. People think that if you learn how to fight then you will fight all the time, but that's not the case. Most boxers never fight outside the ring. First off, you get your fill on work nights. Second, it's just that—work. And third, you know you can take the guy so you've got nothing to prove and if some dumb jerk wants to take it that far then he deserves what beating he gets.

Being in control of anger in the ring is essential. Pop taught us that one while we were still learning the difference between an uppercut and a hook. If you let your anger get the best of you, you can't think straight and you'll lose every time.

I tried to keep that in mind.

Hobbes's gym was a second floor walk-up over a bar and across the street from another bar and a pool hall. Not exactly uptown, but who wants a boxing gym over their tuxedos-and-gowns nightclub?

It was quarter to eleven and there was a light on. I went up the stairs until the sounds of a jazz band playing below became nothing more than a murmur through the floor. The door was unlocked and I pushed on it. It made a loud creak from a rusty spring. The room was like any other boxing gym. A big square with a ring in the middle for sparring and all around the walls of the room were a series of heavy bags, speed bags, and free-weights with mirrors spaced throughout. It smelled the same too—sweat and moldy socks from the fighters, cigar stench and body odor from the managers.

Light spilled into the gym from an office to my left. I heard movement—papers being shuffled, drawers being opened and closed—but I stayed put. It was easy enough to see that me and whoever was moving around in there were the only ones in the place. I let my eyes adjust to the dim light and waited.

After a short while Hobbes came out. He had changed his cardigan sweater for another and was carrying his gym bag and walking with purpose. He crossed the room without noticing me in the dark and stopped a few feet away at a wall switch. He threw the switch and four bare bulbs hanging from the ceiling snapped on, making the room bright in four spots with shadows in every corner. I was centered in one of the bright pools of light and when Hobbes noticed me. He jumped back and let out a tiny yelp like a woman seeing a mouse in her kitchen.

"Fuckin' A you scared me. Where's Jimmy? Do you have the . . ." Recognition flashed across his face. "You're Rex's brother."

"Yeah. And you're Delancey's manager. Let's talk."

Hobbes got all jumpy and threw glances over my shoulder to the door. He started with some fake sympathy. "It's a damn, damn shame what happened. I told Delancey to lay off. I told him to pull up on that right but the kid's got a cannon. He ought to be registered as a lethal weapon."

"I'm not from *The Star* here to get a quote for the bulletin. I just want to know who wanted Rex dead."

Hobbes eagerly shook his head, rattling his jowls. "Nobody. Nobody did, that's the God's honest truth. You think I'd be mixed up in something like that? You don't know me at all, pal."

"No, I don't know you. So I don't know what you're capable of."

Hobbes began to back up almost imperceptibly. I followed him.

"Let's step into the ring," I said. "Do this the way we both know best."

"Wh-what do you mean?"

"I mean we're going to go a few rounds, verbally that is." Hobbes was confused. "Just talk," I added by way of explanation. "We're both men of the ring so that's where we'll figure this thing out."

I climbed in between the bottom two ropes and waited for Hobbes to follow, lifting up the ropes for his easy access. He threw another furtive glance to the door and then tossed his gym bag ahead of him and heaved himself up like a sea lion flopping on the beach. He rolled over on his right side and pushed himself up on one arm and then moved his weight onto his belly, which kept him up but only made him look more like a sea lion or maybe a beached whale. All this effort made sweat rise on his head, his nose grow more veiny and red, as well as pop one of his suspenders from his pants.

I let the ropes down and waited while he gathered himself to standing. I was calm and in control and I could tell this was maybe only his third or fourth time actually inside the ropes of a ring. He felt trapped and that feeling oozed off of him like his glaze of sweat.

"So, I don't think you had anything against Rex. I just want to know who the matchmaker was on this one."

"I don't know what you're talking about, pal."

"I'm not your pal, Hobbes. The name is Ray and you sent your fighter in to kill my brother tonight. You know that much."

"I didn't send nobody in to kill nobody." He stood flat-footed, his loud breath whistling in and out through that busted horn of a nose.

"Delancey acted on his own then?" I asked him, not believing a word of it.

"I guess so. If you're saying it was a fix then it was all in *his* corner. I just send the boys out to fight. Delancey's been prancing around town with society dames and drinking champagne so who knows who's been bending his ear after hours like that. I only know what I tell him when he's here working out."

"So you didn't know he was going to take out Rex?"

"No! I'm telling you that!"

I started moving around in slow circles and Hobbes countered me, but I doubt he realized what he was doing. He was just protecting himself by instinct. Other than the layers of fat to get through I could punch this guy silly without even breaking a sweat if I needed more information.

"Did you see my brother's face?"

"What? No. What do you mean?"

"After the fight. Did you see what your boy did to his face?"

"No. Do you ever go spend time with the guy your boy just beat the hell out of?"

"It didn't look like a face anymore. I grew up with the kid and spent near everyday of my life with him but I wouldn't have recognized him if I hadn't seen it happen right in front of me. Fists don't do that. Even if your kid can punch into next Tuesday, a fist don't do that much damage without help."

"Help from what? From me?"

"Why did you change his gloves after round three?"

"Ray, I don't know what you're goin' on about, but you need to go talk to Delancey about that, not me. I got other guys on my roster besides Kid Delancey. I spend three hours every other day in the gym with them. I don't know what Delancey does when I'm not with him. You know damn well there's a lot of crooked dough in this game and you're goddamn naive if you think it don't get to these kids sometimes."

So help me, I was starting to believe him. I circled around to where Hobbes's gym bag was sitting on the edge of the ring half under the bottom rope. I looked down for a split second, not wanting to take my eyes off Hobbes even though it would probably take him about half a minute to cross the ten feet between us. I saw green nestled in the depths of the bag. I bent down, eyes on Hobbes, and lifted the gloves out. They were heavy, but lopsided heavy. The white stitching in the seams was dark with dried blood.

Hobbes blanched and even his nose drained of color for a moment. I kept my eyes fixed on him. Watch their eyes, not their feet, Pop used to say. Their shoulders will fake you, their hands will fake you, their feet will dance around, but the eyes never lie. I lifted the gloves to shoulder height and dropped them. They hit the canvas knuckles down with a thud and didn't bounce. The buckshot inside had made sure that they would always drop that way, just as if I threw a pair of loaded dice they would always come up snake eyes.

Once the sound of the gloves hitting the canvas stopped echoing in the big square room all that we heard between us was Hobbes's labored breathing. I bent down again and picked up the gloves, this time taking my eyes down and away from him since I knew what I wanted to know and I knew he was no threat. I put them on. The same gloves that killed my brother.

Cool, calm, and collected I crossed the center of the ring toward Hobbes. He backed up slightly and raised his hands, but his real defense was his mouth.

"I'll tell you anything you want to know. Delancey knew what he was doing but he did it too damn well. He wasn't supposed to kill Rex, just take him out of commission for awhile. I'll tell you anything. I'm a songbird for the cops, I spill it all no problem, ask anyone. I'm a regular tenor."

I smashed him across the beak with a right and the blood vessels so near the surface burst, sending a fountain of blood arcing up and then splashing across the canvas as he dropped to one knee. He wailed.

"Where would I find Delancey?" I asked as calmly as I could, but I knew my eyes gave me away. Once I had that first shot out of me it was like a pipe burst and there was no way to stop the flow of violence.

Hobbes said something I couldn't understand through hands covered in blood.

I stood over him and swung down with another right, knocking his hands away from his face and letting loose all the blood they had been holding back.

"Say that again."

Hobbes blurted out an address and I repeated it to myself to make it sink in. I put a foot down on his left hand which was bracing him up on the canvas. I reared back a left and brought it down on his face again. The glove crashed down and some bone gave way with a deep crunch.

"And who was the matchmaker?"

"I don't know," he managed to get out. I think I believed him.

I raised back another right and a disturbing image of my father flashed in my head, but it was too late. I hadn't thrown a punch in anger in years and all that time was surging through my muscles now. Again and again I came down. On his jaw, which gave way easily, and on his cheeks, which became softer and softer as the bones underneath crumbled. He managed to stay up on one knee for much longer than I would have imagined. I put a left directly into his right ear and he collapsed. From there the hitting was more difficult and the blows lacked the same force but I didn't stop. Not until I was done.

I stood up straight, ripped the gloves off and jumped back to avoid stepping in blood. Some of it had spattered on my pants and shoes.

I had no idea if Hobbes had a brother to mourn him or anyone in his life who would give a rat's ass that he was dead.

I had the address for Delancey and another walk would do me good to let my muscles uncoil and my head clear. What I had just done was starting to sink in. Quite often a boxer can't remember details of a fight. Doctors will tell you it's all the blows to the head, but a real fighter knows that it's the zone you get into that blocks out the rest of the world. Maybe it's the only way to do such damage to another man without the guilt running you down. Some sort of deep self-defense mechanism.

A fog was lifting and the image before me was becoming sharper. The gloves, the blood, a dead body—it all looked a little too familiar and I had to get out of there right then.

I was sweating and the smell of that plus the blood made it less like a gym and more like a real fight hall. Neither was a smell I cared for any more.

I made it to the door just as someone was coming up the stairs, taking them two at a time. There was no time to hide.

A skinny young black boy reached the top of the steps and halted when he saw me. I was blocking his view of the ring.

"Who are you?" he asked.

"Who are you?" I countered, angrily. Sometimes the best defense is a good offense. It worked, he backed off.

"I'm Jimmy. I'm supposed to meet Mister Hobbes here." He held an envelope which he suddenly realized was exposed so he put it behind his back. Not the brightest kid to have on the payroll.

"What for?" I demanded.

"Just to . . . well . . . I don't know as I ought to be tellin' you, sir. Mr. Hobbes said it was urgent and not to get distracted talkin' to nobody."

"He meant like at a pool hall or a bar."

"I guess so, sir."

"You one of his fighters?"

"Yes, sir." He couldn't have been more than a lightweight, maybe a flyweight. Didn't have much of the fighter's confidence yet either. Put this youngster in the ring and he'd get torn apart. "Plus I run errands for him sometimes."

"What's in there?" I indicated behind his back.

"Nothin'."

I grabbed the hand that held the envelope and he gave it over quickly when I bent his arm even in the smallest way. It was money. Lots of it. The envelope was stuffed with tens and twenties, so full it wouldn't close. Hobbes had been in on it to the hilt and this was his payoff. I decided to keep the money since it was more likely than ever that I would have to skip town. First it was time to see what Delancey knew.

I shoved the envelope into my back pocket and pushed past the young errand boy and went down the stairs. Behind me, I heard him discover Hobbes.

"Mister Hobbes, sir?" he said to dead ears.

# 6

*Fokoli*

A vertical neon sign hung from the corner building where Third met Whitney Street. "*Boxing*" flashed off and on, red in the dark. This was the private gym and final resting place of Ernest Hobbes, boxing manager and Kansas City's latest stiff. Me and Bob White climbed out of the car and stood on a sidewalk wet with spring rain.

I looked up and down the block, sort of getting a feel for who was out tonight, who looked regular, who looked like they didn't belong. Other than the jazz filtering out of the bar below the gym, it was quiet tonight. A drunk sat huddled in a doorway he'd staked out as his own, clutching the misshapen paper bag that held his fifty-cent bottle of wine. I had half a mind to make one of the street cops standing around arrest him for vagrancy, but our holding cells were full enough. And while some drunks might be violent, this one was doing nothing but taking up space, so it was no skin off my nose.

The prostitutes hanging around were another matter. Cops showing up was like lifting a rock . . . everyone crawled out from underneath and scattered as best they could—but not tonight.

Tonight the ladies hung around, at least a dozen of them, watching the door to the gym. Some of them even hollered at me and Bob as we climbed out of the squad car. "Hey, Copper," one of them called out to Bob. "Let me make a man out of you."

Bob turned red and cleared his throat.

The stench of sweat and full spit buckets spilled down the stairs leading from the gym and out to the wet street. I lit a cigarette, hoping the taste of tobacco and smoke would dampen the smell of whatever else I would encounter up there.

Bob cleared his throat again. "Should we go up?" He

was always doing stuff like that; asking questions with obvious answers.

I ignored him and took a deep drag on my cigarette as I headed up the stairs and pushed through the door, nodding and flashing my ID at the uniform standing guard.

"Barbara's with me," I said, jerking my head toward Bob, who was having trouble getting his badge out of his pocket.

The gym was dim; the walls yellowed by years of cigarette smoke and sweat. It was lit by four naked bulbs at the end of long black cords suspended from a moldy ceiling.

Hobbes obviously hadn't been one for upkeep; he preferred to purse his money.

Rumor had it his house was some art deco number on the edge of K.C.'s high roller neighborhood. Hobbes was the sort of guy who liked to toe the line between law-abiding citizen cum police informant and two-bit number-running thug, anxious to take and make bad bets.

Personally I never liked the guy. But he had a pretty voice when he decided to sing and he'd helped us put away a goon or two in his day.

This was not his day.

There were two or three beat cops milling around, shuffling their feet outside of the ring and looking a little bit like they would rather be outside talking to the whores than in here with Hobbes.

I spied Captain Tolene behind the ring with his hand on the shoulder of a guy I recognized from Internal Affairs. I turned to warn Bob to keep quiet while we were looking around, but he was already making his way over to the captain, arm extended to shake hands.

"Idiot," I muttered.

The I.A. guy glared at Bob before slipping out the back door. Captain Tolene spied me on the other side of the ring and motioned me over. On my way across the gym, I caught a glimpse of Hobbes's body between the feet of the police photographer and the coroner, who had climbed into the ring to evaluate the corpse.

I could see a bit of his holey sweater, splattered with blood. With all the money Hobbes made, one would think he'd buy decent clothes, or even soap. But he was dressed like any other vagrant we cleaned off the street.

"Captain," I said, dropping my cigarette on the floor and stepping on it before shaking his hand. "Looks like a mess." The handshake was a ruse. Everyone knew he wanted me gone.

He shook his head. "It is. It is a mess."

"Leads?"

"None."

Bob had been in homicide for three months and since my partner, Mark, was killed four months earlier, I was stuck training him. He should have stayed put to hear me and the captain hash out prelims of the case, but he'd caught his first glimpse of the bloody sweater and he moved in for a closer look. Captain Tolene and I looked at each other.

"Think this is this revenge for tonight's fight?" I asked, jerking my head in the direction of the stiff.

Captain Tolene pursed his lips a little. "I don't think so," he said. "If I had to make a guess, I'd say Hobbes didn't do what he was supposed to do tonight." Which in cop talk meant this was a mob killing.

Hobbes fancied himself a gangster but, like I said, when push came to shove, he sang like a soprano. Some of the guys at the station called him "No Balls." "Listen," they'd say, "No Balls is singing our song."

Informants generally have a shorter than average life expectancy. Usually, they disappear and wash up downriver somewhere after a few months. One guy, Jasper Deneghy, disappeared after ratting out a pin by the name of Toady Rogers. Jasper made it all the way to the Mississippi River before he washed up in a marsh full of river grass and cattails. He'd been gnawed on by catfish, coyotes, birds, and maybe a cat or two. There wasn't much left to work with.

Hobbes's death had always been a matter of time. Always.

What troubled me was that he was lying dead in the

middle of a boxing ring rather than making his bloated way downriver like a typical mob erasure.

It was clear the same thing was troubling Captain Tolene, or he wouldn't be here with me now. And he wouldn't have been whispering with a guy from I.A. "Inside job?" I asked, wanting to see his reaction.

Tolene just stared at me and I knew enough to keep my mouth shut about it then. "Go take a look at Hobbes," he said. "Then we'll talk."

The uniforms moved aside when I got to the ring so I could get my first clear look of the man that used to be Hobbes.

Hobbes lay on his side facing my direction. His entire head was a swollen, purple mess of bruises and drying blood. Fresh blood still pooled on the canvas where the head wounds had drained and the stink filled the room with a hot, coppery smell that mixed with the sweat and smoke.

I realized Bob was missing and looked around for him. He was standing near the front door, trying to breathe what little fresh air filtered up the stairs from the street.

"Toughen up," I called, crawling through the ropes and then crouching beside the body.

The police photographer was busy snapping pictures each flash lighting up Hobbes's corpse for an instant and giving the room an unreal quality.

The coroner gave me a smile. "Fokoli," he said. "Were you home in bed?"

"I was plowing my wife," I said and that got a big laugh from everyone nearby. It was a lie, of course. I didn't go home much since my old partner died . . . and not since Laura figured out what part I played in it.

I pushed my hat back on my head and studied the body. Hobbes hadn't put up much of a fight. There was no blood on his knuckles, no sign that he'd given anything back to whoever chewed him up like this. He'd gone to fat years ago, his middle hanging over pants that were always falling down. He must have been half crouched during the brunt of the beating. His pants were halfway down his ass; not completely off, but low enough to see that he'd shit himself before it was all said and done.

"Hobbes must have pissed somebody off real good this time," the captain said, lighting a cigarette. He'd come to stand at the ring, one hand holding onto a rope, the other holding the smoke.

"Are you going to tell me which thug you think did this?" I asked, standing and lighting a cigarette of my own.

He shrugged like maybe he didn't want to say too much, like we're not all on the same team or something. I thought about the I.A. guy and I began to wonder if maybe the captain had proof now that I was crooked.

But I could tell there was something more on his mind than just that, so I waited. He smoked the full cigarette and half of another before he said anything.

While he smoked, I noticed a skinny black kid sitting back by the locker room door. He wore street clothes that had been smeared with what I pegged to be Hobbes's blood. He held a pair of gloves to his chest like a small child. A couple of uniformed guys stood nearby, writing down whatever the kid said in little notebooks.

The kid was also crying. And he wasn't crying like a guy who's done something bad and wants to be forgiven—he was crying like a man who's seen something bad and wants to forget it.

The captain finished that first half of his second cigarette just then, and decided to talk. "I'll let you have this case," he said.

"Good." But I knew he was going to watch me through the whole thing; like my career rested on busting this wide open. Since Mark, Captain Tolene was always watching me.

"But you've got to be empathetic."

"Empathetic?"

I'm not sure he was even paying attention to me. He was taking tiny drags on the cigarette, then holding it out so he could examine the glowing tip like it held some profound truth or something. "Hobbes knew a lot of people."

I snorted a little. "Good ol' Hobbes," I said. "He'd rat

out his own mother if he thought there was something in it for him." I kept quiet about the twenty bucks. Everyone bet on fights. Everyone. But it was illegal, so no one talked about it—especially in front of Tolene. "Let me guess," I said, "You think the fight was fixed."

Tolene took another drag and chuckled a little. "Hell yes, the fight was fixed," he said. "Hard to find a fight that isn't in this town. I don't think Rex was supposed to be permanently taken out of commission, but it happens."

Just like that. Like a guy getting killed for sport is no big deal. An image of the I.A. guy with his head bent close to Tolene's danced around my mind again, but I shook it off. My nose was clean—at least it had been since Mark was killed.

"Maybe somebody ought to talk to Delancey," I said.

Tolene frowned. "No known address," he said. "We've got a guy on it."

I opened my mouth to tell him I'd be glad to hit the streets and take a look, but he had other ideas. "I want you to check out Hobbes's house."

I jerked my head toward the kid in back of the gym. "What's his story?"

Tolene blew out a breath. "Hell," he said. "That's Jimmy Scoggins. He's supposed to be Hobbes's up and coming featherweight. The beat cops have been talking to him for the last hour with no luck. Jackass won't stop crying."

"He's just sad he hasn't met me yet."

Tolene gave a small smile. "When you're done with him, make sure someone brings him in. He's a material witness." I started to duck under the ropes, but he stopped me. "And make sure those gloves are boxed and brought in. The way he's holding onto them it looks like they belonged to Hobbes."

I nodded and crawled under the ropes, pausing long enough to pick up a full spit bucket on my way over to have a chat with Jimmy.

Jimmy, in a word, was pathetic. Snot and tears ran down his face, smearing more of Hobbes's blood all over the green gloves. The beat cops doodled in their notebooks and looked bored, having all but given up on the kid.

"Hello there," I said.

Jimmy rocked back and forth, wiping his face on one of the gloves. "He's dead, dead, dead," he blubbered.

"You Jimmy?" I asked.

Jimmy just kept rocking.

I threw the bucket of water and spit in his face.

The shock of it quieted him for a minute. Then his eyes got big and he jumped to his feet. "What the hell did you do that for?"

"Sit down," I said, shoving him back onto the bench. "I need to talk to you."

"Go fuck yourself, *Cop*."

I shrugged. "You can talk to me here or I can put you in a holding cell downtown for the night and you can talk to me in the morning." I made a big deal of looking him over. "Pretty kid like you would have lots of boyfriends in the holding cell."

"I'm a boxer," he said. "I'd tear 'em apart."

I lit a cigarette. "Sugar," I said, "it'd be really hard to box with your arms pinned at your sides and your shorts around your ankles."

His eyes got a little wider. "You're a liar," he said. "All you white cops is liars."

I shrugged. "Suit yourself." I turned and snapped my fingers at one of the beat cops. The beat cop smiled a little and reached for his cuffs.

"Wait," Jimmy said. "Just wait a minute."

The uniform stood there with the pair of cuffs in his hand. Me and Jimmy looked at each other. "What is it?" I asked. "You want to talk now?"

He slid his eyes to the pair of cuffs and kept them there as he answered. "What do you want?"

"Where can I find Delancey?"

Jimmy snorted. "How the hell should I know that?"

I nodded at the beat cop. He let the cuffs dangle a little to show Jimmy we meant business. "You should know," I said, "because you both boxed for the same manager. And my guess is you all stay somewhere nearby."

Jimmy looked at me.

"Someplace cozy," I said. "Where the bedbugs bite and the toilets don't flush." Jimmy's gaze shifted to the ring where the coroner and his assistants were lifting Hobbes onto a stretcher for his final ride downtown. Jimmy's eyes got big and wild again. "He's dead. Hobbes is dead."

Enough was enough. I backhanded Jimmy and his sobs turned to whimpers.

"Last chance," I said. "Where's Delancey?"

Jimmy rubbed his cheek with one hand while he clutched the gloves to his chest with the other. "Don't know. Swear to God I don't know."

I nodded to the uniform who pulled Jimmy to his feet and slapped the cuffs on. The green gloves fell to the floor with a solid thud. I picked them up. "Pretty heavy gloves," I said. "Are these the ones Delancey used on Rex tonight?"

But Jimmy wasn't listening. He was squirming and flailing all over the place, unable to box his way out of the cuffs or away from the cops. "Fuck you," he said.

I shrugged. "Sorry, Jimmy. Captain's orders. You're a material witness."

"Lousy goddamned cop," he yelled as they dragged him outside.

I followed, handing the gloves off to a uniform on my way downstairs. Outside, I stood by the car, breathing deeply. The whores still lurked across the street, curiosity erasing their caution. Bob sat in the passenger seat of the cruiser with a handkerchief over his face. A beat cop, chauffeuring Tolene back to the station, pulled up beside me. Tolene rolled the window down. "What'd you get from him?" he asked.

"Nothing," I said.

Tolene frowned and signaled for the cop to drive away.

I climbed into the driver's seat, started the engine, and tried not to think about the useless partner who sat beside me in Mark's old place.

# 7

*Ray*

I got a few blocks away and the sound of jazz faded. I realized I was hungry. It made me a little sick to feel that way, having just killed a man, but I couldn't deny it and the way my stomach was making noises it was being broadcast for all to hear.

I hopped a cable car at the next corner and sat down to let it do the work of taking me to Delancey's neighborhood. I picked at the dried blood on my pants. Tiny rust-colored flecks. It had soaked into the fabric so the best I could do was wet my thumb and rub it around to smear the dots into streaks of innocent looking dirt stains. Suddenly I looked like I'd been working a factory job instead of committing murder.

The cable car was nearly empty. A drunk slept it off at the end of the bench and a young couple sat entwined in each other, whispering baby talk that made them giggle. The car came to an intersection and I spotted a coffee shop on the corner so I stood up and swung out on the brass railing and did a graceful sidestep onto the street.

It was an all night place and showed the signs of being open twenty-four hours a day for a good many years. The floor was worn away in spots, the tables all chipped in the corners, the ceilings were yellow with tobacco stains, and the man behind the counter was seventy-five if he was a day. His face had every year etched into it from the Lincoln assassination in the year he was born through the trench fighting in the Great War and then back here to the night shift pouring an ocean of coffee and murdering a million eggs for guys who don't want to go home to their wives.

The rag he absently swished across the counter was almost as old as he was. He looked at me and gave a slight nod in the direction of the counter as if to say, "Sit anywhere you like, Bub, just don't bother me."

The booths that ran along one side of the narrow diner were full and the only other patron at the counter was a cop. I hesitated for a moment when I saw him, my foot hanging in midair, but that was the mark of a guilty man so I forced my foot down and sat with two seats between us. Not that he noticed. He was nose down in the newspaper and only unburied his head for frequent slurps of his coffee.

The old man behind the counter set a cup in front of me and started to pour out coffee without me having to ask. He looked at me with tired eyes, sagging and red-rimmed, pleading, "Don't make me ask you, Bub."

"What do you got that you don't have to cook?" I asked.

"Pie. Already made."

"Okay then."

He gave me a grateful nod, then shuffled off down the counter. Someone put a nickel in the jukebox and it started playing "Blueberry Hill" by Glenn Miller. Once the song came on the conversation rose in volume to compensate and there were bursts of laughter to go along with stabs of brass from the record. I kept my back to the booths and stared at the two coffee pots on the counter, simmering away and burning the coal black brew. The old-timer set down a piece of lemon cream pie and I didn't have the heart to tell him I hated lemon cream. I ate it to quiet my stomach, which still gurgled and yawned even as I ate. I had a good long moment to stop and think. All I could think was that I wished I could stop thinking. The sweet crooning on the jukebox, the white noise of laughter and conversations I couldn't follow all helped to make my thoughts a dull fuzz. It probably only lasted a minute but it was the first pause I had enjoyed in my racing thoughts since Rex fell to the final bell.

The cop finished whatever he was reading and looked up from his paper. His thick mustache was still dripping coffee.

"One more will ya, pal?" said the cop.

He straightened his back from his hunched over position and let out a groan as he worked out the kinks.

"I gotta get off this night shift," he said in my direction.

I looked up and acted surprised. With a mouthful of lemon pie all I did was nod and smile then put my head back down.

"Yeah, it's for the birds all right." Now it was a full-on conversation.

"You hear about the fight tonight?" I said. Again, the best defense is a good offense. If you want to land a winning punch you don't do it by hanging back, you have to move right in on them.

"Yeah, I heard something. Young kid took out an old pro. Beat him so bad he never got up again. Permanent." He smiled and his mustache curled up over his lip.

"Yeah, that's what I heard."

"I don't go in for fights. Horses, that's my game. Majestic beasts. Run like hell too."

"Not placing any bets I trust." I smiled an insincere smile but he didn't know the difference and just smiled back.

"Strictly legit. I get my ticket from the betting window, not off some dago in a striped suit. I come for the sport, the history. If I win a few bucks it's just gravy."

"You ought to be a jockey, the way you talk."

"Me?" He pushed back his stool to reveal a considerable gut. "I'd make a horse go swayback in no time flat." He laughed at himself.

My pie was done and I swigged the rest of my coffee. I threw down a dollar and stood up.

"Rub your lucky horseshoe for me, will you?" I said and gave a salute.

"No problem." The cop's refill arrived and he reburied his face in the paper.

I stepped back outside just as the Glenn Miller orchestra hit their final note. The screen door slapped behind me and the Ink Spots started crooning "When the Swallows Come Back to Capistrano" I ran to catch a cable car that was getting away.

The short sprint didn't do my stomach any good for settling the pie and coffee but I got to sit down and rest for a few blocks until I reached Delancey's.

This time there was only one other rider, a woman, crying into a handkerchief. I kept my eyes away from her and let her have her moment. She sobbed even louder as if to try to get my attention.

"Well, Jesus Christ aren't you even going to offer a woman a tissue?" she asked.

I turned. Her face, which had been buried in her handkerchief before, was angry and her eyes inflamed with tears and hate.

"I'm sorry I thought you already had one." I tried to sound soft and comforting.

"This one is fucking well soaked through. I've been on this bucket for an hour already. Not one damn person has offered me a new one."

"I'm sorry to hear that. I don't carry a handkerchief."

"Of course not," she had stopped crying and was just plain mad now. "There's no goddamn gentlemen any more. Everyone is a Neanderthal. Do you even know what that is?"

No, I didn't but fuck her for that tone of voice. I tried one more time with my soft approach.

"I'm really sorry ma'am. I'm just a working stiff. I don't get a call for starched linens all too often."

"Just wipe your nose on your sleeve I bet. Typical man. You're all the damn same."

I averted my eyes and studied my shoes.

"Oh, that's right. Look away. Just ignore me. What kind of animal are you that you can ignore a crying woman?" She went back to weeping into her wet handkerchief.

It was a distraction anyway.

When the car got near Delancey's I hopped off. It wasn't a part of town I'd normally visit after midnight. It was dark and the puddles of strange liquids that pooled in the gutters and potholes reflected no light like they were just black pits to nowhere. All the buildings were painted dark colors and it gave the impression that even if you visited in the bright of day it would still look just as shadowy and black. It was clear Delancey had to travel far from this neighborhood to do his hi-toned socializing.

There were no other people on the street but snippets of conversations and arguments floated by on the cooling night air. Trash blew past, floating above the gutter, carried by the light breeze.

I found the number outside of a four floor walk-up with a basement unit. I breathed in and out five times to calm myself and slow my heart rate. Before a fight Rex would breathe ten times. More than that and you risk hyperventilating.

I stepped up into the vestibule and ran my finger down the row of mailboxes. I found Delancey's hand-lettered name on a box marked 3B. There was only one buzzer, to the landlady's unit.

I had to push it if I wanted to be let in, but I didn't know what I'd say to gain entry and I didn't know if she would call up to Delancey's. If she did I doubted that he would invite me up for tea and cookies.

I pushed the button and, to my surprise, the door buzzed open. I pushed into the foyer and saw the stairwell leading up on the left and a small tarnished brass sign that stated LANDLORD outside the apartment directly to my right. The door did not open, but from behind it came a shrill and crone-like voice that made me picture the Bride of Frankenstein.

"Whaddaya want?"

"Delancey in Three B."

"Go on up. Third floor."

Some security.

As I climbed the steps and my eyes became level with the worn carpet of the third floor I could see light from beneath the door of Three B.

I knocked without thinking too much about it first. The bell had rung and the round was underway. I couldn't stand flat-footed and dumb or I'd get my block knocked off.

No one answered. I knocked again.

"Go away. You got the wrong door," came from inside.

I tried the knob and it turned. Even if it'd been locked, a good shove would have forced the flimsy door open. The layers of old paint were probably tougher than the wood it was made out of.

I pushed open the door but stayed standing in the hall, wary of walking into a trap.

The room was decent sized or maybe it just looked that way because all it had in it was a small bed shoved against one wall, a sink, and a chest of drawers pushed up against the other wall. A heavy punching bag hung from a chain suspended from a bolt Delancey had drilled into the center of the ceiling. Other than that the room was barren. No rug on the floor, no art on the walls.

This seemed like the kind of place Hobbes would hole up one of his fighters and it also seemed like the kind of place a hungry kid like Delancey would want to get out of. That might make him real receptive to a guy in a sharp suit waving money and society dames at him in exchange for a little dirty fighting.

Delancey was up and he may have been pacing. He didn't smoke but he looked like he should have been. He wasn't overly surprised that I had opened the door.

"Who the hell are you?" he asked and he acted entitled to an answer.

"I'm Rex's brother. Rex was the man you killed tonight." I figured I'd put a point on it for him.

"No shit?" Now here was that boxer's confidence I was talking about. He showed no fear. If I was there to kill him he knew he could defend himself. But I was just there to talk. Honestly.

# 8

*Fokoli*

Bob got himself together, for the most part, by the time we got to Hobbes's house. But he was still a little weak-kneed. A couple of squad cars sat in the drive with their lights flashing. I'd kept the lights on my car off because Bob said it gave him a headache. Christ, he could be an embarrassment sometimes. I opened the door and helped him out. He stumbled up the curved driveway and got sick in the grass. I dragged his sorry ass back to the car.

"Oh, Jesus," he said. "Oh, God."

"What's up, Bob?" I asked, trying like hell to keep my temper in check. He was starting to remind me a little of my wife on a bender.

"Don't know, Dean," he said. "Bad clams or something."

"First rule of police work, Bob, never lie to the guy training you. It's bad form."

One of the uniforms wandered over and I flashed my badge so he wouldn't chase us off. "Is he all right?" He didn't want to get too close to Bob.

I shook my head as I lit a cigarette. "Says he ate bad clams."

"Shouldn't eat clams in K.C., son."

Bob retched again.

"Plus," I said, leaning against the car, "He's part girl."

That got a laugh from the cop.

I kept the cigarette pinched between my lips as I helped Bob into the car. I made him roll down his window, thinking the night air would help.

"I'm sorry, Dean," he said. "His face was . . ." He looked like he was going to get sick again, so I motioned for him to keep quiet. Bob had seen bodies before, like anyone in homicide. But he was still new and the bodies he'd seen so far had usually been killed with a gun. He'd seen head shots, chest shots, gut shots. He'd even worked a case with me where a wife used a car to kill her cheating husband. He was pretty much severed in half. But his face was recognizable. His legs were easily identified too. It was just the stuff in the middle that was all mushed up.

Hobbes was different. Hobbes's head was brain pudding and what was worse—someone had done that with their fists. It was the sort of violence that was up close and personal. Some of us aren't able to handle the up close and personal stuff. The fact that I could left me a little cold inside.

I thought about the bloody gloves . . . and Jimmy Scoggins holding them close to his chest, wondering if those gloves were what crushed Hobbes's face. Then I thought about Chicago and what it meant if those guys were in town whacking our informants. Guys like Hobbes did a little business with both sides. The cops knew about it. Chicago wasn't supposed to. If this was a Chicago job . . .

Thinking like that gave me a headache, so I stopped.

I left Bob in the car and told the uniforms I was going in to have a look around. "He's got good beer in the icebox," one of the cops said. I figured he was joking. Hobbes hadn't seemed like a beer man. He was more of a wine from a brown paper bag sort of a guy. But if I was wrong about it . . . well, it wouldn't be the first time.

Another uniform sat inside the front door. He'd dragged what looked like a dining room chair out to sit on and he was thumbing through a girly magazine, ogling a blond in a two-piece bathing suit. I flashed my badge and he motioned me past with a grand gesture. "Don't work too hard," I said.

He grunted and went back to picturing himself with dames he'd never stand a chance with. The foyer was small, with a narrow stairway on my left leading to the second floor. To my right was a set of white pocket doors. I slid them open and poked my head inside. Living room, real uptown; white carpet, white furniture, white brick on the fireplace. I gave a low whistle and felt nervous about stepping on that carpet, so I backed out. The cop in the foyer had managed to plant his fat ass right in front of another door. I got him to move over so I could check it out. It opened to a narrow corridor leading straight back to the kitchen with a small bathroom opening off to the left, under the stairs.

The cop outside had lied about the good beer. There was nothing but a bottle of milk in the icebox. A coffee pot sat on the stove and I peeked inside, half expecting to find a wad of cash. Just old coffee.

I made my way back to the living room and stood just outside the big double doors. I figured this was the place he tried to impress people and as I stood there I even tried to imagine Hobbes in a suit, swirling brandy in a snifter as he talked it up with the big boys. But it didn't fit. Nothing here fit. My guess was that Hobbes wanted to own this place just so he could say he owned it. And I'd be willing to bet he used it for a tax break somehow too. Maybe he trained boxers in the basement or something.

At any rate, I needed to check it out, so I made sure my shoes were clean and I headed in. If being in that room made a guy like me feel clumsy, I couldn't begin to imagine how it made Hobbes feel.

Hobbes had invested in only one piece of art. And he hung it above the fireplace. I looked behind it to make sure it wasn't hiding a safe. It wasn't.

I tossed the cushions and looked under the furniture. Nothing. Looked like Hobbes hadn't used this place much. I backed out and made my way up the staircase to the second floor. Three bedrooms and only one was furnished—with a dirty mattress on the floor. My guess was that Hobbes didn't have many guests, overnight or otherwise.

What clothes he had he kept in piles in the middle of the floor. The carpet here had been white once. Time, as well as Hobbes's filth, had worn it to a dull gray, making me more certain that Hobbes rarely used the living room. There were more girly magazines like the one the cop in the foyer was reading scattered here and there. What was the saying?

"Those who can, do. Those who can't, look at dirty pictures?" Something like that.

"Radio call for you, Detective." It was the guy from the foyer.

I headed downstairs again and took the radio the uniformed cop handed me. "Yeah," I said. I walked into the kitchen.

"We've got a line on Delancey's place." It was Captain Tolene.

"Is Delancey talking?" I asked. I was opening kitchen drawers, looking for some sign that Hobbes had been part human. I found only loose cigarettes, spilled coffee grounds and dirty silverware.

"Don't know yet."

"Where's he live?"

"He's in a flophouse over on Elm—the kind of joint that rents rooms by the week."

"No kidding," I said, looking around Hobbes's fancy kitchen and thinking the guy was a bastard. So this is what he did with the kid's winnings. I always knew it. Hell everyone in K.C. knew it. Boxing managers were as crooked as my grandma's spine. But it was another thing to have the crookedness of it stare you in the face.

I'd been on Elm Street a time or two.

It was a bad place.

"There's a squad car on the way," he said. "If they find Delancey they'll hold him until you get there."

And I thought, yeah, great—a squad car on the way, running lights and sirens loud enough to make everybody on Delancey's block disappear . . . including Delancey. It didn't matter if any of them did anything wrong. When anybody over on Elm saw a cop, they ran. I always thought it was funny that the streets over in that neck of the woods were named after trees: Elm, Oak, Pine, Poplar, Ash. Prettiest names. Ugliest streets.

Tolene hung up and I settled back into my search of Hobbes's place, wanting to get done soon so I could check in on Laura before swinging down to Delancey's. She'd been falling asleep on the couch with her bottle lately, head thrown back, mouth wide open. If she got sick in the night and choked—well, let's just say I didn't need another death on my conscience.

I opened cupboards, shoving aside glasses, dishes, wadded up bags and dirty linens. What were linens doing in the kitchen cupboards?

"Everything okay in here?" The beat cop said from the kitchen door.

"I'm in a hurry. You want to help with this search."

His eyes lit up. He put the magazine on the kitchen counter. "Sure. Beats looking at what I can't get."

I didn't say anything to that. "Start upstairs in Hobbes's bedroom."

I heard his feet on the stairs and finished my search of the kitchen. The bathroom off the kitchen was nothing more than a sink and toilet and I figured that the main bath must be upstairs. I washed my hands in the sink but there was no towel to dry them on, so I used my jacket. The beat cop was standing in the middle of Hobbes's bedroom when I walked in. "You notice how bad it stinks in here?" he asked.

"You ever smell Hobbes when he was alive?"

He gave a half smile. "This smells like animal."

My sense of smell isn't that great, but I took a whiff. What do you know? He was right. I drew my gun. A guy could never be too careful, right? Hobbes was just the kind of guy to keep a bear to help his boxers train.

We backed out of the bedroom and made our way toward the other two. I took a quick peek in the bathroom. Clear.

The second bedroom was clear. The third bedroom was locked. "You check this yet?" he asked.

I shook my head and pulled my gun. He drew his too. I stepped back to kick the door in, but the over eager son-of-a-bitch shot the knob off.

"Jesus Christ," I said.

He shrugged. "Sorry."

A mad scuttling sound came from inside the room and I

pushed the door open, now able to smell the full extent of the filth on the other side. "Hell," I said.

"Oh God," the beat cop said, holstering his gun and covering his mouth with both hands. "What are they?"

"Chinchillas," I said as I watched gray wads of fur scurry over the shit encrusted floor. "I'd say about fifty grand worth." I holstered my gun and backed out of the room.

"What do we do?" he asked.

"You stand here and hold the door closed," I said. "Don't let any of them out." I grinned. "Shouldn't have shot off that knob. It would have been easier to keep it closed."

I handed him the gun he dropped. "Try not to shoot any. They're evidence."

I whistled as I made my way downstairs and outside into the fresh air. Chinchillas meant fur. In K.C., no one was set up for this sort of thing. Fur meant mob. It also meant Hobbes was probably axed by crime goons he cheated out of a fur hat and stole set.

I did a little jig as I made my way out into the driveway and climbed into the car. "What are you so happy about?" Bob asked.

"Mob killing," I said. "We'll never solve it."

"So?"

"Less paperwork."

I didn't bother stopping at home to check on Laura. I'd swing by Delancey's, ask a few questions, get tough when he didn't want to give answers, teach Bob White a thing or two about technique. The night was winding down. I'd be in bed by three o'clock. Four at the latest.

Sometimes I can be so wrong.

# 9

*Ray*

Delancey's face was puffy from the fight but not bad like someone who usually had gone the distance with Rex. He stood his ground while I stepped into his room. The door swung shut behind me on crooked hinges.

We sized each other up for a second.

"Real sorry about your brother, y'know?"

It was almost sincere. He talked in that rural Midwest twang that told me he was from a wheat farm in the west of the state, not a Kansas City native.

"What happened?"

"What happened!? You were there, you saw what happened. The ref should have stepped in earlier. I'm no judge of how much is too much. That's what he's there for."

He stopped short of saying, "Don't blame me."

"Who set it up? Who gave you the gloves?"

"What gloves?" He straightened up to his full height, a good four or five inches taller than me.

"The weighted gloves. The ones that killed Rex."

"Look, I don't know what—"

"I just came from Hobbes," I cut him off. He stayed cut off. "I know it was a fix. I don't guess you wanted Rex dead since we've never seen you before so I want to know who did."

We both stood firm in our spots on opposite ends of the room, a room shaped like a boxing ring.

He let his shoulders slip a little and lowered his voice to friendly. "Look, it wasn't supposed to go like that. The ref came in too late. I was supposed to . . ." He hesitated before spilling it. "I was supposed to just take Rex out for a little while. There are some big fights going on over the summer to make a play for a new state champ and they didn't want Rex to screw it up."

"Who is 'they'?"

"I don't know a damn thing. Hobbes set it all up. Honest."

He was adamant but not pleading. I was grateful to him for giving me some answers. I knew Hobbes was too small time to set up something like this without it being an order from somewhere higher up. I wasn't sure how much I could get from Delancey but I had to try.

"You're up late," I said.

He nodded, unsure of me.

"You waiting for Jimmy?" I remembered the name from when I surprised Hobbes. It was worth a shot.

"Jimmy who?" he countered.

"Jimmy with the money. Your money. Your cut."

He had no answer for that. I reached into my back pocket and took out the envelope. I was letting my guard down but he took his eyes off me and laid them onto the cash like a hungry man seeing a steak. Watch their eyes, always the eyes.

"Where is Jimmy?" he asked.

"With Hobbes."

He nodded at the envelope. "Is that for me then? You're delivering it?"

"Not exactly." I put the money back in my front pocket this time; harder for him to swipe it. I felt the handle of my razor in there, grateful to have it with me. In case. "If you tell me who hired you to use the gloves on Rex then you can have it. This was Hobbes's share so I'd bet it's more than what you were promised."

He reached up and touched the swelling on his cheek from the fight, thinking.

I said what I thought he wanted to hear, "I won't go to the cops. I want to know for myself."

"I honestly don't know who set it up. It was set up before I got involved."

"Any name will do."

"I'm telling you, it was supposed to be another fighter. An old nigger who's no good for nothing except taking a fall these days. But they saw Rex fight and decided they needed someone better otherwise Rex might knock him out before it even got to the glove switch. Plus, it had to be probable for someone to hit him that hard. That old nigger didn't have the arm anymore."

I hate that word. I hate people that use it. I bit my tongue.

Delancey was oblivious. "So they brought me in. They think I might have a shot at the title someday," he said with some pride. A sin.

I knew about an older black fighter called the Dive Bomber since he hadn't fought a legit fight in a decade. He was of Pop's generation. I knew his boy Velvy, about Rex's age, from when we were kids. I doubted if it was the same guy, but it was a place to start anyhow.

"You don't know his name by any chance, do you?"

"No. Just some old nigger."

I bit my tongue again. Delancey was an idiot. He was being used by the Chicago boys. He got talked in to this deal with Rex and didn't know when to hold back. He was a bigot and a prideful son-of-a-bitch. But he had answered my questions. Maybe I was tired or maybe I just didn't like the way Hobbes's death was sitting with me, but I decided to let him alone.

I reached down and got out the envelope again. I picked out a few bills and tossed them on the floor. "You didn't give me much to go on but that's okay. It's clear you don't know much." I doubted he caught the dig.

"But that's my money." He ignored the bills on the floor and pointed at the envelope I tucked back in my pocket.

"It's Hobbes's money. Your share might be in here, but I bet it wasn't much more than that." I indicated the scattered bills on the floor.

Delancey couldn't argue too hard with me. He wanted to say that he had earned it, but he earned it by killing my brother. He kept quiet and clenched his right fist.

I turned my back to Delancey, holding my breath and listening for any indication that he was going to jump me.

He hadn't moved an inch since I walked in.

I took a step toward the door.

"I hope you find that old nigger. I'd hate to think what I'd do if I saw my brother killed. 'Course if Rex had better form on his defense I wouldn't have been able to beat him to death. It all could have gone to plan. He'd have a hell of a headache but he'd still have a head."

I tensed. Was he baiting me or was he just that stupid? Rex's defense was my best work. He was flawless. It was so rare for another fighter to score a head shot on Rex he could have fought wearing glasses.

Delancey kept talking. "It's kind of his own fault. I told them they didn't need to worry about him, I could beat him fair and square any day of the week. I'm the best there is in this state. And if I wasn't yesterday, I sure as hell am today with him gone."

Fighter's confidence. Cockiness. He was using it to needle me. He was making a mistake.

I couldn't take Delancey in a fight and he knew it. He was too big. There was a lot of ground to cover if I spun and attacked and he'd be ready so I took one more step to the door and put a hand on the knob, still holding my breath.

That's when I heard the clomping of his feet across the bare floor. Flat-footed, just like I told Rex.

I spun and he was aiming at me like a howitzer, his right arm drawn back in firing position and all four knuckles white in the grip of his fist. As I spun I came out with my razor and thumbed it open. He got to me first.

I faded right and his huge fist, much bigger up close and personal, glanced off my shoulder and ricocheted into the door. I thought I heard a hinge split. I held the razor and swung my arm around and slashed down across his back through his t-shirt. The split in the fabric oozed red.

Delancey spun, fist still clenched. He sucked air through his teeth, trying to fight off the pain of the cut on his back. He threw a big roundhouse right at me that was easy to dodge. I jabbed with a left to the body to keep him off balance and then slashed down again with the razor to his right arm. I caught him across the triceps and felt the razor slow with the friction of the cut. This time he cried out.

He came at me again with a right and I put up both arms to block. He knocked my arms back into me and then jabbed with a left to the body. Sparring with Rex had gotten me used to curling up in a defensive position to wait out the storm. This storm was short.

I opened back up and swung out with the razor. He put up a hand to defend and I slashed him across the right palm. Blood splattered on the dirty wood floor.

With a grunt he rushed me and wrapped me up in a clinch. He pinned my arms down by my sides so I couldn't slash at him any more. He rammed us both back and I hit the door frame hard. We were face to face and I could feel his breath and spit hitting my cheek as he huffed. His eyes were wild, wilder than in the fight with Rex, and they gave away how much pain he was in. But still he kept fighting.

He managed to get one hand inside my pocket and he latched on to the envelope of money, then he let me go. He stepped back holding the money in his good hand. I chased him, no point in hanging back against the ropes now. He raised his right hand again, and again I cut him. The second cut ran right across the first, making an X on his palm that drooled blood down his fingers.

He punched out with his left making a fist around the envelope and caught me on the cheek. I leaned back with it but I knew he had gotten me pretty good. I also knew he couldn't counter with his right so I had him until he could recover and wind up again with his left. I came up and forward with the razor and caught him at his left ear and pulled down. The razor dug in and cut a deep path across his cheek and, with a twist of the wrist, down along his jaw right through the dimple in his chin.

He bellowed and grabbed his face, pushing the envelope of money up against it. He was no longer on the attack. I readied myself in a stance, prepared to defend or to hack and slash more if needed, but he staggered back and his right foot slipped in the pool of blood on the floor. He went down flailing like a grizzly bear trying to use ice skates.

Delancey sank back to the bed and sat down hard, dropping the envelope and letting the cut on his face open. Bone peeked through.

He was weak from the blood loss and had that look a fighter gets when he knows he's lost the fight. Trouble was, Hobbes wasn't here to throw in the towel.

"It wasn't supposed to go this way," he said in a whisper.

I stayed in my stance, not wanting to be rope-a-doped. Blood dripped from his palm and down his fingers, his arm ran rivulets of blood onto the floor, blood from his back soaked the bed sheet and his face drooped and hung open.

"I didn't kill him," he said.

"Yes, you did," I replied, arms up, fists closed, feet moving by instinct.

"I didn't mean to."

"I know."

He leaned back and flopped on the tired springs of the bed. His right arm hung loosely at his side. He brought his left hand up and clamped it to his cheek, pushing the loose flap of flesh into place. I could see his heart was still beating by the steady pulse of blood pushing from his many wounds. It wouldn't be for long.

I moved to the bed, unable to avoid getting blood on the soles of my shoes. I picked up the envelope, pulled out bills not soaked with blood, and stuffed them in my pocket. I dug a towel out of Delancey's gym bag and used it to wipe most of the blood from my feet.

I didn't mean to kill Delancey. I thought on the irony of that as I cleaned up. He hadn't meant to kill Rex; I hadn't meant to kill him. It made my head spin. Delancey attacked me. I had to defend myself. But now I was really in the shit. Two dead because of me and I still had more work to do.

I heard movement downstairs. The buzzer rang; the old crone's voice penetrated the floorboards. I had to get out of here.

I slid out the door and went up one flight, knowing there

was some commotion down below. Once on the fourth floor I headed for the end of the hall and out onto the fire escape, scrambled down the four flights, and into the alley behind the building. I crept up and peered around the front and saw just what I didn't want to. Cops.

I beat it back down the alley, on my way to Negrotown to look up an old friend.

# 10

*Fokoli*

There's something about an empty cop car—lights flashing, siren quiet—that thickens my blood and turns it cold. I could tell the sight affected Bob the same way. "Uh-oh," he said, and I thought he might as well have said something like "Gee whiz," or "Golly," because "Uh-oh" was just about as dumb a thing as a cop could say.

I told him to shut his trap and double check the address.

"1215 Elm," he said. "Like I already told you."

I pulled the car over and cut the engine. The abandoned squad car had been pulled into the curb at an odd angle, so its back end stuck out into the middle of the road. I stood beside it, and looked in the window. Car Fourteen. The one Tolene had sent to check things out. I swiped a hand across the back of my neck and looked up toward the crumbling Victorian monstrosity sagging in the middle of a brown lawn. Sickly yellow light shone through every window, piercing ripped shades and spilling out into the dark.

"Maybe something happened to Delancey," Bob said, once again pointing out the obvious.

I kept quiet and walked back to our car to pull the keys from the ignition. No sense leaving it to be stolen. Even a cop car wasn't safe in this neighborhood.

A toothless man in a torn shirt and shorts stood on the porch, gesturing for us to hurry, hurry, hurry. His fly hung open, allowing a withered penis to spill out the front and dribble urine down his leg.

"Oh, Christ," Bob said as we reached the top of the porch steps and I poked him. Hard.

The old man put a hand on my shoulder. "Bad in there, boys. Bad. You tell your mother she's late." He muttered more crazy gibberish but we didn't have the time to listen. I patted his hand and moved to walk past him into the house, but he stopped me. "Spare a dime?"

I looked at Bob. "Give him a dime," I said. I would have, but I didn't have one. Five months ago I'd have shoved the old man out of my way and moved past. I guess a man can change. Right?

I had my hand on the peeling wood of the screen door when the inner door was pulled open and the screen kicked into my face. I reeled back a step and almost knocked the man with the penis off the porch.

Bob helped me regain my balance. I think he helped the old man too because his hand was wet and smelled like piss. "Back off," I said.

"Who the hell are you?" Her voice was deep. Like Mae West with balls. I only saw her silhouette, dark in the artificial brightness of the doorway. But I saw enough to tell me she was big. Tits like bowling balls at one time. Age had pulled them down to the level of her waist and I couldn't help wondering if she was related to the old man with the gaping fly and the shiny new dime courtesy of Bob.

I flashed my badge. "Detective Dean Fokoli. This is my partner, Bob White."

The woman backed up a step and let us in. "We're looking for a boxer," I told her, letting my eyes wander around the house. Papers and laundry littered the floor. What wallpaper was left on the wall was torn in places, leaving long, jagged scars stained brown underneath.

"Yeah," she said, fishing for a cigarette in her sweater pocket. Or maybe she was scratching one of those low hanging tits. I hoped Bob wasn't getting turned on. She pulled out a smoke and a match and lit up. Her hands were stained brown and she smelled like cat shit. Or maybe there was chinchilla on my shoe. I didn't know and I didn't care. The day was starting to catch me. It would overtake me soon and I was starting to feel bad about not going home to check on Laura yet.

She jerked her head toward the stairs. "He's upstairs with the cops." She dropped the match on the floor and squinted at us with one eye while she inhaled. When she spoke again, her words spewed out in a yellow cloud. "Son-of-a-bitch bolted a one hundred pound bag to my ceiling. Do you have any idea the damage that can do to a place?"

Me and Bob looked around a little, wondering if she really cared.

"Someone's going to have to compensate me for that," she said. "I got rights." She started up the stairs and motioned for us to follow.

I went first.

She had brown streaks on her legs.

Cat shit.

Dear God, please let it be cat shit.

"Goddamn boxers making noise all times of the day and night."

"You have other boxers living here?" I asked.

She didn't answer. We were at the second floor landing and she was losing her air. What breath she had left, she used for the cigarette as we made our way up to three.

The two cops from Car Fourteen were in the room. Gunderson and Samms. "There's the mess that's left of your friend," she breathed. I told her to wait in the hall and me and Bob went inside.

Gunderson winked and shook my hand. He was on the take and I could tell he thought I was still the same old Fokoli. Samms hated me so he stood back where he didn't have to look me in the eye. "Fokoli," Gunderson said, ignoring Bob. "We got here too late."

There was blood pretty much everywhere. "These your shoe prints?" I asked him, looking at the crimson stains tracked to the bed and out the door.

Gunderson laughed like we were old friends. "Not ours."

I looked over my shoulder at Bob to make sure he wasn't going to cheese it on me. He was steady. He'd seen blood like this before. We all had.

"What's the story?" Bob asked.

"Nobody broke in," Samms said. "Landlady heard a knock about an hour ago. She buzzed whoever it was inside and we showed up awhile later. Scared him off, I think because nobody remembers seeing him go out the front door."

I was only halfway listening to him. Delancey made it to the bed before he died . . . like maybe he knew he was hurt but thought, If I could just lay down for a minute I'll be fine.

He had laid one hand over his left cheek, like he was resting. His face, his arms, his chest, and the entire bed were soaked with blood. I stepped closer. His knuckles were a little bit bruised, but whether from the fight with Rex or from the go-round with his killer was hard to say. Other than the blood, the bed, and a boxer's bag, the room was empty. There was a rust stained sink hanging onto the wall by some crumbled plaster and a rusted pipe, and a duffel bag on the floor.

And a wad of bloody money on his chest.

I used my handkerchief to pick it up. The way it was folded, the way the blood stains stopped sharply in places, made it obvious there had been more.

"Why do you suppose they didn't take all the money?" Bob asked. "I'd think the mob wouldn't care about blood on their money."

"Yeah, you'd think so," I said. "Let's roll him over." I was looking at the bed sheet, saturated with blood beneath him. The place smelled like Hobbes's gym. I preferred the smell of gun powder.

Bob and I turned Delancey. Gunderson and Samms helped. We got a good look at his right palm then—filleted to expose the bone inside.

"Defensive wounds," Bob said.

And then we saw his face. As we rolled him, his hand fell away from his cheek. He'd been cut wide there, again, all the way down to the bone. The skin hung in a thick flap. Even Gunderson turned away and he had bigger balls for this sort of thing than anyone I'd ever met.

We looked the back over—criss-crossed with slices. "Looks like a straight razor," I said.

Bob agreed.

"You're handling this better," I said.

"His head still looks like a head," Bob said, but his face faltered a little and I could tell he was still bothered by Hobbes.

We moved away from the body and into the heart of the room, next to the punching bag. "Any rumors about new mob hit men?" I asked.

Gunderson and Samms shook their heads. Samms still wouldn't look me in the eye but I knew him to be an honest cop. He was telling the truth.

"Any skirmishes between families we should know about?"

Again, they shook their heads, but they looked nervous, like they were thinking the same thing as me and Bob. The goons in K.C. were small time. If this was mob it was big. And God help us all.

"Maybe someone in the neighborhood wants a little more power," Samms said, his voice soft.

I nodded and said, "Could be."

I went back out into the hall to talk to the landlady. She was scratching her tits, smoking another cigarette. Six or seven butts littered the floor around her feet. "You about done in there?" she asked. "A gal needs her sleep, you know?"

"When did Delancey rent this room?" I asked.

She blew a cloud of smoke in my face and said, "Last year. I don't know the date."

"You keep records?" Bob asked.

She snorted. "Most folks stay a week or less, son. And if I started asking questions of every Joe that takes a room here, this place would always be empty."

"When last year?"

She shrugged. "How the hell should I know? Some fat guy in a sweater set it up for him."

Hobbes. But we already knew that.

We took the landlady's name, Georgia Lynch, and phone number and headed back out to the unmarked car we drove.

"Want to go file these reports tonight?" Bob asked.

I nodded. Tolene would expect it. And Jimmy Scoggins

had spent a little time in lock-up by now, so maybe he'd be a little more loose-lipped.

I was dead on my feet and still thinking about Laura. But she'd have to wait.

# 11

*Ray*

I stopped to wash my hands in a leaky standpipe about a block away. The blood was starting to dry and I had to scrub to get rid of it. I washed off the razor too and nearly cut myself trying to get blood off the blade. My shoes and pants would have to wait. I'd have to do my best not to get stopped by a cop or I was done for. Two different blood types on me, Hobbes and Delancey. It was like serving up a Thanksgiving meal to the coppers, only I was the turkey with all the trimmings.

My adrenaline kicked in. I started to sweat and my hands got a little shaky. It happens that way when you learn to control yourself for the ring; it's after when it all hits you. I killed two people tonight. Oh my God.

The row with Delancey was ugly. I reviewed the play-by-play in my head and I didn't like what I saw. It was self-defense, sure, but unless you were there in the room you wouldn't buy it. Delancey all hacked up and blood all over the place, like he was just a side of beef on the wrong side of a slaughterhouse. It looked like I went there for a reason.

Pop always told us that if you get into a fight outside of the ring you don't want to play it for the decision. You hit that guy until he goes down and you hit him so he'll stay down. Only thing worse than a guy who is pissed off enough to come at you in the first place is a guy who's doubly pissed because now you hit him. Put him down so that when you walk away, he can't get up and follow you. I guess I did that with Delancey.

Two people. Damn. I washed the blood off my hands, but I still had blood on my hands, you know? Didn't make a whole lot of sense but I wasn't exactly thinking straight at the moment.

I had to get across town and hope that Velvy still lived at

the same address. I hadn't heard that he struck it rich or anything so there was no reason for him to move, but I hadn't heard much of anything about him in a few years so anything was possible.

We used to pal around when we were kids. Pop and his dad used to fight on the same card quite a bit so us kids would always be hanging out in the locker rooms together. We didn't know from black and white. Under the bleachers it's all the same. I guess I always wondered why we never left out of the same door, but I just figured we lived on opposite sides of town.

Velvy was Rex's age and I kind of looked after both of them when Pop was in the ring or when Velvy's dad, Clark, was fighting. I think they only fought each other once. Pop won. He hit Clark in the fifth and I didn't even think it was that good of a shot but Clark went down and stayed down. When I was thirteen I didn't know what taking a dive looked like.

Rex and I used to go over to play on Velvy's street. There were always tons of kids outside playing stick ball or making up games that we didn't have equipment for. We used to get nickels and go see the matinee shows. We loved the Our Gang shorts. They always had black kids and white kids playing together so we thought it was like that all over, but none of Velvy's other friends seemed to know any white boys.

Velvy was skinny and fast and funny as hell. He had the craziest expressions for things. "Nigger talk," Pop would call it and Mom would slap his hand. It was Mom who told us that there was no real difference between a black man and white man. She told me something that stuck with me as a truth that I couldn't deny. She said if you look at the world from above, like God, all men look the same. Just like little ants. If you get up close like you or me then all men, every man, looks different and if everyone is different then nobody is any more or less different than anyone else. That seemed true. Then she said that if you look even closer, like a scientist would or a doctor, we're all just molecules and atoms and we all look exactly the same again. I don't know if it makes a whole lot of logical sense, but it made sense to me and I still believe it.

When I got to the edge of the Eighteenth and Vine district, what they called Negrotown, I stopped for awhile to catch my breath. It wasn't written on a map anywhere the way Chinatown was but everyone had always called it Negrotown and it was well understood what streets defined the borders. It's like having a funeral parlor in your neighborhood, everyone can tell you exactly where it is but you never see anyone going in or out and when you walk past it you find a reason to look the other way. White people, adults anyway, almost never went inside the confines of Negrotown. I'd stick out like a snowball on a coal pile but I had to find Velvy and try to get him to take me to see Clark.

My heart slowed, the adrenaline faded, but the weight of what I had just done to Hobbes and Delancey wasn't any lighter on my shoulders. Right then, though, I had to ignore it and keep moving forward.

I went up the street, turned left and made for the apartment building where Velvy used to live.

It was late but people were awake and music floated down from open windows. Arguments were loud and echoed sharply between buildings. Two boys who couldn't have been more than ten crossed the street in front of me and both did double takes at the white man in their neighborhood. They should have been home in bed.

At the next corner were three guys hanging out the way men do. These fellows were drunk, that much was obvious. They noticed me in all my obviousness too.

"What the fuck...?" one of them said out loud and even rubbed his eyes to make sure it wasn't just the cheap wine playing tricks on him. He had dandruff in his hair that made it look like someone had spilled a salt shaker over his head.

The tall one in the middle turned and nearly spit out his mouthful of wine with laughter. He choked it down but some drops clung to his bushy mustache.

"What the hell are you doing here, Cracker?"

"You lost or something?" said the first dandruff-covered guy.

"Just looking for a friend." I kept on walking. They followed but not without some difficulty. The third, portly one almost didn't make it across the street he was stumbling so badly. I didn't figure him for a hangover tomorrow though; you have to stop drinking for that to happen.

I led the trio as they stumbled behind me like Keystone Cops. I really didn't want another fight tonight.

"Hey man, what friend you got who lives over here?"

I couldn't see which one was speaking. I just kept on walking.

"Shit, Cracker here is looking for pussy."

"Is that right?" another voice called after me. "Are you here looking for pussy? That the kind of friend you was talking about?"

"Nope. Just a friend." I kept my stride up and things started to look familiar. I knew I was on the right block. I used to play stick ball right on the sidewalk. I saw the fire hydrant we used as first base and the lamp post that was home base.

"Maybe he came around looking for dope."

"That's most all the white crackers who come here are lookin' for. Pussy an' dope." They all laughed. I heard back slapping.

I knew I was on the right block but none of the specific buildings looked familiar. The stickball landmarks I remembered, but I didn't know if I was ever even in Velvy's apartment. Two white kids in Negrotown was one thing, but getting familiar enough to go inside an apartment? Velvy would catch shit about that for sure after we left. Probably from these three goons who for all I know I used to play stickball with. But I needed help so I had to ask.

"Any of you boys know Velvy?"

"Did you just call me boy?" the tall one said, stretching erect to look intimidating and brushing off his mustache.

"You guys, you fellas. You know Velvy Dane?"

"What the fuck you want with Velvy?"

"I told you he's a friend of mine."

I got scrutinized up and down by six eyes, all bloodshot. I guess I passed the test.

"Three doors down. One-seventy-eight. Number three. I guess you ain't such good friends you don't know where he lives," said Mr. Dandruff.

"I guess not," I said.

I turned and went to the address and rang the buzzer for number three. The trio stayed behind and watched me, commenting to themselves.

No one answered. I buzzed again but I knew it was useless.

"Try the Eight Ball," the mustache yelled.

"Cracker," Dandruff added.

I looked back to them and they were pointing straight to the next corner. When I turned that way I could read the neon sign of a pool hall.

"Thanks," I shouted back.

The only thing more obvious than me walking the streets around here would be me stepping into a pool hall that was full and noisy, but if Velvy was inside I'd find out in a hurry.

I took a deep breath. I don't even play pool.

I pushed through the doors and the music didn't stop, the conversation didn't go silent. I got a few looks but mostly people were busy doing their thing and didn't seem to care if I was there or not. I scanned the room but it was dark except for the harsh squares of light over the pool tables, of which there were six, and it was smoky so I couldn't see to the back of the room. The jukebox was playing a Big Bill Broonzy record but I couldn't tell you the name and it was hard to hear over all the conversations, loud and loose with alcohol.

I don't frequent bars. It doesn't fit with the training regimen. Plus, whenever Rex and I did go out to celebrate a victory in some small town, if it came out that Rex was a fighter then some young hot shot would step up and try to prove himself to his girl and pick a fight. That's where I did most of my punching. The last thing Rex needed was to break his knuckles on some drunken loudmouth out to prove the size of his dick to a woman who already knows the sad truth of it.

I stepped up to the bar figuring the bartender always knew what was going on in his joint. He looked up at me and for a second I think he thought I was a cop but then he saw my outfit and realized that couldn't be true.

"Yeah?" he grunted.

"You know a guy named Velvy Dane?"

"Who wants to know?"

"My name's Ray. I'm an old friend of his."

"So you already know him. Why do you care if I do?"

I couldn't blame the guy for being suspicious. "I need to find him. Can you tell me if he's been in here tonight?"

"I didn't even say if I knew the cat or not."

A couple next to me moved away. Thankfully they took their lit cigarettes with them.

"I need to speak with him. I'm not a cop." That didn't impress him.

The trio of drunks all pressed through the door at once, causing a minor pile up. They were looking for me and I wasn't hard to spot. They all three stumbled forward in a clump. The tall one with the mustache put a hand on my shoulder to steady himself.

"Find your pussy, Cracker?"

"All right, get the fuck out," said the bartender. Dandruff dropped white flakes on the bar where they stuck to pools of vanishing beer foam.

"No, no," I protested. I did not want to make enemies. "These guys are drunk. I'm just looking for Velvy. Have you seen him or not?" Mustache had a firm grip on my shoulder and I wasn't going anywhere until he thought I should.

"Who's gonna fix up Cracker here with some pussy?" he shouted to the establishment. We got a few crooked glances and a few laughs. I needed to get out before things got ugly.

"Guys, I should go now." His grip was still hard like I was the only thing holding him up.

"I thought you was looking for your friend," said Dandruff. I could smell the wine on his breath—tonight's wine and the wine from the last month. I tried to lift off Mustache's hand without being obvious. The third of the trio finally spoke up as he stumbled in front of Dandruff to be heard.

"He don't know no Velvet. I don't know no Velvet. Just what the hell are you doing down here anyway?" His breath was as angry as he was.

"Listen, fellas . . ."

"Stupid Cracker." I got a shove from Bad Breath. The bartender tried to head off a scuffle.

"All right, take it outside."

"Look, these guys are the trouble, not me."

Dandruff stepped even closer to me and put a foot on top of my foot so I couldn't move now from two points, the hand on my shoulder and the boot on my foot. I really didn't want to have to throw a punch.

"Just say you want some pussy, boy, and I'm sure there's ten fine ladies in here will take your money, long as it's green."

Dandruff brought his wine bottle up and it smashed on the brass railing of the bar. Whether that was intentional or not I don't know, but it made more people look and even paused the game at the nearest pool table. Now Dandruff gripped a broken bottle neck in my direction and the bartender was reaching down for something. I hoped it was a baseball bat and not a shotgun.

Most bar fights start off slow. The guys don't really want to fight but each wants the other to back down, so there is posturing and posing and it lasts until someone backs down or a punch is thrown. There was no posturing with this fight. It started in a flash.

The first punch came from nowhere. Funny thing was it landed on Dandruff. It was quick as lightning and it retracted and then shot out again at Mustache. Both shots hit right on the nose and both men staggered back. In their staggering they bowled over Bad Breath and he went down without ever being hit. I turned and found myself face to face with Velvy.

"Where've you been?" I asked him, smiling.

"Where've I been? Where you been? I haven't seen shit from you in six, seven years."

Dandruff was back to moving forward with the broken bottle out in front. I lashed out with a right jab that made his head nod back and forth a few times. When he didn't go down I swung wide with my left into his gut and that dropped him.

My hopes for the bartender's weapon didn't come true. He held a shotgun leveled at me and Velvy.

"I see you still telegraphing your left," said Velvy, smiling at me. He took my arm and led us both outside.

# 12

*Fokoli*

Captain Tolene was a strategist. He considered himself familiar with Freud's philosophy about the human psyche—there's a sexual reason behind every action. Combine that with the old saying, "For every action there's an equal and opposite reaction," and you've got one sexually deviant world to patrol. And in the past I'd loved every minute of it.

"Fokoli," the captain shouted as I walked in, thinking about Laura, wondering if she was all right. "What have you got?"

"Not much," I said. "Delancey looks like filet mignon without the bacon. There was a wad of money on his chest. Bloody footprint at the scene. Lab is checking on that. The coroner wasn't there when we left."

He laughed and slapped me on the back and I thought maybe he was being just a little too friendly; but then, I'd trained myself to be suspicious of everyone lately.

Bob followed us into Tolene's office.

"Gentlemen," Tolene said, sliding into his chair and gesturing to the chairs across from him. Me and Bob sat down. "What else did you find?"

"Hobbes's place was full of chinchillas," I said. "I'm guessing fur trade through Chicago, but I can't be sure about that. If that is the case, we're going to need to get Chicago P.D. involved so we can have them watch the river for transport."

Tolene laughed about the chinchillas. He thought a roomful of rodents was funny. I figured it was only funny if you didn't have to smell them. He leaned back in his chair and laced his fingers behind his head. "You don't think they're carried over land?" he asked.

I shrugged. "Probably a lot easier to dump a load of chinchillas in the river if cops are after you than it is to turn them loose in the middle of Illinois."

"Exactly," Bob said.

Tolene nodded and touched his chin. "We'll transport the animals to a farm outside of town. From there, they'll be transported to the nearest chinchilla farm." Apparently, he liked saying chinchilla.

"You're not going to use them as bait for the bad guys?"

Tolene shook his head. "If Hobbes's death was due to mafia, and if mafia was behind the fur, then they already know about Hobbes' death. Fifty-thousand dollars worth of fur is small time to these boys. They'll let it go. They won't be happy about it, but they'll let it go anyway."

I nodded even though I didn't agree with him. I figured the fur would have been to Chicago mafia what sugar was to an anthill. But when Tolene got something in his head there was no arguing with him. I was also nervous because whoever whacked Hobbes and Delancey was streetwise and when streetwise gangsters start whacking each other, it's like tossing a lit match into a powder keg. When the blowup happened, it brought a turf war with it.

But there were those gloves clutched to the chest of a bawling black kid to think about too, and a manager with a dead brother to question—loose ends that didn't tie into the mafia theory.

"Jimmy Scoggins been processed yet?" I asked.

Tolene nodded. "Sure. But you and me got more to talk about." His eyes narrowed when he said that, so I knew it couldn't be good.

The last thing I wanted to do was talk to Tolene about anything other than the case. I tapped Bob on the shoulder. "Let's go talk to Jimmy." We both stood.

Tolene's face was red. "Just a goddamn minute," he said.

I opened the door and tried to meet Tolene's eye but I couldn't. I was losing my edge. "I'll be back," I promised.

But I could tell Tolene was angry.

Jimmy Scoggins looked small and scared in the dim

interrogation room. Some small part of me felt bad about that, but I had a killer to catch. The captain was thinking about fifty grand worth of stinky chinchillas, and Chicago mafia and I was thinking about how I was going to have to stop a mob war between Kansas City and Chicago if we didn't get this sorted out.

Me and Bob sat down at the steel table across from Jimmy.

"What do you want?" he asked. He had dark circles under his eyes and he was holding his neck at a funny angle, like maybe he'd been punched around a little in holding already.

"How's the holding cell?" I asked. "You got a boyfriend yet?"

"Fuck you."

I lit a cigarette and offered one to him. He just stared at me with black eyes full of hate—not only for me, but for every white man who ever wronged a black man. No one could stand up under that scrutiny, and after a minute I dropped my eyes under the pretense of looking for the ashtray.

"Delancey's dead." I let him chew on that for a minute while I watched his expression.

"I didn't have nothing to do with them chinchillas," he said. He was looking at Bob, like maybe Bob was more likely to believe him.

I felt Bob look at me. He hadn't quite mastered a poker face yet. Jimmy was nervous and his balls were shriveling. If we played it right, he'd start singing a nice little tune for us . . . that is if Bob didn't mess it up. For now, I ignored Bob's stare.

"What do you know about the chinchillas?" I asked.

Jimmy looked away and slouched in his chair, letting his head move a little too far in one direction and crying out when it caught on the kink.

"You get roughed up in holding?" Bob asked.

Jimmy didn't answer.

"Tell us about the chinchillas," Bob said. "Was

Delancey in on it?"

Jimmy sat for another minute and I decided to offer him a cigarette again. This time he took it and the deep drags he sucked in told me he wasn't as serious about his training as he'd like us to believe.

"Delancey didn't do much with them, I don't think. He spent time with Hobbes at the house, though." He shook his head. "Delancey was Hobbes's boy."

I didn't give a shit about the chinchillas. Stinky balls of fur. And it took about a million of those little suckers to make any sort of decent coat. But chinchillas were all we had right now, at least until we could put the screws to Jimmy to give us more.

"So you deliberately withheld what Hobbes and Delancey were doing from the police?" I asked.

Beads of sweat broke out on Jimmy's upper lip.

"Let's table that for a minute," I said. "Who killed Hobbes? You going to blame that on Chicago too?"

He kept his head cocked at that unnatural angle while he stared at his hands resting on the table. "It wasn't Chicago." He rubbed his thumbs together a little bit. The steel table was starting to get wet from the sweat coming off his palms.

"Who was it?" Bob asked. "Local guys, angry about the fight? Did Delancey mess it up?"

Jimmy shook his head as much as he could. I looked at Bob. "Get him some aspirin," I said.

Bob looked a little worried about that, like maybe it would be a bad idea to leave Jimmy alone with me. But he knew better than to argue. After he slipped out, I looked at Jimmy. And Jimmy looked at me.

"Fuck you," he said right off the bat.

"You see anybody leave the gym before you got there?"

He just stared at me.

I put my cigarette in the ashtray and rested my hands on the table. "We managed to get our hands on this shipment, but I'm pretty sure there were others. And I'm also pretty sure those other shipments were transported across state lines."

"Fuck you. I didn't raise no fur."

"That makes it a felony." I stood and paced, stuffing my hands in my pockets like I was real deep in thought. "You've had a rough couple of hours in holding." I made a show of looking him over. "Imagine what prison would mean for you."

I strolled over and pulled out my pack of cigarettes again. He readily took one and inhaled greedily when I lit it for him.

"I talk and he'll come for me," he said after a minute.

"Who?"

Jimmy shook his head.

The back of my hand was starting to itch and I wanted nothing more than to beat the shit out of the puny kid sitting there with his stiff neck and his "fuck you's." But sitting in lock up for a little longer would probably do just as well to loosen his tongue.

Bob came in with the aspirin and some water and I let Jimmy dose himself. "You got anything to say?" I asked. "Last chance."

"Fuck you."

I waved the guard in and he escorted Jimmy and his crooked neck back to holding.

"You get anything?" Bob asked.

I said I hadn't and we made our way back to Captain Tolene's office.

The I.A. guy was sitting across from Tolene. He stood when me and Bob walked in. "Gentlemen," he said. "This is Carter McWilliams from internal affairs."

We shook hands. There was no way he could know anything about me. Laura was the only one with any proof about what went down with Mark. And the shooter, whose name I swore never to mention, not even in my sleep, would never talk because I had more information on his life than on my own; and it was information that could send him upriver for a long time.

My balls started to sweat anyway. Another bead of sweat started between my shoulder blades and made its lazy way down my spine.

Captain Tolene motioned for us to sit down, which we did. That left Carter without a chair, so he sat on the edge of Tolene's desk and stared down at us. I didn't loosen my tie even though I wanted to—more than anything.

Carter's stare was intense. "How much did you win on the fight?" he asked.

"What fight?"

He stood and put his hands in his pockets. It was a gesture I'd made just a few moments earlier with Jimmy and I didn't like being on the other end of it. It made me feel like a suspect. He paced a little, then stopped at the window and looked out over the parking lot. He rubbed his chin and said, "You boys bet on the fight? The one that ended in Rex getting killed." He turned and looked at me and Bob. "I'm too tired to play games."

"We bet on the fight," I said.

Bob was pale. He nodded at Carter. "We did."

"How many of you bet on Rex?"

I was the only one who bet on Delancey. I was the only one with a dirty past. Everyone knew about my dirty deeds. No one could prove anything.

Except Laura.

"I bet on Delancey," I said. "Everyone else bet on Rex. I won twenty bucks. It was supposed to be forty."

I looked at Tolene. He wouldn't meet my eye. Guys bet on fights all the time in the precinct. This was a shakedown. Directed at me and only me.

"Forty, you say?" Carter asked, arching his eyebrows like this was shocking news.

I blew out a breath thinking that it would be a screaming shame if I went down for a bet I didn't even get the full amount for. "I bet Ted double or nothing that Delancey would hit Rex hard enough so he wouldn't get back up."

"My, my," Carter said. "How . . . *omniscient* of you."

I stood up fast and hard enough to tip my chair over. "Look, you," I said. But Bob was there, putting himself between me and McWilliams.

"Careful, Detective," Tolene said. And there was an edge to his voice I'd never heard before.

I picked my chair up and sat back down, angry, frustrated, and guilty. Shit.

"I'm trying to find the killer," I said.

"Delancey's the killer," Carter said, smiling.

"I mean I'm trying to find Delancey's killer," I said.

"Then by all means, go and find him," Carter said. "Bob," he gestured to my partner, "has agreed to keep us informed of all your progress."

Bob flushed a deep shade of red.

"That's all," Tolene said. "Get to work."

He still wouldn't look me in the eye.

# 13

*Ray*

Out on the street away from the smoke I could breathe again. I turned to look at Velvy. He looked the same. Skinny, grinning and sly. His pants were a little short for him, like he'd been wearing them since before his last growth spurt. His shoes were barely holding on at the seams and his shirt was stained with something other than what was smeared on the tie he wore loosely as a gesture to any ladies who might think he was down on his luck. But in his face he still looked like the same ten-year-old kid who used to outrun me, tell better jokes, and knew ten different ways to get a stranger to give you a dime. We smiled at each other.

"Thanks for that," I said.

"Easiest fight I've ever had. Now next time I'm out I can tell a woman about the time I fought three guys at once."

"With my help."

"You ask around in there and already there's nobody that saw you at all."

He laughed and we joined together in a hug. From behind us the door opened again and this time the bartender was hustling the three drunks out. He left the shotgun behind. He threw the trio down in a heap on the sidewalk.

"Get out and stay out!" he yelled needlessly as he turned to go back inside. Velvy and I parted and readied for round two of the fight but it didn't happen. The three drunks rolled over and looked around like they'd been dropped out of the sky from the Land of Oz. They didn't even see us there and each one mumbled something and staggered off in a different direction to go sleep it off.

Velvy slapped a hand on my shoulder. "C'mon, man." He led the way back down the block to his apartment.

"Hold it Velvy. I need to tell you why I'm here."

"I figure you're in some kind of trouble. If we don't get

off the street you're liable to be in a heap more."

"I need to find your dad. If he's home I should warn you that I have some tough questions for him."

"Shit, Dad ain't lived at this apartment for a long damn time. He got money enough to get a house. It's a piece of shit but it's a house. Paid for by taking naps on a canvas bed."

"So you know where I can find him?"

"Course I do. I go over to see Mom once a week. But first I want to hear all about your trouble. And you interrupted my drinkin'. Come on up. I'm buyin'."

On the third floor was the two bedroom apartment Velvy grew up in with his dad, mom and two brothers. Velvy lived alone there now. It was worn out and sparse like the Kansas prairie fifty miles out of town had been brought indoors. There was even a dead plant in a pot by the window. I figured it for a suicide.

I guessed that Clark took most of the furniture when he moved and Velvy didn't have the cash or inclination to buy more of it. The place smelled like a wet dog but I didn't see one around. I felt a little sorry for Velvy. He deserved better.

He went into the kitchen and snapped on a bare bulb, the only kind of lighting in the place.

"What can I fix you? I got rye or I got whiskey. Both of them are shit."

"None for me, thanks." I looked around for a place to sit, but the edge of his single bed was the only choice so I stood. Seating was the only reason I can figure why he kept his bed in the parlor room.

"So tell me," Velvy said from the kitchen, "what's this trouble? And why ain't Rex helping you out that you gotta call on your old friend Velvy?"

"Rex is dead." It was easier to say with him in the next room. The sounds of drink pouring stopped. It was so quiet I could hear the roaches behind the walls move.

Velvy stepped out of the kitchen with no drink and suddenly very sober.

"What happened?"

I told him how I'd kept myself busy since I left the Excelsior. I told him that I had killed two men that night. I told him about Rex's ruined face lying on that locker room table. I told him everything.

"So I need to find your dad and see if he knows who gave the order from above. I know it wasn't his idea."

"I don't know that," snorted Velvy. I could tell the anger toward his father stung his throat worse than the burn of that rye waiting for him in the kitchen. "That dumb nigger would do anything for a buck and another 'good boy' from the fuckers that pay him to take dives. He dives more often that the donkey at the carnival that jumps off that high platform. And that ass does six shows a day for nickels."

"I've heard rumors . . ." I tried to be delicate.

"Rumors? Fuck. Stone facts, Ray. It's not like when we was kids. I grew up. I saw what he was, what he did. I used to think my dad was a hero. Better than Joe Louis. Now I can see that he's a drunk and a cheat and a coward. He'll roll over like a bitch dog for anyone with a twenty dollar bill and a jug of wine. Son-of-a-bitch smacked me up and hit on Mom. Goddamn coward couldn't fight a decent bout in the ring these days but he can beat up on his kids and his woman. Now the sorry S.O.B. has dirty money that he spends on whiskey and betting on his own crooked fights. He's gone fat too. Not a man, woman or child can't see a dive comin' from the first bell when that out of shape nigger steps in the ring."

"But how do you really feel about him?" I asked sarcastically.

Velvy smiled, breaking his scowl. The smile faded and he looked me square in the eye the way a real man and a true friend does. The way that lets you know he is speaking no bullshit. "I'm sorry as hell, Ray. Sorry as hell."

"Thanks."

We sat and stared at the ground for awhile. Sounds of an argument echoed between the buildings from out the back window. It sounded like someone threw a flower pot or something that smashed in the alley.

"So what now?" Velvy asked.

"So now I find Clark and see what he knows. I just have to keep going up the ladder one rung at a time I guess."

Velvy chewed the inside of his lip. "You really killed two dudes?"

I nodded.

"I didn't figure you for the type."

"Me either," I said. Velvy moved back to the kitchen to resume pouring his drink. I stayed put leaning on the wall, only a thin layer of plaster between me and a colony of bugs and probably rats too.

"I can help you out but you got to do me a favor."

"Sure, anything," I said.

There was a pause as I heard him finish a long pour of liquor into a glass. "Kill that mother fucker."

I guess it was easier for him to be in another room too. I didn't respond. I stayed where I was and let him come to me. When Velvy came out of the kitchen the glass was in his hand but it was already empty. He looked straight at me in that way again.

"I should have done it years ago, before he left." Velvy's voice was quiet. I could tell this was a talk he'd had with himself here in this room at night many times before. Now it was hard to say it out loud after so many times just playing the conversation in his head but he went on, eyes locked with mine. He had listened while I spilled my guts and now it was my turn to listen to the darkness inside my friend.

"That cowardly son-of-a-bitch started to hitting on me and I didn't give a shit. Most everyone up and down this block has had a good beating more than once. It makes you a man. But when he started hittin' on Mom . . . I should have done it then. Poor woman gave her life for us kids and what does she have to show for it? Two no good crooks, one in jail and one pimping, and me, a goddamn coward who can't do what needs to be done. I need your help, Ray. You said yourself you need to blow town when all this is done so what's one more notch in the belt, am I right?"

"I hadn't exactly planned to make a career out of this

when I started."

"But you know you got it in you now. Those other two fellas, they did you wrong and you did them right. Now it's time to take care of another man who's doing wrong."

"I just don't know if I can do it, Velvy. With Hobbes I was half-crazy and with Delancey . . . well if he hadn't jumped me it never would have happened so . . ."

"All right, all right. You go to Clark. Find out what you need to know. Then just make him leave. Just disappear. I want my mom to have a chance. If he gives you a name then he should get the fuck out of Dodge anyway. Just make it persuasive. But make good and sure he gets the hell out of Kansas City and never comes back."

I stood and thought. I saw the water in Velvy's eyes get heavy. He was serious. I started to see how this apartment was a trap for him. Every night having to live in the scene of a crime. He was paralyzed by it. He couldn't get a steady job. He barely made ends meet, that much was obvious, but he was never going to move forward until this burden was off his mind. And I didn't want him to go and do something stupid.

I'd followed my impulse to kill and I knew how stupid I'd been and how I would take it all back if I had the chance even though the thought of Delancey and Hobbes sleeping side by side at the city morgue did give me an inner smile. I had come to him for help in the middle of the night and I expected him to be there for me and now how could I say no to him when he was asking the same of me?

And then there was Pop. I had given myself that same speech Velvy gave, alone in a dark room at night just like I know Velvy had said it all to himself before tonight. I wished I had done something when I first saw Pop take a swipe at Mom. I wished I had done something the second time or the third but I didn't. Then he punched Mom silly and we never got her back the same way again. Pop left town and robbed me of the satisfaction. Yeah, I knew how Velvy felt.

"Okay, I'll make him get out of town. But that's it. First

things first . . . I need my information."

"Ray," he put a hand on my shoulder and squeezed. "That's mighty white of you." He smiled a tight lipped grin that didn't show any teeth. Even now he was trying to crack me up.

"It's one o'clock in the morning. Where you gonna sleep tonight?" he asked.

"I wasn't thinking I was."

"Bull shit. You can't go knocking on nobody's door at one in the morning. He'll meet you on the doorstep with a pistol. Stay here, get a few hours sleep. He'll be drunk and sleeping it off until noon so you got time."

"What about the cops?"

"Cops don't come to this part of town. You know that."

"Okay, what about a bed?" I looked over to his one single bed with a tired mattress about as thick as a newspaper.

"I got another mattress in the closet. We used to sleep three brothers in one room you know."

"I still don't know how."

"You and Rex didn't have your own floor with a butler as I recall it."

He had a point and I had another reason to think about Rex. We didn't say much else as he got out an old mattress left over from when he and his brothers were just kids when they spent the night farting and drooling and having wet dreams. It didn't excite me to sleep on it, but as soon as I lay down I realized how tired I was.

Part of me hoped that when we both had time to sleep on it Velvy would call off the favor and just let me ask Clark the questions I needed answers to. I tried to shut out the long day's events as the gentle tapping of rat feet in the walls lulled me to sleep.

# 14

*Fokoli*

Bob and I typed up our reports on Delancey. By then it was four thirty and my eyes were gritty with fatigue. If Tolene expected me to go out on the beat again, he could fuck himself. I needed to sleep. I called it a night.

Me and Laura lived on the second floor of a two-story walk-up. It was nicer than what most of the guys on the force could afford, even the homicide guys. After the thing with Mark, I wanted to move to someplace more amenable to my real salary, since that's all I decided to bring home after it all went down.

Mark dying—no—scratch that. My part in Mark dying set me straight but by then I was in pretty deep and Laura knew everything. She knew everything and she threatened to use it if I moved her out of the walk-up.

So I worked long hours, afraid to go home, afraid to stay away. And Laura stayed home and drank.

The sun was rising an hour and a half later when I opened our front door Laura was in the wingback chair in front of the fire. Her stockings had rolled halfway down her legs, which were pushed together at her knees. Her skirt was halfway up her thighs. I stood and stared at her for a minute . . . maybe two. She still had beautiful legs for a woman her age.

She'd dropped the bottle, half of it spilling near the chair and I couldn't tell if the booze smell was from what splashed on the rug or what was coming off of Laura. Seemed it was harder to tell a lot of things these days.

I opened the living room drapes, taking a little pleasure in seeing her grimace as the glow from the rising sun slammed into her face like a fist.

"Jesus," she mumbled, and flopped forward like a rag doll, resting her chest on her legs. Then she threw up on the rug.

I blew out a breath and picked her up in my arms. After Mark, when Laura started drinking so hard and I had to start putting her to bed, she weighed around 120. I had no idea what her weight was now, but I could feel every bone through the dress she hadn't bothered to change out of last night. Normally I would have put her in bed, but she was covered in vomit and I thought I even saw a little blood in it this time.

"Let's get you a shower," I said.

She struggled a little. "Put me down, you lug. Put me down. I hate you." But her eyes weren't open as she said it.

I sat her on the toilet while I started the shower. I took off my clothes and then undressed her before managing to drag us both over the edge of the tub to stand beneath the hot spray. In the harsh light of the bathroom, I could see the effects of the hard drinking written on her skin. Deep bruises spread over her arms and abdomen, and the whites of her eyes were deep brown now. I'd seen drunks on the street get that way when their livers were shot. If Laura's liver quit working, it wouldn't be long before she quit working too.

I thought about what it would be like to live without her while I washed her hair and cleaned her up. I didn't know how I felt about it. Laura and I had been together for fifteen years . . . most of them good. But I didn't know her anymore, and she knew me a little too well.

I wrapped her in a towel and carried her to bed. I didn't bother to get dressed. I cleaned up the living room rug and then climbed in beside her and held her close because she was shivering. Lying together like that, naked, right after a shower, felt like old times. Laura smelled the way she used to smell and it was easy to remember good things about being married to her. I let myself drift off . . . holding my wife, thinking good things.

The phone ringing jolted me awake. I was still naked. And I was cold, despite the late morning sun that streamed through the window. Laura was no longer beside me. And she clearly wasn't answering the phone. I staggered to the living room and picked up the receiver.

"'lo," I managed.

"Rise and shine, Sleepyhead." Christ, I hated Bob.

"What time is it?" I looked around and spied Laura sitting at the kitchen table with a mug in front of her. She was in a flowered robe and her hair had been combed, falling over her shoulders. I didn't figure it was coffee in the mug.

"Ten," Bob said. "Captain wants you here. We need to go over the case and develop a strategy."

Laura stared into her mug.

"Strategy?" I asked. She was crying.

"Couple of thugs exchanged shots at the docks last night. There's rumors about a mob war. Someone's got to swing for Delancey and Hobbes, or all hell's going to break loose."

There was no mob involved in this, but I'd never get the captain to believe that . . . or the Kansas City mafia for that matter. I wondered if I could get anybody in internal affairs to talk to me about what they wanted with the Hobbes case. Did they know something? Was it just coincidence they were at Hobbes's gym? Was I under the microscope? Would Laura talk if they pressed her? "I need an hour," I said to Bob.

Laura didn't look at me when I sat down. She stared at the mug and wiped her nose. I would have offered her my handkerchief, but I was still naked.

"Laura," I said, taking her hand. She didn't pull away and I was grateful for that. I slid the sleeve of her robe up a little so she could see her arm. "See these marks?" Her eyes wandered over and rested on the bruised flesh. "These show that you're sick. Too much booze. You gotta stop."

She pulled the sleeve down and hid her hands in her lap.

I rested my arms on the table. I felt a little cold, but it was the first time I'd really seen her in days and I didn't want to lose the chance to talk to her by going to get a robe. "You didn't sleep long," I said.

"I can only sleep when I'm drunk."

"I can move out," I said. "You can keep this place,

Laura. You can have it and I'll get out of here and you can start over . . . find yourself a decent man."

She smiled a little bit. "You'd like that, wouldn't you? To see me entrenched in another marriage so that if word leaked out about what you've done then I'd be ruined too?"

"How would you be ruined?" I asked.

"Do you think anyone would want me after they found out I was married to a murderer?"

There was venom in her words. But there was also truth. I hadn't pulled the trigger on Mark, but I'd set him up for the fall. So I could be with his wife. And that was the real rub—the needle in my underpants that kept poking me in the ass. Even if I wanted to patch things up with Laura, I couldn't. Because she felt not only the burden of having a crooked cop for a husband, but also the burden of knowing I'd been unfaithful with—and killed for—another woman.

Me and Sylvia had talked about getting rid of Mark for a long time. He was a little rough sometimes and if he ever found out Sylvia wanted a divorce, well, there was a chance he'd have killed her. At least that's what I let myself believe.

So we planned things out. I kept volunteering me and Mark for more and more dangerous cases; the ones where we'd be likely to draw fire if we caught up with the bad guys. Mob cases.

And I knew a lot of guys in the mob. I greased the wheels for them, hoping it would open doors for me. It did. After awhile I put the word out that if me and Mark came looking they should shoot first and ask questions later.

One night I got lucky. I had a stoolie call in a fake tip that an armored truck, stolen earlier in the week, had been spotted. The stoolie said the cargo was being divided and transferred into sedans for delivery to small banks across the country. Me and Mark set up a stakeout in the alley, ready to pounce when the transfer was done. We tried to stay back undercover while we watched, but I'd worked it so that one of the grunts who worked for Chicago would off Mark when I gave the signal. And the signal was simple: push Mark in the open and watch while he got shot.

After the funeral, I went to see Sylvia. Only she was sick about it all by then. To tell the truth, so was I. But she and Laura were good friends so Sylvia told my wife. Everything.

There's no jury so tough as a scorned wife, I think.

"I'm trying, Laura," I said, wishing she'd look at me. "I've been good. I'm not on the take anymore." I tried to touch her hand again.

"Please don't," she said.

I picked up the mug and carried it to the sink. "You've got to stop this. You'll kill yourself."

"I think that would make you happy."

"To see you dead?"

She nodded.

I walked back to the table and knelt in front of her. "Help me make this right," I said. "I'm trying Laura."

She cried again. "I don't know," she said. "I don't know."

I didn't know what more she wanted from me. And didn't know how much more I wanted to give. I left her sitting there alone while I went to shave and get dressed. She had the mug in front of her again when I walked back through the dining room. I thought about taking the bottle away from her, but I'd tried that before and she threatened to tell what she knew. So I let her be.

"I'm going to work now," I said when I was ready, but she just stared at the mug.

# 15

*Ray*

I woke up from a deep but fitful sleep. All night long I watched movies of the previous day's events over and over and saw myself running, running, running down dark alleys and dead ends.

I snapped my eyes open and found myself staring at the barrel of a gun that Velvy was holding. Not really how I wanted to wake up. I wanted to be back in my own bed with Rex in the bed next to me. We still shared the same room like we had ever since we were kids. Even after Mom died and the whole house was ours to spread out in as we pleased we stayed together just out of habit.

But back to the gun.

Velvy's gun was old and black and looked like it may have fired a few shots in the Civil War but it was lethal nonetheless. I stayed still waiting to see if Velvy was going to shoot me or not.

"Take this," he said.

He was up early and showed no signs of a hangover. Either he had already indulged in a little hair of the dog or the alcohol from last night was still seeping out his pores to make a one hundred proof cologne that drifted down to the floor where I lay on the pancake mattress.

He wanted me to take the gun for my visit to Clark. So much for him having a change of heart once he had slept on it. He was back to me killing his father.

"I won't need it," I replied as I sat up.

"It's for your protection. He keeps a shotgun and who knows what else around the house. Some white guy comes to his door he'll shoot first and ask questions never."

"I'll be okay." He still tossed the gun down on the mattress next to me.

I showered off. I'd seen cleaner showers in locker rooms

of backwoods fight halls in Podunk towns in Missouri. Velvy had strong coffee brewing when I got out and that was a welcome smell.

When I came into the kitchen to get my cup there was a pair of pants draped over the chair that I assumed were for me so I could go out in the daylight without blood stains all over myself. They were tight but with all the exercise and the skipped meals of the past day and a half I fit into them well enough. Velvy and I didn't say much to each other. We said it all last night.

While I was in the shower Velvy had moved the gun onto the kitchen table and it sat there on the chipped green finish, all black and weird angles like one of us spilled our coffee cup. I ignored it. I finished my coffee and stood up to go.

"You go see him. You find out what you want to know. You find who done Rex. Then you make him get the hell out of town and never come back, you hear?" Velvy said this with his head down staring into the blackness of his coffee.

"I'll do that. Thanks for everything, Velvy. I knew I could count on you."

"You keep on counting on me until this here is done. Nobody does Rex like that and gets away with it for free. That boy was like a brother to me. More than my own brothers most times. Hell of a fighter too."

"Hell of fighter," I said. The outside noises hadn't started yet. It was still too early, only a little after nine thirty. I had the address of where to find Clark and I had a certain clarity now in what I was doing.

I had killed two men, that couldn't be undone, so it was time to keep on with it. Find where the order came from and deal with that, whatever that meant, and then move on out of town.

To make that happen I needed to move forward all the time. Keep up the offense but have enough sense to know when to use the defense. And conserve my energy. This one might go the distance so I needed to be ready. I couldn't count on a knockout so I had to keep using my inside moves and keep wearing my opponent down.

I left Velvy with a firm handshake that he pressed five dollars into. I handed it back.

"Money's not an issue."

"Well then, hell, can I borrow fifty bucks?" Velvy smiled at me. Always trying to crack me up. I wished to hell I could just forget it all and invite Velvy out on the sidewalk to play stickball.

Those days were over.

Clark had bought a house on the outskirts of Negrotown near Twenty-Seventh Street. It was rundown, the lawn was mostly dead and brown, but what green patches did grow were high and had puffs of dandelions sprouting in bouquets. There were iron bars on all the windows and an iron fence surrounding the front yard. The gate was missing so it did nothing for security.

The house was a dump but it was a house and it was more than most people who grew up like Clark would ever get. Clark had lived hard, growing up in a life I didn't know any details about but even if I did I am sure I couldn't relate to. I heard once that his father had been lynched and that Clark had watched the whole thing happen when he was just a boy and I think that colored his feelings toward white people. He saw taking their money for dirty fights as a kind of revenge. He loved taking money for not fighting. It felt better to him than to give them the satisfaction of sitting in the bleachers and screaming out for his Negro blood to be spilled. He'd hit the floor with a pansy blow and then laugh all the way to the bank. The only thing that bugged him was hearing the bigots in the crowd crowing about how it just proved that no nigger fighter could ever beat a white boy.

Clark would take the occasional unfixed fight just to prove that he could still go to town on a young cracker when he needed to. And he did need to. All the dives and fixes didn't satisfy his need to punch people in the face. It was a dry hump after a lot of heavy petting. The need to hit things, to feel the connection of a fist with a solid object bottled up and when it overflowed it came out against his kids and his wife. Clark had genuine rage and being a boxer is the best and worst thing for a man like that. He gets a place to release all that hate but he also gets a taste for the feeling of a fist connecting with a jawbone that snaps or he learns just where to land a kidney punch that would leave an opponent pissing blood for days. But if that release didn't come then whoever was nearest when the steam reached boiling point was going to get burned.

Clark's non-fixed fights were few and far between these days and he probably hadn't had one at all in a year or two that I knew of. He wasn't any spring chicken and his rage was his fighting style more so than any real technique. He was a sledgehammer fighting younger, faster guys who could dance better and punch quicker.

I walked to the front door at about a quarter after ten and I knocked. I waited as I heard someone moving inside. Something crashed to the floor and I heard a loud but muted, "Motherfuck!"

The door opened and both barrels of a shotgun poked out into the morning light. Clark was still in the darkness of the indoors.

"The fuck are you?" He cleared his throat violently after he spoke, as if speaking the words had dredged up something vile deep within his lungs. I heard him spit inside on his own floor.

"Clark Dane?"

Somehow just me knowing his name satisfied him. The gun lowered, the door shut briefly as he unlatched the chain lock and then swung open again. I saw Clark retreating into the house with a tattered burgundy bathrobe on and the shotgun down at his side. I assumed this was an invitation so I stepped out of the warm morning sunshine into the dark recesses of the house.

Clark led me into the kitchen. He set the shotgun down on the countertop and picked up an open bottle of whiskey. He tipped it upside down and tried to get any last hint of liquid from deep within. He brought the bottle down and licked his lips, shifting his eyes around the room in search of a new one.

The robe hung open and he was shirtless and wearing only under shorts dulled to a dirty gray color. He didn't look like Velvy at all, or I guess it's the other way around. It made me wonder if Velvy's mom had a secret she was keeping. Maybe it was just the years of taking punches and chasing it with whiskey by the case. He had pitch-black skin and a cauliflower ear. Remnants of the last thing he ate were collected in the scrubby three-day beard that scribbled its way across his chin. His eyes stood out against the blackness of his skin and tiny red veins slashed across them making me want to rub my eyes just looking at his.

"Well, just leave it on the table there and be on your way, boy."

There was self-satisfaction in the way he called a white man boy.

"I'm sorry?" I said.

He spoke slowly and deliberately like I was a mental case.

"Put. The money. On. The table. Then get. The fuck. Out." He turned and started his search for the morning bottle of liquor.

"Mr. Dane, I'm Ray Ward. You knew my father. Me and my brother used to be friends with your boy Velvy."

Clark turned and studied my face for any sign of recognition.

"You don't got my money?" he asked.

"No, sir." Sir. Old habits die hard I guess.

"Ray?" he studied me like a doctor would examine a new species. "Brother Rex you say?"

"Yes."

"Well, shit, yeah I know you boys. Rex turned himself into a bulldog of a fighter didn't he now? Yes, yes, yes I see his name in all the columns. Fists that could break concrete so they says."

"He's dead."

There was a tiny flicker of shock but no real surprise. He

knew the fix was in; he just didn't know the final scorecard would show Rex dead.

"I'll be goddamned," he muttered for my benefit. I stared at him and instinctively started shuffling my feet side to side. Verbal sparring and the real thing weren't too much different.

"I'm here to ask if you knew anything about the fight last night."

"Last night you say?" Stalling.

"Last night was when he was killed. A fighter named Delancey. Young kid."

"White boy?"

"Yes."

"Pretty boy?"

"Not any more."

Clark stayed silent. I was fairly sure he knew what that meant. He turned as if he had just gotten a great idea and made a direct line for a cabinet high above a rusty icebox and retrieved a full bottle of dark brown liquor with no label. Homemade bathtub hooch. The kind that makes you blind if you drink too much of it.

He took a swig. Modest. He knew how to drink this stuff. How not to over do it and how to make it last.

"I don't know nothin'. Now if you ain't got my money you need to get the fuck out."

I decided to go a little aggressive but I was ready to back down if it went badly. "You act like you aren't glad to see me," I said with that fighter's bravura.

He swigged again and he didn't even react to the burn down his throat, if he could even feel it anymore.

"Listen, boy, memory lane is a dangerous street to walk down sometimes. What happened last night, last week, last year is gone and it ain't comin' back. Best to let it lie."

"I heard that you were supposed to fight Rex. It was your fight but they took it away from you because they said you were too old and it wouldn't look right for you to fight a guy as young and talented as Rex. Everyone would know it was a fix from the start." I kept dancing side to side but I could tell I was pushing him toward the ropes. "Besides, if you were expected to knock him out of the game for a few months, they doubted you could do it any more. I doubt it myself. Of course if you'd had the weighted gloves that Delancey had . . ."

Clark slammed the bottle down on the counter. He wiped his mouth with the back of his hand and it cleared away some of the old food sticking to his whiskers.

"What do you want from me? I wasn't in the ring. I didn't do nothing to your brother. I never killed nobody in the ring." Interesting that he felt the need to qualify that statement with "in the ring" but all I cared about was Rex.

"I just want to know who handed down the order to knock Rex out of the way. I know it wasn't supposed to be a hit, but it turned out that way and I'd really like to know who is behind it."

Clark gave me a stare I could tell he had been perfecting from across the ring for twenty years. It was intimidating, I'll admit, but I knew it was a put on so I stood my ground.

"I'm not here to make any trouble, Mr. Dane. I just want to do what's right for my brother."

His stare softened.

"They killed him, huh?"

I nodded. "Died in the ring."

Clark shook his head. The plight of a fallen comrade had gotten to him. Suddenly his memory got better.

"You two used to come over and play ball with Velvy, I remember. Two young cracker boys playing in the street. I'd have to explain it to all the neighbors and tell them you were okay." Then he looked away from me. "I get all my fights from one guy, Baxter. Promoter. He lays most of the fixes in town. He gets them from up on high though. I don't know who. He's the one who gave me the fight and then took it away. Said the big man needed a fresh new face. Guess this old nigger is 'bout to be put out to pasture."

"Baxter. Any idea where to find him?"

"He contacts me. But look for a fight on the down low, the crookeder the better, and he'll be there."

I remembered the guy in the suit who sat ringside at the fight.

"He a big guy? Likes to dress up and smoke cigars?"

"Has a cigar but never smokes it. Too cheap. Don't want to spend the nickel for the next one."

That was the guy. Clark took another swig.

"For the record, boy, I'm glad I didn't get that fight. I couldn't have done it to Rex. Besides, you're right, that boy could punch the black right off of me, fixed fight or no."

"Thanks Clark." It made the next part a little harder. "I need to talk to you about something else."

"What now, boy? Don't you see I got drinkin' to do?"

"It's about Velvy. He wants you to leave town. And not come back." There. I said it. But not with fighter's confidence. I felt like a ten-year-old asking for a free peppermint stick from the guy who runs the five-and-dime. I knew he wasn't going to give it to me.

"What the fuck for?"

"You'll have to ask him."

"Fuck that. He'll have to ask me. Pussy little bitch. Why don't he get the fuck out of town?"

"You said yourself you were being put out to pasture."

"That don't mean I want to go to live in a real pasture!"

"I think he's mad about you hitting him." I swallowed hard. Clark was getting upset and I was close to entering a fight that wasn't mine.

"Fuck lot of good it done. That boy is still a pussy little bitch. You tell him to go fuck himself." Clark leaned forward and when the rest of him caught up inertia took him out of the kitchen to the living room where he flopped on the couch which looked like a nest of newspapers and old clothes. This was his sleep-it-off spot which had now become his bedroom. "Fucker ain't even my kid," he mumbled.

So I wasn't the only one who noticed.

I felt good that I had tried to do Velvy his favor and run Clark out of town, but I wasn't going to make any more of it. Don't get in the middle of two dogs fighting or a father and son fight. That's square advice.

I had a name and I knew what the man looked like so I could start my search for Baxter. Then I did something stupid. I followed Clark into the living room.

"Can I use your bathroom before I go?" I asked.

"Do whatever the fuck you want, boy."

He waved the bottle behind him to indicate the vague direction of the facilities. I went there innocently enough.

# 16

*Fokoli*

Bob didn't say anything to me until we got into the car and drove five blocks or so. "Where you going?" he asked when I headed toward the golf course.

"Back to Hobbes's house," I said. I was bleary-eyed from lack of sleep and concern about Laura and I wanted to fix it. I didn't know what it was. Laura? Mark? My job? Me? I wanted to fix something. I'd have to settle for the case. "Maybe I missed a clue somewhere."

We drove in silence, Bob feeling guilty for reporting my every move to the captain, me wondering if Laura was going to die soon.

"I don't ever tell them much," Bob said. When I didn't respond he continued, "It wasn't even my idea. Some of the guys—"

I gave him a sharp look, one that matched the feeling of the knife in my gut. Some of the guys. Some of the guys who'd been friends with Mark and knew I straddled the fence. Some of the guys who watched me sit in the front row at Mark's funeral next to Sylvia. Some of the guys was really all of the guys. Including Captain Tolene and Carter Fucking McWilliams.

It was time for Laura to move over. I was circling the drain right along beside her.

I said to Bob, "Do your job. Do whatever they tell you. Keep your nose as clean as you can." It was the only advice I could give him.

There was one patrol car in Hobbes's driveway. The driver was asleep. I banged on the window with my wedding ring. It was still good for something. He snapped awake. "Jesus," he said and me and Bob laughed because we could hear him from outside the car. He rolled the window down when we flashed our badges. Then he decided he'd better not talk to detectives through a window, so he opened the door and got out.

"Nothing new to report," he said.

I looked him in the eye. "How would you know?" I held out my hand for the house keys, which he handed over with a scowl.

Me and Bob went inside and he gave a low whistle. "Man, oh man," he said.

"I forgot," I said. "You haven't seen this yet." I gestured wide with my arms. "This is how fat, disgusting, crooked boxing managers live."

"Nice."

We went straight upstairs to the room where we found the chinchillas. It was a waste of time, I knew, but as long as Bob was babysitting me, I didn't feel good about following my gut, even though my gut was starting to tell me something was weird about all this.

The door to the chinchilla room stood open; the filth visible in the darkness beyond, the stench so fierce you could almost touch it. I stepped inside, tasting the smell. Dried shit and urine stains covered the floor. A dark mat of hair clung to the top.

"What are we looking for?" Bob asked, covering his nose.

"I have no idea." There was no furniture in the room, only filth.

"Jesus," he said after a minute.

We turned and left, stopping at the office at the top of the stairs. Hobbes wasn't one for keeping records of any sort, not even the kind assholes like him usually kept around so they could blackmail anyone who pissed them off. The office was cluttered with dirty dishes and laundry. There was a desk, its drawers stuffed with newspaper clippings featuring stories about Delancey and some of Hobbes's other fighters. Nothing on Jimmy Scoggins. Go figure. There were no financial records and no personal files of any sort.

"Maybe back at the gym?" Bob said.

I knew he was right. We'd have to head back there and

take a look. Sometimes being a cop is like being on a merry-go-round, passing the same places over and over again, hoping you'll see something you didn't see before.

Me and Bob didn't know where our killer had gone. All we could do was hope that, if it was Chicago, their work was done. But like I said, my gut was singing a different tune and I didn't know all the notes.

There was a strip of yellow tape across the door to Hobbes's gym. The smell of sweat still carried out to the street, but it wasn't as strong. The whores and drunks had crawled back undercover someplace. Despite the emptiness of the street, me and Bob still looked out of place.

A uniformed cop named Doyle was at the door to keep an eye on things. He was one of the cops that took my statement when Mark died. That night, he stood there with one hand in his pocket and the other scratching his chin, like he didn't quite believe things went down the way I was telling it.

He was looking at me the same way now.

"We need to get into the office," I said.

Doyle raised his eyebrows. "What for?"

Bob jumped in. "We're detectives working a homicide," he said. "If you don't want to be written up for interfering, then I guess you'll open the door."

Doyle shoved his tongue in his cheek and rocked up on his toes a couple of times, but did what we asked.

The gym's office was as bad as Hobbes's home office. There were papers everywhere.

Bob gave a low whistle.

"Stop doing that," I said.

I sat at Hobbes's desk and gestured for Bob to sit across from me. "What are we looking for?" he asked.

"I already told you I have no idea. Look for anything to do with fur. Anything from a Chicago owned company. Anything handwritten. Anything that looks interesting."

"Is there anything we aren't looking for?"

I ignored that and started making my way through the

papers, thinking it was a waste of time, thinking our killer was out there getting away with murder.

After an hour, Bob went out for sandwiches. Doyle came into the office and asked how it was going. I figured Bob sent him in to watch me. Or maybe I was just getting suspicious of everyone. I told myself I had reason to be suspicious. I.A. was after my job now and it would be easy enough to get clean guys from the department to report any ass scratching I did.

Let's face it. Everyone hated a cop killer and that's basically what I was now to anyone that mattered.

"It's going fine," I said. "Want to help?" I tried a smile but it didn't feel right so I kept digging. Doyle didn't say anything, just stood in the doorway and watched me.

I dug a little more, trying to ignore Doyle, and found a handwritten note. It said PEREZ, DOCK 3. Why did these assholes always meet at the docks? I palmed the note so Doyle wouldn't stick his big nose into it and kept sifting through papers.

After awhile, Bob showed up with sandwiches and coffee. We ate in silence with Doyle at the door, watching me, even though Bob was back. It was then I figured out that I.A. and not Bob had Doyle in my face. This was how it was going to be. Every asshole on the force was after my badge. Well, fuck them.

"Let's go out for a smoke," I said to Bob after we finished our sandwiches. We walked down the steps and into the sunshine. Doyle stayed in the gym.

"What's up?" Bob asked. He held his hand up to shade his eyes.

I showed him the note.

"You guys cops?"

Bob pocketed the slip of paper and we both looked at the guy who'd just wandered up to stand beside us. "Yeah," I said. "We're cops."

He had a pair of boxing shoes hanging around his neck by their laces, and a large gym bag over one shoulder. "Can I get into the gym yet?"

"What's your name?" Bob asked.

"Clete. Clete Travis."

We knew the name. There was a poster of him hanging in the locker room at the station. His nose had been broken since then, and his cheeks were more angular. "You box for Hobbes?" I asked.

He shrugged. "Not sure anymore."

Bob lit a cigarette. "What's that mean?" He offered one to me and to Clete.

Clete said no to the cigarette. "He's a little behind on paying my cut."

I lit the cigarette Bob gave me. "Fixed fight, Clete?"

He backed up a step. "I'd better get going," he said, but Bob stopped him.

"What's your hurry, Clete? We're just talking here."

I took a deep drag and blew out a cloud of smoke. "It's a helluva lot nicer here than downtown," I said. "Jimmy Scoggins has been there since yesterday. I bet he could tell you stories."

Clete's eyes widened a little. "What's going on?" he asked. His Adam's apple bobbed up and down a lot, like we were making him nervous.

"Hobbes got whacked," Bob said. He'd found some backbone in the last day. I tried not to smile.

Clete shook his head and swallowed some more. "No," he said, like he couldn't quite believe it.

"What can you tell us about Hobbes's friends?" I asked.

Clete snorted a little. "Nothing to tell. The asshole didn't have friends. He cheated everyone. If I didn't keep track of what he owed, he'd skim off the top and leave me short." He shook his head. "Every goddamned fight." His fists clenched a little at his sides. "He still owes me for last Saturday."

He was wearing a wedding ring and he stared at it now, like he was thinking really hard. "Some of the guys are talking union," he said.

I laughed a little. "A boxing union?"

"Why not? Everyone else has a union. Why not us?"

"Sure," I said. "Why not you? Who's the mastermind

behind the unionizing of the boxers?"

Clete's eyes were vacant. "Huh?"

"Who's getting it together?" I said.

"Guy by the name of Rich DeLuca."

Bob wrote the name down, but he didn't need to. I'd done a little business with DeLuca in the past. I'd never met him in person, but in the old days, when I finished a job, I knew it was his money being shoved in my pocket. He lived in Chicago but came to K.C. on occasion to do business. I tried to lose track of him after Mark died.

"Where do we find him?" I asked.

Clete was starting to sweat a little bit. "Look," he said. "I don't want no trouble. Mr. DeLuca is a good guy. He's a good guy."

I grabbed Clete by the shoe laces dangling around his neck and pulled him closer. His eyes widened and his fists clenched, but he knew enough not to punch a cop.

"We aren't going to say anything that will get you into trouble," I said. "But we'd really like a word with Mr. DeLuca." I let him go and he stumbled back a step.

He licked his lips and looked up and down the street. Still quiet. Not a stool pigeon in sight. "I meet him at Smiley's," he said. "It's where all of us meet. Those of us who want to talk about a union."

"You pay dues for this union?" Bob asked.

Clete shook his head.

Bob smiled. "Good. Keep your money in your wallet."

Clete nodded and I watched that Adam's apple bob up and down a little more. "Can I go now?" he asked.

We told him sure.

Smiley's was a bit of a misnomer. The guy behind the bar was really a dame but she was dressed like a man. And she didn't smile. "What'll it be?" she asked.

Me and Bob flashed our badges. She smiled then. "Looking for Rich?" When we nodded, she jerked her head to the side. "Back there," she said. "But for the record, everyone here thinks unionization is a good thing."

There was a door cut to blend in with the paneling along the back wall. We listened for a minute. "Pool table," I said after hearing the clacking of balls, and we walked in.

The room was cloudy with cigar smoke. There were four or five guys, all Italian, all in shirtsleeves, suspenders, and fedoras, chalking up their cues and laying money on the table.

"We're looking for Rich DeLuca," Bob said.

"Yeah? And who the hell are you?" a tall, skinny, greasy-haired kid asked.

We pulled out our badges. "I'm Detective Bob White and this here is Detective Dean Fokoli." Nobody heard my name because they were too busy laughing about Bob's name.

Four guys moved forward to block our path to a man who looked to be in his early thirties, good looking, but slick. DeLuca. A little different than I pictured him, but still a slimeball. "It's okay, fellas," he said. "I'm curious. I've not had the pleasure of meeting Kansas City's officers yet."

He pushed his friends aside and extended his hand. Bob shook it. I didn't. DeLuca's eyes were hard. "Let's sit over here."

He went through the motions of ordering drinks and lighting a ten dollar cigar before settling into talking. "Now then. What can I do for you?"

"We're here about Hobbes," I said, to see his reaction. He looked puzzled.

"What about him?" Either he was very good or he really didn't know Hobbes was dead. The only ones who did know were the cops and Jimmy Scoggins. As far as I knew it hadn't gone out on the newswire that morning.

"I heard he was against this union you're trying to start up."

He rolled the cigar between his finger and thumb. "Many of my Kansas City friends are opposed to the idea of a union," he said. "I'm sure they will come around with time."

"And persuasion," I said. DeLuca shrugged.

"Has Mr. Hobbes run to the police with this dispute?" he

asked.

"We've just come from his gym," Bob said.

DeLuca blew out a breath and put his cigar in the ashtray in the middle of the table. Then he leaned forward and rested his weight on his elbows. "I have had many meetings with Mr. Hobbes regarding this issue," he said. "It might interest you to know that Hobbes is the criminal here. He cheats his fighters. And he cheats me."

"You?"

"Yes. I own his gym, after all."

I felt like an ass. It hadn't occurred to me to see how deep into Hobbes's pockets the Chicago boys were.

"You own a lot of businesses here in K.C.?" Bob asked.

DeLuca laughed. Something else to check on.

Hobbes had four boxers working under him. Delancey, Jimmy, Clete, and another guy by the name of Franky Farfle. Lousy name, mean left hook. Delancey was dog meat. Jimmy was parked in holding, we'd just had a talk with Clete. That left Farfle to check on. But he'd have to wait. There was too much on my plate already.

"You know about Rex Ward?" I asked.

His mouth drew into a hard line. "The fighter Delancey bounced? Yeah. I know all about Rex."

"You don't sound pleased," I said.

"I'm pleased if I'm the one fixing the fight. I had nothing to do with that. And I lost five thousand. No, Detectives, I am not happy. I assure you, I'm taking appropriate action."

"No need," I said. "Hobbes is dead."

He looked amused by this. Then he turned and snapped his fingers at one of his friends on the other side of the room. "Charlie," he said.

"Don't bother sending your men to Hobbes's place," I said. "We've got the chinchillas." DeLuca changed his mind about talking to Charlie.

He picked up the cigar again. "So I take it this wasn't a health related death?"

"Somebody beat him to death," I said.

DeLuca's eyes narrowed. "What did you say your name was?"

I told him.

He picked up the cigar and leaned back in his seat, smiling a little. "I know about you," he said. "You've worked with my guys before." Then he nodded to Bob. "Does your friend deal too?"

When we didn't answer, Rich continued. "I want that fur. You know I'll pay well."

I ignored that. "Who else in Kansas City would have fixed that fight?" I asked.

But DeLuca was done talking. He stood and walked back toward the pool table, taking his cigar with him. Five big men stood and rolled up their sleeves.

Bob and I left before things got dicey.

When we were driving again, Bob said, "You're a pretty good detective, Dean." I didn't say anything to that because what could I say?

I was driving and figured we should head for Dock Three now to see who Perez was. My guess was he was the barge operator hired to carry the chinchillas upriver. We were going in all the wrong directions.

"I think we're going in the wrong direction," Bob said.

My hands tightened on the wheel. Was Bob reading my mind?

"No," I said. "The docks are this way."

He shook his head. "No. I mean with this case. Doesn't this feel wrong to you?" I looked at him as he continued. "Two bodies. And we're chasing chinchillas that belong to the mob? Who the hell would kill over chinchillas?"

I didn't have an answer for that. I said, "I could think of some people who would be angry enough to kill if the boxers unionized."

"True. But not Chicago. Chicago wants the union. That's why they're here."

I pulled over so we could talk. "Tell me what you're thinking, Bob."

"I think," he said, "I want to know the names of the men

in that pool room with Rich DeLuca. I'm willing to bet they are some heavies from Chicago. So why are they here?"

"The union."

"Exactly," Bob said.

"They wouldn't have known about Rex and Delancey's fight until it happened."

"And they sure as hell wouldn't have killed Hobbes the way they did. They'd wait until he had the full purse. And we both know it can take a day or two for all the bets to come in."

"True," I agreed, relieved that Bob was thinking what I'd been feeling.

He looked at me. "You've been thinking the same thing," he said.

"Look," I told him. "There's a good chance I won't have a job with the department after this case. The why of it doesn't matter anymore. Like I said before, I think you should keep your nose as clean as you can."

"I want to catch a killer, Dean."

"We will," I promised.

# 17

*Ray*

I passed back through the kitchen of Clark's rundown house and out the other door on the far side which led to a small bathroom. I opened the door and it caught on a small rug that was bunched up and not moving. I shoved a little harder and it folded in on itself and the door opened enough to reveal her. I instantly wished the door had stayed jammed and I never would have set foot in there.

Clark's wife, Velvy's mom—I never knew her name as a kid, always just called her Mrs. Dane—was on the floor lying on her side with her knees pulled up almost to her chest and her house dress riding high enough to be immodest. Dried blood surrounded her, sticking the dress and her hair to the floor. It was obvious she'd been there a few hours at least. I didn't know whether she was alive or dead and I wasn't sure if she had passed out there or had managed to fall asleep, which I doubted because of all the blood and bruising.

Her face had been beaten and I was sure if I lifted her dress I would find more bruises and cuts to match the collection on her face. Her left eye, the one closest to the floor, fluttered and struggled to open. So she wasn't dead. That seemed like a mere formality at that point. She had to strain at her eyelid to get it to break the seal of dried blood cementing her lashes together. Her right eye was swollen shut and it wasn't opening any time soon. My instinct was to take out my razor and cut it open for her to reduce the swelling but the feeling passed.

She got the left eye open and looked up at me. There was no recognition, only relief that it wasn't Clark. The rest of her started to move in small ways and it was unclear whether it was voluntary or not. I realized I was just standing there, staring. I had never seen anything like it but mostly because I hadn't hung around Hobbes's gym long enough to evaluate the damage I had caused last night. It may have been selfish in the moment but I thought about how I had inflicted this same punishment to another human being.

She made no sound and didn't appear to be trying. Her right hand was on the floor, spread out with all five fingers laid flat and as she lifted it she left an outline of her hand in dried blood like a child's finger painting project. Her hand rose a few inches but then flopped back down and sat in a ball on her knuckles this time.

I bent down and looked in her good eye.

"How can I help?" It was an honest question.

She said nothing. A blood vessel had burst in her eye and it bloomed red on one half, making the tiny sliver of white on the other side the only thing on her body that wasn't black or blue. I noticed two teeth frozen in blood beside her mouth. Her cheek was still glued to the floor with the blood. It seemed that much of it had flowed from her mouth.

Clark did this to her the night before, and he sat out there drinking without giving her another thought. I doubted he even remembered doing it. I didn't know which was worse, to do something like this and not even know it or to have done this and ignore it. What I did to Hobbes and Delancey never left my thoughts for a second. Clark had been far more concerned about where that next bottle was located.

Mrs. Dane was always good to us boys. She had a firm hand and wouldn't let us get away with any nonsense on her watch but she kept us in peach cobbler and shoofly pie so we didn't mind. She had an enormous laugh that shook the rafters.

I barely recognized her.

"Mrs. Dane? I'm going to call an ambulance. You stay here." As soon as I said that last part I felt silly. Of course she wasn't going anywhere. Maybe never again.

It occurred to me then that Velvy and I shared more than childhood play times. We shared no good bastards for fathers. I was being given a second chance to right a wrong that I hadn't acted on before and as reluctant as I was last night, now that I was face to face with it I felt the heat of rage start at the back of my neck and burn its way up into my brain.

That could have been my mom. It was my mom at one point. I had never seen her like that but now I knew exactly what I had been missing. Pop had done this to my mother, to his own wife. I was glad that I was here to see it and not Velvy. I had made it this far just fine without knowing exactly what happened to my mom and I wanted him to have that luxury. After the past twenty-four hours I'd never be that lucky again. What I saw I couldn't unsee, so what's one more vision to haunt my sleep?

I stood and turned to exit. A fly buzzed past my ear, drawn into the room by the smell of coagulated blood.

I crossed back through the kitchen. My eye caught the shotgun still on the counter. I kept moving past it and into the living room again.

Clark was taking another gulp. The bottle was already half empty.

"You still here boy?"

"Where is Mrs. Dane?"

"What?"

"Where is your wife?"

"The fuck I should know? She's a grown-ass woman. She can do as she pleases."

"Can she?"

"Boy, you better get the fuck outta here or I'm gonna go get my shotgun up again and make you go."

No remorse. No recognition of what he had done.

"Did you and your wife get into a fight?"

"A fi—? Who the fuck *are* you?" He shifted on the couch as if he was going to get up, but the deep nest and the effects of the alcohol on his equilibrium kept him in place.

"Did you beat up your wife last night Mr. Dane?"

"I beat on my wife, I don't beat on my wife, I beat on my kids, hell I beat off on my own dick ain't none of your concern. Key word in all that shit is *mine*. Now I'm gonna go get *mine* shotgun."

He pitched forward and let the momentum take him which seemed to be his main method of transportation. It got him off the couch but he ended up on his hands and knees on the floor in front of it.

I thought back to a time when me and Rex went to see Velvy. It was a split second thought but the whole memory was wrapped up inside that split second. Velvy came to the door with a shiner and when you can see a black eye plain as day on a black man's face you know it's bad. I'd seen guys go ten rounds and have better looking eyes than that. He stood behind the door and never opened it fully. He said no to stickball that day and for a week after. It was before Pop starting hitting on us so we didn't think much of it. Now I saw it for what it was. It was Clark. For years he'd been doing this. Velvy was squatting in a shitty apartment afraid to live his life because of this old man. Now this monster's wife was dying alone on a bathroom floor and he couldn't even goddamn acknowledge that he put her there.

I reached down and grabbed the scruff of his neck like an old dog. He grunted in surprise but was powerless from his position on the floor to do anything about it. I yanked him forward, keeping his hands and feet on the ground. His bottle of homemade spilled out on the floor and mixed with the years of other spills and mysterious stains.

I dragged him on all fours through the kitchen and to the open bathroom door.

"Look!" I shoved his face inside and lifted on his forehead to raise up his eyes. They were scared. It was a look a boxer should never have, even one past his prime.

He saw his wife. I could read the recognition rush across his face like blood flowing back into a vein after it had been tied off. He tried to scramble back but I held his face forward and just said, "Look!" again.

Mrs. Dane moved her body slightly and I saw her face start to peel up off the floor with the dark rusty blood holding her cheek down until she pulled hard enough to rip it off like a bandage. The strain of lifting her head was too much though and as soon as she had torn her skin loose she laid it back down again.

I tugged at Clark's neck and brought him back into the kitchen. With my free arm I grabbed the shotgun off the counter and we went back to the bathroom. I threw him down and gave him a kick so he was sent backward into the room. It was a small space even without the body splayed on the floor. With Mrs. Dane there, Clark had no choice but to land partly on her. He sat up quickly as if she was electrified. With one hand I held the gun and with the other I reached into my pocket and got out my razor. I bent down onto one knee, set the butt of the gun down in front of Clark, unfolded the razor and pressed it to his neck.

I leaned in close to his cauliflower ear and spoke low so she couldn't hear me. "You take that gun, put it in your mouth and pull the trigger."

He didn't react except to start shaking like he had the DTs. I pressed a little harder with the razor and a thin trickle of blood started to form.

I leaned the barrels of the gun up to his forehead. I kept watch on his hands to make sure he wouldn't make a grab for the gun to use it on me but Clark's days of fast reaction time and the element of surprise were behind him.

He kept his eyes shut tight but tears still leaked out of them like water straining at a kinked hose. His eyes eased open. He rolled them to the side—careful to avoid turning his head for fear the razor would slide across his throat—and looked at his wife. Three more flies joined the first to feed off the fragrant layer of blood leaking from her body and pooling on the floor.

I tapped the gun barrels against his forehead. I didn't want to have to repeat myself. Clark reached out a hand and it brushed the stock of the gun but he didn't grip it. He seemed too weak to grab anything, like his fingers had suddenly stopped working. He was sobbing now. A drunk sob; sloppy, spit covered and vocal. The kind that got no sympathy because everyone who heard it instantly knew it was just some drunk crying in the gutter about his lost youth or his dead dog from twenty years ago.

I picked up his hand and put it on the barrels of the gun and pushed it down off his forehead to his chin.

"You do it," I said through gritted teeth. "I ain't gonna do it for you and you ain't making it out of here alive."

I stood up quickly to make it to a defensive position before he could turn the gun on me. As I stood the razor slipped across his throat a little bit. The thin string of blood had turned to a rope of red, pulsing out and down his neck, stopping to form a small pool in his collarbone before flowing south over his chest and being absorbed by the bathrobe. He didn't seem to notice, the weeping was so intense. I stood, half crouched, waiting to either leap forward with the razor to cut him or lunge out of the way of a shotgun blast.

Clark was shaking, crying, and drooling. He didn't look like he was going to follow my instructions any time soon. I stood rocking back and forth in my crouch trying to be hyper aware but also spend some of my brain power on trying to come up with another plan to get him to pull the trigger when I saw it from the corner of my eye. It was the way you see a faint shifting of your opponent's feet that tells you when to take the big shot or catching your manager on the ringside as he gives you one quick hand signal saying, Go in for the kill.

It was Mrs. Dane's right hand. It hovered over the dried blood outline it had left earlier and had a kind of blood halo around the edges where it had been stuck to the floor for so long. Her index finger was extended and was reaching for the trigger. All she had to do was steady herself enough to slide it in the small opening and then let her hand drop again and the weight of it would set off both barrels.

I shifted my weight and jumped sideways into the kitchen. As I hit the floor the gun went off. The shot came through the thin wall and sprayed plaster and cheap tile into the kitchen. Little flecks of red came through the wall as well. Clark. Soon to be coagulating himself.

Silence followed the deafening explosion as the dust

settled and my ears rang from the intensity of the blast.

I stood up and brushed off. I looked at the razor in my hand. I threw it into the kitchen sink. I never wanted to see it again.

I stumbled out into the living room and made for the door.

Spectators, drawn to the sound of the blast, gathered out front. I walked out with purpose but no one tried to stop me at all.

"Call an ambulance," I said to the small crowd.

I heard someone say, "Shit, ambulance don't come around here."

# 18

*Fokoli*

They called him Nickel Whip Perez because of the five cents worth of licorice whips he kept in his front pocket. When he got the urge to smoke, he'd eat a piece of licorice. "My wife can't stand smoke," he told Bob and me because Bob asked him about it.

From the look of it, Perez ate a lot of licorice . . . and it had rotted his teeth down to dark black nubs. He didn't feel too talkative after we showed him our badges. "Fucking cops," he said, with a bit of Mexico in his voice. "Always sticking your dicks in holes they got no business going. Take your dicks someplace else, man. Leave me alone."

"Come on, Perez," Bob said, pulling his hat off. "Just a few questions."

"Yeah, sure, sure," Perez said. "It's always just a few questions. Then it turns into a few more and then I end up downtown."

"Look," I said, but Perez wasn't listening. He was writing something down on his clipboard and whistled at a couple of guys standing around near another cargo container. "Dock Two," he said, jerking his head to the next dock over. Dock Two jutted out farther into the water than Dock Three and a Carolina skiff floated there, ready to make its way upriver.

"What's in the boat?" I asked.

Perez's face got a little red and he pulled a piece of licorice from his pocket. "None of your goddamned business."

"Chinchillas?" Bob asked.

"What do I know from chinchillas?" Perez said.

We couldn't search the cargo hold without reason and I didn't figure Bob had the balls to do anything dangerous . . . plus I needed Bob to keep on the straight and narrow right now . . . so I did the next best thing. I grabbed Perez by the shirt collar and shoved him against the corrugated metal wall of his "office," which was nothing more than an emptied out freight container.

"Listen, you," I said, "I got other places I need to be. I'd like to get to those places as soon as possible, see?" Bob politely turned his head. "My partner and I have a few questions for you and if you know what's good for you, you'll answer them."

Perez didn't look scared. He looked angry, but still he gestured to the cargo box that stood empty except for a card table and two chairs and a rusty metal cart with a hot plate on it. A coffee pot simmered on the burner. Bob made his way toward the coffee pot. "You don't touch my coffee, damn cop," Perez said.

Bob hid a smile and took one of the wobbly chairs. Perez took the other. That left me to stand, which was fine.

"We're looking for some fur," I said.

"You want a whore, you go to Third Street."

"Fuck you, Perez," I said. "I mean fur. Hobbes was killed before the fifty grand in chinchillas he was hoarding in his house could be transported."

Perez's face blanched just a little.

Bob leaned forward in his chair. "So are you the one who ships the fur out on that Carolina skiff over at Dock Two?" His voice had an edge I hadn't heard before. Maybe Bob's balls were dropping. It made me feel better about the way things were going for me, knowing Bob would be okay.

"I don't know what the fuck you're talking about," Perez said.

I pulled out a cigarette and cupped my hand to get it lit. "You know a guy by the name of DeLuca?"

He started to sweat and I could see the wheels turning in his head, wondering what he should do. Right now he could lie to the cops, knowing full well we could make life hell for him, or he could admit to knowing DeLuca and risk getting fitted for a pair of cement boots. Me and Bob kept quiet while he thought it over.

"I gotta get back to work," he said after awhile. "Got things to do." I could tell he was scared now. And that was good. Dangerous. But good.

Bob stood up and we made our way toward the opening in the cargo container. "We'll be sure and give DeLuca your best," I said.

Me and Bob made our way back to our car, which was on a street running parallel to the main walkway of the K.C. Docks. From the car we could see Perez hurrying along to Dock Two and barking orders at the men on the skiff, his arms gesturing madly.

"You think he ships the fur?" Bob asked.

"Hell yes," I said. But we looked at each other and shrugged.

"So DeLuca's furrier is dead," Bob said.

I nodded. "And we have the fur, so he's out fifty grand."

"And Hobbes was cheating his boxers . . ."

". . . who were talking union even before Hobbes got killed."

Bob clenched his fists. "How's DeLuca going to fund a union with no money?"

I shook my head. "Oh, DeLuca's got money. Lots of it. But that's not our problem. Our problem is that the K.C. mob thinks Chicago whacked Hobbes. And the Chicago mob thinks the K.C. mob did it. If there's a street war over this, so be it. I just want to catch the real killer."

I already knew who finished Hobbes. And I think Bob knew it too. But with me simmering in a nice pot of hot water, we couldn't just run off after the murderer . . . especially when we didn't know how to find him. Our job was to pretend we thought a gangster from Chicago killed Hobbes and Delancey, no matter how unlikely it was.

We pulled off at a small diner shaped like a torpedo and ordered coffee and toast. While we waited for the food, I called the station to fill Tolene in on Perez's dealings at the docks.

"What?" he said. Didn't sound too happy.

I told him about Perez. And Clete. "I don't know if there

will be a turf war over all this or not," I said. "If Chicago thinks a middle man here in K.C. whacked Hobbes and Delancey, then there will be more shootings."

"Already had one today," Tolene said. "Somebody just shot up Carlisle's Restaurant." Carlisle's was a hangout for the Chicago boys when they were in town. I used to be a regular when I was peddling information and taking bribes. Carlisle could make a mean plate of spaghetti, but there wasn't a straight customer who set foot in his front door. And I ought to know.

The captain's news was bad. We weren't going to stop a turf war. The best thing the cops could do was get out of the way, let the bad guys shoot each other until numbers on both sides were sufficiently thinned and Chicago went back home.

Tolene got tired of waiting for me to say something. "Get over to Carlisle's, Fokoli," he said. Then he hung up.

I gave Bob the news, then I ate a piece of cold toast and set it afloat with two cups of coffee. I couldn't help wondering of Laura had eaten yet, or if she'd invested the twenty bucks I left her in another bottle or two. I shoved an extra piece of toast in my pocket to take home to her. Maybe I'd stop and get a cut of meat for dinner if I got away from the office early enough.

The street in front of Carlisle's was busy with the usual daily traffic but the restaurant itself was quiet . . . just after lunch and too early for dinner. The front window had been shot out, and the glass on the front door was shattered, but the joint was otherwise in good shape. Carlisle figured bullet holes gave the place character, so he didn't really want us to pursue an investigation. "Leave it alone," he said. "Nothing much you can do."

Me and Bob nodded and Carlisle gave me a bottle of wine. "For your wife," he said. I gave the bottle to Bob in the car. I knew he wasn't married, but he had to have a girl stashed someplace, and Laura didn't need the wine.

"Dead end," Bob said about Carlisle's.

"Did you expect anything different?" I asked.

I wondered if Hobbes's killer was aware of the trouble he'd managed to stir up. Right then, I'd have given just about anything to find out.

# 19

*Ray*

I moved away from the growing crowd of gawkers outside Clark's and retraced my steps back to Velvy's apartment. I walked quickly but never heard sirens. No one called an ambulance. No one called the cops. I knocked hard on Velvy's door before I gave myself too much time to think. I didn't know what I would say to him but I figured I'd just spill it all out and let Velvy pick up the pieces. It's what he wanted anyway. But I knew he wouldn't be happy to hear about what Clark did to his mom.

He was shirtless when he answered the door and he looked a little hazy-drunk even though it was barely past noon. I could smell the alcohol on his breath from out in the hallway. He had showered and shaved though. He kept clean and that gave me hope that he wasn't lost to the bottle. Once this news hit him I had faith he could turn things around for himself and maybe get out of this rat hole once and for all.

"It's done," I said.

A smile crept up on his face and cocked one corner of his mouth up where it stayed for the rest of the time I was there.

"You did it? He's gone?"

"Real gone," I said, hinting.

"Shit, Ray . . . gone, gone?"

"Dead."

Velvy looked down at the floor and I thought for a second he might cry. Tears of joy, not sadness. He held it together and swung his eyes up to meet mine; sober as the day he was born.

"You really did it?"

"Sort of. Your mom pulled the trigger. You should call an ambulance. She's hurt pretty bad."

"'Cause of him?" Just as I thought, there was no surprise

in his voice.

I nodded.

"You got a dime?" he asked. I fished one out of my pocket and handed it over. He stepped into the hall leaving his door wide open. Two empty liquor bottles stood on his table.

Velvy placed a call to the hospital at the pay phone in the hall. He didn't mention the dead body they would also find, just gave numbers and street and said his mother's name.

He hung up and looked at me. We stayed in the hallway.

"You find out what you needed to before he passed?"

"Enough," I said.

"Good. You do right by Rex. He was a good kid."

Rex was only two months younger than Velvy but the hard lines on Velvy's face made him seem much older than that. I liked it that he called Rex a kid.

"Will you be okay?" I asked.

"Never better. I feel like I'm livin' an old time gospel tune. I once was lost but now I'm found. You done me a great, great thing Ray. I'm in your debt. You call on me when you need me and I'll be there."

"You already were, Velvy. Thanks."

We embraced and slapped each other's backs hard and the sounds echoed down the hall and went out to the street where they mixed with the shouts of kids playing stickball without a care in the world.

I stepped onto the streets of Negrotown again and got the double takes and long stares out of the way. I contemplated where to start my search for Baxter. "Look for a fight," Clark had said. Not much happening in the fight game on a Sunday afternoon. Fighters are a Jesus-loving bunch and tend to take that day of rest thing seriously. Rex and I always did our hardest workouts on Sundays, figuring it gave us an edge over the other guys. I guess God finally got back at us for all that sinning.

I set out for the Excelsior, figuring that if a fight was going to break out it would happen there as well as anywhere, seeing as they had the seats and the ring and everything.

A return to the scene of the crime.

I was lost in thought. I've lived my whole life surrounded by violence but always a controlled violence. A referee was there to keep it above the waist. A timer was there to ring the bell. The newspaper men were there to put all the blood and sweat into flowery words to make it seem like what we were doing was more than just two guys slugging each other. They compared us to Greek gods and quoted Shakespeare. Horse shit, but I ate it up with everyone else who read the fight column on Monday morning. It was enough to make you remember it differently.

"Remember in the fifth when you brought down that right like an oak tree falling in an old-growth forest?" I'd say to Rex. "No," he'd say. "Well, I do. It was a mighty blow that sounded out across the hall like the bells of Notre Dame and when that oaf hit the canvas the earth shook like Krakatoa had awakened again."

"Crack a what-a?" he'd ask. I'd have no answer but boy, it sure did sound grand. That's the kind of ideas those writers can put in your head.

"Cracker ass mother fucker!" The voice shook me back to the present. It came from behind and I turned to see my three friends from the night before; Dandruff, Mustache and Bad Breath were all walking toward me. It wasn't the most intimidating sight because I could tell they had already been well into their wine but three-to-one odds meant that I would take at least a few shots just by law of averages. I picked up my pace.

I guess moving any faster wasn't an option for them or maybe they just weren't that into the chase but a wine bottle was sent sailing my way. It smashed on the ground and tiny green shards hit my feet as I came to the edge of the street that defined Negrotown.

Another bottle was launched my way and I had to side

step to avoid it. This one even had a few good sips of wine still left in the bottom so I knew these boys were pissed off at me. I couldn't say I blamed them much. I bet they woke up with worse headaches than normal that morning.

I crossed the street and I guess Mustache was feeling left out of our little game of catch because he sent his bottle flying as well. It was a high, arcing toss that I watched fall to earth for a long time. It was so off target that I didn't need to adjust my angle of crossing. The bottle spun end over end with little rain drops of wine shooting out the neck as it rotated. Watching it drop lower on the horizon I saw what I should have seen sooner if I hadn't been so involved in the flight path of the bottle—a cop car.

The bottle smashed violently on the street about five feet in front of the cops. I turned to see what my three friends would do when they saw the police but they had seen it way before I did and suddenly got a burst of speed because I couldn't even see them anymore.

The cop car skidded to a halt making a more dramatic squeal of tires than was really necessary. I stopped, knowing only guilty men run.

"Shit," I muttered to myself as the cops both sprang out of the car as if the bottle had been a bullet and as if it was intended for them and not me. I went through the list of things I would say to Rex in the corner just before a fight.

Don't panic. Stay light on your feet. Stick to the fundamentals and you'll be just fine. Think defense, not offense until you see what they're showing. Even of it gets bad you're only one swing away from winning.

The driver stepped up to me. His partner was looking across the street from where the bottle had come. The driver got closer and I could read his name tag—Kaminski. I knew a fighter named Kowalski once. Big brute of a guy. Dumb as a bag of hammers. The boys all had a lot of fun telling Polish jokes at his expense. Kowalski was dumb enough to make the jokes more true than funny.

"What the hell was that?" asked Kaminski.

"A wine bottle I believe," I replied. Apparently he

thought that was a smart ass answer and he put one hand on his night stick.

"I can see that," he said. I wondered why he asked.

"You fightin' with them boys?" asked the partner. By "them boys" he seemed to mean any and all of Negrotown, as if everyone who lived there was interchangeable with one another. I could see why the three of them ran.

"I guess they were mad about something." I stood still and kept my cool. Kaminski kept rubbing his chin and looking back and forth from me to the smashed bottle on the ground, to the front end of his car which didn't have so much as a drop of wine on it, and then to his partner, as if this was a highly confounding crime scene and he was just scratching the surface of it all.

Inside the cop car the radio crackled and a woman's voice came on.

"Car twenty-four you still on patrol?"

The partner leaned into the car and picked up the hand set and replied to her.

"Yeah, Shirl. Still here." He didn't mention the highly tense and dangerous situation he was in currently. I smiled. Shirley continued.

"You got a one eight seven over on twenty-seventh. Woman shot her husband after he beat her silly. Some blacks said they seen a white guy leaving the house though so they want us on it."

Kaminski and his partner stared each other down across the divide, planning their next move.

"We got a . . . uh . . ." the partner struggled for the right words to excuse them from the murder scene. "Uh, a situation here. We may have a suspect in custody. Any description?"

They both looked at me waiting to match me to whatever Shirley said.

"They said white guy, that's it. To them we all look the same."

"All right, Shirl. We got a guy we'll bring in for a lineup. Send car eighteen to the scene."

He tossed the handset back into the front seat without waiting for Shirley's response. Kaminski drew out his handcuffs and approached me.

"Care to take a ride?" he asked as he cuffed my hands behind my back.

"I don't seem to have much choice. You don't really think I did it, do you? You just don't want to go over there."

"Look, pal, if we go over there we're gonna find fifty angry blacks telling us we came too late and then some hot shit homicide guy is gonna show up in his suit and tie and shut us out because we're only lowly uniforms like he was never in one. I take you in and I get to have some coffee, relax a bit and maybe, just maybe, you're my killer. At the very least you were disturbing the peace with this bottle throwing shit."

"But I didn't throw the bottles. They were thrown at me."

"Well, then you disturbed someone awful bad to make them want to chuck bottles at you. I don't know what you did, fucked some colored guy's wife or what, but we all three of us get a free ride down to the station and I'll tell you what, the coffee is on me."

He ducked my head as he pushed me into the back seat. I could have done worse with two cops who gave a crap. These two didn't. Time to just keep the feet moving and lay back, play defense for awhile. Keep the guard up and wait for the bell.

# 20

*Fokoli*

We got half a block before I saw Carlisle dart out of his restaurant and signal to the goon he had stashed across the street. "We're going back," I said to Bob.

"What's up?"

"Carlisle duped us."

Bob craned his neck around so he could see the man in the black trench coat cross the street and disappear into the front of the restaurant with Carlisle.

"What's it mean?" Bob asked while I turned the car around.

I didn't answer him. Carlisle was banking on me being a crooked cop. That's why he sent us away. And I was too tired and stupid to put up a fuss. But the goon hiding across the street was a bad omen. It meant he'd been inside the restaurant when the shooting happened. Goons are like dogs; they travel in packs. If he was inside, there'd been others inside and my gut was telling me they'd been hit in the drive-by.

I turned at the next block and circled around to the alley in back of Carlisle's so we could punch our way in the rear. After I parked the car we climbed out and drew our guns. I willed Bob to keep his mouth shut and his eyes open. He didn't have much experience with closing in on a joint and after his reaction at Hobbes's gym I didn't know if I could count on him holding it together.

The door leading in from the alley was ajar, swaying in the breeze and creaking on hinges in need of a good oiling. I crab-walked a little closer and motioned for Bob to stand aside so he could take on anyone who got past me.

I couldn't see inside but I knew the layout from previous visits. A short, narrow hallway opened up into a large kitchen. The kitchen had a tile floor with a drain in the middle. I'd seen that drain used a few times for things besides mop water.

I thought about entering but I had no way of knowing what Carlisle was doing in there, who he was with, or if maybe me and Bob should call for backup.

The sound of labored breathing and grunting came from inside. Someone was heading in our direction. Bob and I crouched lower, ready to lunge at whoever was getting ready to push their way into the alley.

Carlisle backed out first, struggling to stay upright under the weight of the corpse he was helping to carry. His fat hands were wrapped around of pair of scrawny ankles that were connected to a pair of size thirteen feet stuffed inside size twelve shoes. The goon we'd seen trotting in the front door emerged next, carrying the stiff's shoulders.

"What's your hurry?" I asked, leveling my gun and touching it to the back of Carlisle's neck.

Carlisle started a little and almost dropped his half of the body. Now that I could see the goon with the shoulders up close I recognized him as one of the guys in the pool hall with DeLuca.

"You're having a busy day," I said, watching him struggle with the dead man.

Bob said, "Set him down, boys. We'll need to report it."

Carlisle dropped the feet and backed away, pressing up against the grimy brick wall.

"Anybody else inside?" I asked.

Carlisle shook his head.

I looked at the goon. "You got a name?"

He lifted a corner of his mouth, like this was all real fun for him. "Name's Chuckles," he said. I remembered then; DeLuca had called him Charlie. I looked at the stiff. I didn't recognize him.

"Chuckles?" Bob asked.

"Yeah," the goon said with a sneer. "'Cuz I'm so much fun."

"Drop your friend," I told him and he did. Bob frisked him, pulling out a .38 special, a set of brass knuckles, and a knife from his pocket.

"Where you boys headed?" I asked. Carlisle looked at me like I was a stranger; wondering why I didn't remember our "working" relationship. Word about my change in heart hadn't spread this far downtown, I guess.

"To church," Chuckles said, nodding to the stiff. "Last rites."

The banter was getting old and my feet were tired. I still had a piece of toast in my pocket for Laura. I wondered what time it was. Had she eaten yet?

We cuffed Carlisle and Chuckles and stuffed them in the back of our car, then we radioed in for backup. I left Bob with the car and went into the kitchen to check for any more bodies.

There were two.

My heart did a little skip. They had to have been plugged while standing out in the dining room and dragged in here when the shooting stopped. The fact that Carlisle was going to keep it quiet meant Chicago was planning revenge. No cops meant no newspapers. It was mafia style all the way. Keep the killings quiet and the other side wouldn't know when revenge was knocking at the door.

Shit.

I pushed through the kitchen and stood in the dining room for a minute staring at the blood on the floor. Carlisle's boasted a long bar on one side of the room and I took the opportunity of being alone to fix myself a Scotch. Then I sat at the bar and thought about the case. And about Mark. And about Laura.

It was fifteen minutes before anyone showed up. Two uniforms. Younger than me and even Bob. "What do we have here?" one asked, his hand on his gun.

My badge was on the table and I pointed to it with my empty glass. "Ah," he said. "You're Fokoli." He said it like he knew it was a bad thing to be me. Which it was.

"Yeah," I said. "I'm Fokoli. You bring the meat wagon with you?"

His partner shook his head. "They're coming."

I stood and put my glass on the bar, thinking again about Laura and the bruises on her arms. We needed to work the scene before we could leave. It would be at least another hour before I could get away to check on her. In the alley, Bob was leaning against the side of the car, his arms folded over his chest.

"Two stiffs inside," I told him. He wasn't surprised.

I pulled out the piece of toast and showed it to him. "Mind if I disappear for a little bit?" I asked.

His jaw worked a little. We both knew my time on the force was coming to an end, so if I left now to check on Laura it wouldn't really matter. But Bob would know about it and knowing about it might cause him problems with Tolene down the road. He thought it over. "Go on. Get out of here," he said.

I told him I'd be back in thirty minutes, but I didn't know if that was true or not. I didn't know if he'd tell the captain I'd left the crime scene at Carlisle's or make up some other excuse. It didn't matter. It ended up being a family emergency.

Laura loved baths. In summer, she'd bathe twice a day, an hour each time. That's one twelfth of her life she'd spend soaking in water. On purpose.

I, for one, looked at bathing as necessary and functional rather than something of a luxury. So it was a rare thing when I joined her in the tub. When I did, I confess, my purpose had nothing to do with washing behind my ears.

She hadn't indulged in baths much since Mark died, since she found out about my part in it. But I could smell her soap the minute I opened the front door. I stood there for a minute, hesitating. An empty bottle had overturned beside the couch and it was clear what she had used the twenty on. I took a deep breath, shut the front door, and headed for the bathroom.

Her head was above water. That was something anyway. But the color of her skin was worse, a deep brown mottled with purple. I knelt beside her, patting her cheeks and saying her name, my sleeves and my tie soaking up the water.

"Laura," I said.

I saw a pulse winking at me from her neck. It was faint, but it was there. I smiled a little, surprised at the relief I felt. Always I had wondered how I would feel if she died. Would it be better for us both if she was gone?

For now, there was that pulse—that tiny, flickering pulse and I felt nothing but an overwhelming sense of happiness.

I scooped her up and carried her to the bedroom, rolling the bedspread over her.

I rode with her in the ambulance, holding her hand and whispering in her ear. "I love you, Laura."

When we got to the hospital, they took her away, down a long hallway, and told me I couldn't go along. It was just as well. I didn't know how to help her.

My suit was wet and smelled like her soap. I held my tie to my nose in the taxi as I made my way back to Carlisle's.

Tolene had been and gone by then and Bob had taken Chuckles and Carlisle back to the station. The coroner was finishing up with the corpses in the kitchen. A photographer snapped my picture as I walked in the back door. I felt like punching him, but the effort to lift my arms would have been too great.

I turned and left, catching a cab back to the station, ready to talk to Bob and Chuckles and Carlisle if I had to. Mostly, I wanted to find the boxer's brother, Ray Ward, and let him know what he'd started. Maybe I wanted to make him pay for it all; for Hobbes, for Delancey, for Laura. I don't know. The urge to find him had become palpable and it pushed against me from all sides, like water in a dam.

By the time I reached the station, the dam was ready to burst.

# 21

*Ray*

The ride to the police station was less than comfortable because of the handcuffs pinning my hands behind my back. Kaminski and his partner talked and laughed about life outside the force. If I hadn't been there against my will it would have been a pleasant drive. At least they left the window open for me and a cool breeze blew in. It filled my ears with a steady rushing sound that blocked out most of the conversation from the front seat so when they finally did acknowledge me I didn't notice at first. By the time I heard Kaminski he was shouting.

"Ward! I'm talking to you!"

"Sorry, what?"

"I asked if you had a record. Ever been arrested before?"

His partner spoke up. "We need to know for the report. Makes it easier on us if we can just pull your file."

These two seemed to be all about making the job easier. Kansas City's finest.

"No. Never." The boys in blue looked disappointed and went back to ignoring me.

Rex had gotten busted once. I bailed him out of a jail cell in an Iowa town called Burlington. He was up there for a fight at an Elks' lodge and before the fight even began an Elk, I think he may have been the Big Cheese or whatever they call the head Elk, started in on Rex. This guy had already guzzled about sixteen beers as far as I could tell and Rex had very little tolerance for drunks. Even less than I do.

He ranted about how there had never been a decent fighter to come out of the Midwest. Rex argued that Max Baer was born in Omaha and that Joe Louis got his start in Detroit. This didn't seem to hold any water with the Big Cheese and he started in calling Joe Louis all kinds of names. He seemed to hate just about everyone. He called

Primo Carnera a dirty wop and Max Schmeling a kraut. This guy was an equal opportunity offender. Not sure if you ever saw them fight but Schmeling and Carnera are guys you do not want to insult. They would have taken this Elk and mounted his head on the wall in a library.

The other Elks seemed to get a kick out of the Big Cheese, though, and they laughed up a storm and spit beer out of their noses when he came out with another insult to a boxer who could have torn him apart, all five foot five and two-hundred-thirty pounds of him—two-thirty-three if you added in all the hair grease he wore..

It was when he said that Rex didn't stand a chance against the fighter they had lined up that night, who happened to be the Big Cheese's son-in-law, that the shit hit the fan. To make his point the Big Cheese said Rex would have better luck against a dame. Then, to better make his point, he socked one of the girls serving drinks. He didn't punch her hard but he was sloppy enough about it that the tray of beers she was holding tipped over, spilled on her dress, and smashed at her feet making her slip. She landed with one knee down on the broken glass. That was too much for Rex.

He pulled his arm back and hit the Big Cheese with an uppercut that broke more than a few teeth. I could tell because he spit them out high into the air like he was performing some sort of bar trick. The other Elks rushed in but they were out of shape and too drunk to punch so Rex tossed them off with a single punch each until he had a pile of drunken Elks at his feet like Popeye in a cartoon. I got a few shots on the back row fellows that tried to join in but I concentrated on getting that girl up and out of there.

Rex gave me the nod to take care of her so I turned and ushered her out. By the time I got her to the hospital, her stocking had filled up with blood and the doctor said her knee needed more stitches than his Grandmother's quilt which I assumed was a good amount.

I made a call to the local police station and my hunch was right: Rex was there. I'm not sure if it was because the cops were dumb or it was such a small town that they only had one cell but they threw Rex right in with the pack of drunks he had just beaten up. When I got there to bail him out there were six drunk Elks with shiners on one side of the cell all crowded onto a cot and Rex alone on the other side leaning against the bars. That was our only real run-in with the law.

Kaminski and his partner hauled me out when we got to the station. I think they were making a show for the other officers because they started acting real tough and shouting profanities at me. I just shuffled slowly where they wanted me to go and didn't make a fuss.

I couldn't believe that for both of the murders I had committed, I was being brought in for one I didn't even do. I only hoped to be out of there in time to get back to finding Baxter.

At the front desk Kaminski made a big deal of announcing me to the desk sergeant.

"Here he is, Cooley. Your Negrotown killer. All wrapped up nice and pretty for you. We got him running back into our part of town."

"Issat right, Pete?" Cooley drawled. He sounded like he was taking a nap. "Well now, you jus' take him right on in and set him right on down and we'll make sure he's mighty comfortable."

I was taken to a simple room with no windows and only a table with a chair on either side of it and a lamp hanging down making harsh shadows. They left my hands cuffed but put them out in front of me so at least I could sit more comfortably. That meant I was going to be there awhile.

There was a clean ashtray on the table but that was all that passed for decoration.

"Time for us to do some paperwork, Ray. You sit tight." Kaminski left and I heard him laughing down the hall. I knew I'd never see them again. They were done for the day. The paperwork would take them the rest of their shift.

I sat for a long time. Hard to say how long since the room didn't have a clock, but if I had to guess, I'd say at least an hour. With my finger, I traced some initials carved into the table by some other man in custody who had come before me. I let my fingers wander beneath the table and felt more etchings, but I couldn't make out the letters. I bent down to read what my fingers could not discern and saw FUCK YOU in big letters.

Some beat cop hadn't done their job and let a prisoner sit down with a sharp instrument. Could have been Kaminski or it could have been any other cop on the force trying to cut their shift short with paperwork. Easier to avoid getting shot at when you're in the station house typing. I touched the letters again. If the guy who carved them had kept a pen knife hidden I'd hate to think what he did with it when someone finally came in to interrogate him.

The door opened. No knock. A detective came in.

"Ray?" he asked but I knew that he knew my name. I nodded. "I'm detective Bob White. I'd like to ask you a few questions."

Detective White was a pudgy guy and he looked like he spent his whole life in a suit jacket, maybe even slept in it, but it was never going to make him look any better than just a Midwestern cop who had graduated to homicide because there was an open slot, not through any real skills he had to offer.

There goes my fighter's confidence. Sizing up an opponent and knowing just how much better I was than him. In my mind I had already won this fight.

"You spend a lot of time in Negrotown, do you, Ray?"

"Not a lot."

"But some?"

"Some."

"Okay." He wrote that down. I'd given him a non-answer but made him feel like he had dug it out of me so he felt enough of a sense of accomplishment to make a record of it. This was going to be easy. So I kept telling myself. Truth is, the back of my neck was getting hot now that a real detective was here sniffing around. If the questions all stayed with Clark's murder I could do this no trouble. If Delancey or Hobbes came up, I'd have to do some fancy footwork. I had no idea if I was a good liar or not. Until now I hadn't known I was capable of killing someone.

"What were you doing there today?" he was poised to write down my answer.

"To visit a girl." What the heck. I had already been accused of that anyway.

"What girl?"

"Any girl."

Detective White got a flash of understanding. He wrote it down.

"A whore," he clarified. I nodded. "You like 'em dark skinned like that?"

"I guess so."

He felt as if he made a real break through.

The door opened and another detective stepped in. The way detective White yielded I knew this was the guy who was really in charge. He carried himself differently. Beaten down but tougher for it. Punched out but smarter from it. The lines of experience criss-crossing his face were made deeper by the harsh lighting.

He didn't say anything at first. Smart. Let your opponent come to you. Detective White filled him in on his notes in a sidebar off in the corner of the room. The new guy kept aiming looks over White's shoulder to me in my chair. I rattled my cuffs on the table and then worried it made me seem nervous—which I was.

The conference ended and the new guy stepped into the pool of light.

"Ray, I'm Detective Fokoli. I'm sorry about your brother."

I wondered if he was a fight fan or if he just read the report from the homicide squad. I nodded.

"Let's talk about why you were really in Negrotown today."

Gloves up Ray. Stay on your toes. Defense. Keep moving.

## 22

*Fokoli*

Tolene called me into his office the minute we got back to the station. "You disappeared," he said. I opened my mouth to tell him about Laura, but closed it again. The thing with Laura was private. So I told him what I thought about the shooting at Carlisle's and how I figured if we could get Hobbes's killer and prove it wasn't a mob job, we could avoid an all out war.

He listened to me with his chin cradled in his hands, like this was some kind of bedtime story. When I was done talking, he pinched the bridge of his nose. It was clear he didn't plan to do a fucking thing. About any of it. I'd blown my wad for nothing.

I pulled Laura's piece of toast out of my pocket and dropped it in the trash.

"You do a little dining at Carlisle's?" Tolene watched the soggy piece of bread fall into the garbage and I wondered if he would use something as flimsy as a lunch break as an excuse to get rid of me.

"It was for Laura," I said.

His mouth twisted a little. "I imagine she's hungry."

I didn't say anything to that, just thought about her on the gurney disappearing down the white hallway.

"We've got the brother," Tolene said.

My fists clenched. "Ray."

"Yeah. Ray. Seems he was strolling out of Negrotown a couple of hours ago at the same time we got a call about gunshots. Found a dead guy in a bathroom and a woman beat nearly to death right next to him."

I didn't know what to say to that so I just asked if there was a report yet.

"Kaminski brought him in. He's typing it up." Tolene smirked a little as he looked at me. "I figured you'd want to have a crack at him."

I shrugged, feeling the weight of that statement. Sure, I wanted a crack at Ray. I wanted a lot of things. But right now I was circling the drain and I didn't know if I had the strength to keep my head above water much longer.

Tolene stared at me. "Get out of here," he said. "Question Ray. Try not to fuck it up."

I let Bob go in first, mainly to let him get his legs under him. Bob was still at the stage of the game where he was scared of suspects. Never let a suspect see your fear. I told him that over and over, but the only way for Bob to get over it was to sit in a room on his own.

I smoked part of a cigarette while Bob did his thing. Then I went in.

Ray was a hard cord of a man, muscles coiled tight enough to fire bullets without a gun if needed. His hands were cuffed together and rested on the table in front of him. Like the cuffs would do me and Bob any good if Ray decided to pounce.

Bob wiped the sweat off his forehead when he saw me and led me over to the corner to tell me what he'd got so far . . . which wasn't much. "Says he was looking for a girl."

"Whore?"

Bob nodded.

I moved back over to the table and told Ray I was sorry about his brother—and that was the truth. I was sorry about a lot of things and his brother's death was just one more on the list. "Let's talk about what you were really doing in Negrotown."

His fists clenched a little when I said that, the tendons of his wrists straining against the metal of the cuffs. "Get those off him, Bob," I said.

Bob looked like he wanted to argue, but he took the cuffs off and stepped back, like maybe he'd let a tiger out of the cage or something. Ray just nodded and sat there, not giving in to the urge to rub the raw spots.

"You want a cigarette?" I asked.

"Don't smoke."

I shrugged. "So how about it? What were you doing there?"

"What makes you think I'm lying about the girl?"

"I think you've been too busy to think about girls."

He was silent.

"Tell me about the fight."

Ray didn't say anything. He met my eyes and I could tell he was a man who'd seen a lot in the last couple of days. It occurred to me that maybe he knew what it was like to be circling the drain too.

Bob cleared his throat and shuffled his feet and looked like maybe he wanted to say something, but I held up my hand and he backed off. I couldn't fault Ray for not wanting to talk about the fight and I sure as hell didn't want him going ape on me and Bob.

"Fine," I said. "Fair enough." I made a point of looking at his hands. Bruised, raw knuckles.

"Let's talk about Hobbes."

A muscle worked a little bit in his jaw. "What do you want to know?"

"Why'd you kill him?"

"Who said I did?"

"No one yet, but there's a pretty boy in lock up who says he saw someone leaving the gym."

Ray shrugged. "How do you know it was me?"

"My gut tells me."

The corner of his mouth curved up a little and I thought how he was probably a handsome enough kid when the world wasn't crushing him like it was just then.

"That's some gut," he said.

"Yeah. So how about it? Tell me about Hobbes."

"Can't tell what I don't know."

He acted tough, and he was, but beneath it there was a sadness that touched the tough part of him. I bet he couldn't tell where the one feeling ended and the other began anymore. Or maybe I was just seeing myself in him.

I sat down in the chair across from him, leaving Bob to lean against the wall behind me. "Delancey killed your brother."

The muscles in Ray's forearms moved beneath the surface of his skin, but his hands stayed curled on the table . . . the perfect picture of self control.

"Yeah," he said after a minute, "he killed my brother."

I figured he had a raw nerve exposed now. So I did my best to step on it. "I heard the fight on the radio." I shook my head. "When a guy goes down that fast, you gotta figure the fight is fixed."

The muscles moved and his fingers looked like maybe they wanted to clench a little now. "Really," I went on, "these days seems like all fights around K.C. are fixed. It's the way of it." I leaned back and lit a cigarette and acted like I was putting some pieces together in my head. "But you and your brother never played that game. Right?" Ray looked me in the eye. "So the fight would have to be rigged in such a way that Delancey's victory was a sure thing." Ray put his hands flat on the table. "And the only way to make sure that was the case was to cheat." I watched him a little longer. "We've got the gloves, Ray. A man gets hit enough with a pair of lead gloves and he'll never get up again. I can see how that might piss you off a little."

Ray looked down at his hands and I thought for just that instant he was going to break and tell me everything. And I thought how disappointed I'd be if he did.

I pulled out a cigarette and stood with one clenched between my lips for a minute while I watched Ray. After a minute I called outside for a clerk to bring us some water. Ray drank like he'd gone days without anything. I sat down again. "So they didn't call the fight and your brother died."

"That was a tough break," Bob said, then shrank back against the wall when me and Ray glared at him.

"I'm guessing you tracked Hobbes down first so you could figure out where Delancey lived. Sometimes these managers don't like to flaunt the whereabouts of their fighters . . . don't want other managers luring them away."

Ray played with his water glass.

I leaned back in my chair. "You opened a whole can of

worms for me when you killed Hobbes," I said. "You started something that's going to get a whole lot uglier in the next few days."

He still didn't say anything, but his hands moved away from the glass and relaxed on the table again.

"You wanna know why it's so obvious you did Hobbes?" I asked. "Because his head looked just like they said Rex's did after the fight. Brain pudding. That's what they said."

Rex stood up fast enough to knock his chair over. Bob jerked away from the wall, his clumsy hand reaching for his gun. I just leaned back and stared into Ray's eyes, thinking he was capable of revenge, thinking I knew he killed Hobbes and Delancey, but knowing we'd never get him to break and tell us the truth. Ray was tough, hardened by years of . . . something.

The door opened and Kaminski dropped a report on the table. "Here you go, Detective," he said. "These are the notes on the Negrotown arrest."

I pushed back from the table. "Stay here, Bob," I said, ignoring how stricken he looked at the order, and followed Kaminski into the hallway. "What's the Negrotown story?" I asked when we were out of the room.

Kaminski shrugged. "We got a call about gunfire and were in the neighborhood."

I flipped through the report . . . a one page summary filled with typos. "You actually saw the dead man and the beaten woman?"

Kaminski looked down and shuffled his feet. "Well, no. Not exactly. I phoned the sheriff's department when we got back to the station. They filled in the blanks."

I rubbed the back of my neck. "Jesus Christ."

"Look, Fokoli," he said, "Negrotown is county business. Everyone knows that. They have black deputies who can go in without getting shot. This precinct stays clear."

I shook my head. Ray had been picked up blocks away from a crime scene our cops didn't bother to investigate. Now I'd have to go to Negrotown myself, bribe a deputy or two, as well as the sheriff, and track down the woman who was beaten, if she was still alive.

I called Bob out of the room then. "What?" His feelings were hurt.

"Put Jimmy Scoggins in a cell by himself. We're going to take Ray for a walk in a minute."

Bob swiped a hand over his face. "Shit," he said. But he moved off toward holding.

I took the report Kaminski gave me and joined Ray again. I lit another cigarette. "Want to tell me about Negrotown?" I asked, pretending to look the report over. "It says here a guy named Clark Dane lost the top of his head there."

Ray sat still and silent.

"If I'm not mistaken, he was a fighter once. Wasn't he?" I took a deep drag and blew the smoke out, wanting to just let this kid go . . . wanting to go and check on Laura. "Did you know him?"

"As a kid."

"Did you kill him?"

"No."

"Did you kill Hobbes?"

He didn't answer.

I leaned forward. "Look, Ward," I said. "What happened to your brother is rotten. But killing Hobbes has brought Chicago into town and we're bracing for a street war the likes of which K.C. has never seen before."

Ray looked at me with those intense eyes. I could tell he knew how deep he'd gotten himself into this mess. If he confessed to the cops and went to jail, the mob would whack him from inside the joint for what he might know about anything in the fighting world . . . or anything about anything for that matter. If he kept quiet the street war he'd brought to Kansas City would get lots more people killed. If all those people were gangsters, fine. But the thing about street wars was that they had an unfortunate tendency to take out innocent folks right along with the guilty.

Ray was thinking hard.

We stared at each other for a few minutes, each turning things over in our minds.

There was a sharp knock on the door and Bob poked his head inside. "Ready," he said.

I gave Ray a tight smile. "Let's take a walk," I said. I jerked him out of his chair and slapped the cuffs on him again.

He didn't put up a struggle. Me and Bob led him down the hall and through a door that led to single holding cells.

Jimmy was in the third one on the left. His eyes were swollen like he'd been punted around a little bit.

"Hello, Jimmy," I said.

"Yeah, fuck you." His lip was bleeding.

I looked at Bob. "You do that?"

He shook his head. "He's been in holding for awhile."

"We'll get you out of here today," I told Jimmy. "Just tell me if you recognize this guy."

Me and Bob shoved Ray out in front of us. He met Jimmy's eyes with cold calmness. Jimmy looked frightened for a minute, but then he squared his shoulders and I thought, We've got him. Case closed.

But Jimmy looked me in the eye and smiled. "Fuck you," he said. "I never saw this cracker before in my life."

I blew out a breath. Bob lunged at the bars, like he was going to brutalize Jimmy or something. I pulled him back by the collar. "Relax," I said. "He's not gonna talk. Put him back in holding." I let go of his shirt.

I pushed Ray ahead of me, ignoring the stares we got from everyone we passed. The desk sergeant gave me a cold stare. "What do you need?"

"Get Mr. Ward his walking papers. Then get him out of here. And let Jimmy Scoggins go too."

Bob joined me and we stood by and watched while Ray signed a couple of forms and disappeared out the front door. Me and Bob headed for the car.

"What now?" Bob asked.

I took a deep breath and thought about Laura. "We follow where he leads."

# 23

*Ray*

I was glad to be out of the station. Detective Fokoli knew what was going on but he couldn't prove anything. I wasn't dumb enough to think he was done riding my ass but I got the impression that no one was going to miss Hobbes or Delancey and certainly not Clark Dane, so at least I had that going for me.

And that Jimmy kid . . . lucky for me he already had a bad relationship with the K.C. police. I could see in his eyes that he remembered me and I know that detective saw it too. I guess he had more against whoever gave him that fat lip than he did with me. All I did was kill the manager who'd been ripping him off.

Out on the street I rubbed my wrists to ease the pain from the handcuffs. I twisted and scratched until they were numb. It takes awhile to get your hand used to being laced into boxing gloves, but eventually you do. Handcuffs were nothing I ever wanted to get used to.

My search for Baxter took on a new urgency. Find him and find him quick, but also keep one eye peeled to see who else was tagging along for the ride. I preferred the life of the ring where it was one man against another and if someone was intent on doing you harm you could damn well see him coming. Plus, if things got really out of hand, there was always the bell to save you. On the other hand, the rules of the ring hadn't worked for Rex.

I thought about hailing a cab but I saw a cable car rumbling out from a stop at the corner so I sprinted to catch it, getting a hand on the back railing just in time. A woman clutched her handbag closer to her when I leapt on. People weren't usually afraid of me but I guess they had reason to be now. A killer, hunted by the police. Goddamn, where did I go wrong?

I thought about Drake, hoping he was at the Excelsior today. One fight promoter should be able to get me closer to another one, right? I could still see Baxter, sitting in the audience at Rex's fight: The cheap suit, the unlit cigar, the pot belly and that leer.

I sat near a window so I could feel the breeze in my hair. The interrogation bothered me more than I wanted to admit. I knew there was no way I could handle prison.

I thought about Fokoli. He knew. He tried to get to me, talking about Rex. I shouldn't have jumped up like that. Maybe it made me look guilty. I wouldn't have thrown any punches. I knew that before I made it to my feet. Still, my reaction looked bad.

So there I was, on the lam and yet sort of not. All I knew was that I had something to finish and a man to find. I'd spilled a lot of blood and none of it made me feel any better about Rex. I wasn't sure if finding the right guy and spilling some of his blood would do the trick but it was too late to go back now. Might as well go all the way.

As the cable car rumbled along, I ran my tongue over the tooth Rex chipped during our sparring match. That tooth had always been a reminder of Rex's talent; a symbol of my hope for the future. Now it brought back memories and made me sad. I remembered what a tough kid he was. Hard to believe anyone so young could punch so hard. I remembered him smiling. That was the face I wanted to remember, not the one I left behind on the table of the locker room.

There were no fights scheduled at The Excelsior that night, but the doors were unlocked and janitors were hard at work cleaning up from the last night's bouts. Never do at midnight what you can put off until tomorrow at three in the afternoon.

I rapped on the door and a skinny black janitor opened it for me. He spoke with a rasp like a radio with its tubes on the fritz.

"Mornin' Ray. Didn't think you'd be back so soon."

I felt bad I didn't know his name. "Just passing through."

He swung his mop around and got back to work. He knew I wasn't there to see him.

I found Drake in his office, last night's money out in front of him in neat piles. He was doing his customary third count. When I walked in he held up a finger to warn me not to speak so he didn't lose his place. His fingers flew and his lips moved, whispering the count as fives and tens piled up in front of him.

He put the last bill on the pile and made a note of the number with a stubby pencil on a pad smeared with lead and then finally looked up. He was surprised to see me.

"Ray. How the hell are you? What are you doing here?"

"Good to see you too, Drake."

"It's not that . . . I just . . ."

I stayed standing. "You know a guy named Baxter? Promoter. He was here with Hobbes the night of . . . the other night."

"Yeah I know Baxter. You lookin' for him?"

"No, I wanted to send him a Christmas card. I'm getting my list done early this year."

Sarcasm wasn't usually my thing but then again, neither was murder.

"You shouldn't ought to mess with Baxter, Ray. He's bad news. A real sonofabitch."

"Doesn't stop me talking to you." The sour new attitude didn't suit me any better than my new identity as a killer.

"I'm just saying, Ray, he's connected. To Chicago."

"I know he's connected, he's connected to Rex's death and that's what I want to talk to him about. I don't care who he knows in Chicago or Peoria or Cincinnati. I just need to talk to him about why my brother is dead."

"You all right Ray?"

Drake looked genuinely concerned. I guess he could tell I wasn't myself as much as I could. I let out a deep breath.

"I'm working toward that, Drake."

He leaned back in his chair leaving the money unprotected which was rare for him. I knew he was serious then.

"'Cause I heard some things, Ray."

"Things?" Drake nodded slowly.

"Things like Hobbes is dead. Face beaten to a pulp they say. Things like Delancey is dead too. Throat slashed as I heard it."

He left those two notions to hang in the air between us. He wasn't judging me, just letting me know that he knew why I was going to see Baxter.

"I just want to talk to him, Drake. I swear."

"The way you talked to Hobbes?"

"They were mistakes. Things happen. He wasn't cooperative. Look, I don't have to run down the where's and why's of it. You got to trust me on this one Drake. You know I'm not that guy. If things get out of hand, I'll defend myself. If things aren't set right then I have to defend Rex too. He's not exactly around to do it for himself anymore."

Drake huffed out a breath. He looked very grandfatherly and he spoke like one too, like he was giving me a life lesson or something. "I'm on your side Ray. Hobbes was a son-of-a-bitch and that kid he ran was headed that way. I don't doubt that someone has to pay for Rex and I'd just as soon do it myself but you put yourself in a lot of danger here Ray."

"No one knows that better than I do. I'd love to tell you I know what I'm doing, but I can't. All I know is I'm going to do right by Rex."

Drake exhaled again, resigned, and his breath made the piles of money flutter. He sat forward with a great creak of his chair but still didn't stand.

"Baxter can be found wherever the crookedest fight in town is. He don't much care what it is as long as he has his hand in the pocket of everyone watching." He scribbled on a piece of paper with his stubby pencil. "Try this," he said. "There won't be much action until after sundown." I studied his childlike scrawl, figuring he probably hadn't gotten too far in school. The paper contained the name of a downtown intersection.

"There'll be something in that neighborhood," he said.

"Look around. But dang it Ray, just watch yourself will you?"

"Sure thing. Thanks for this." Yeah, thanks for nothing.

"Just follow the smell of blood and money and you'll find him."

I stuffed the paper in my pocket and headed out, grateful to be rid of the sweat and beer smell. Blood and money didn't sound much better.

I took a cable car near the address Drake had given me and hit up a lunch counter for a bite to eat. I didn't realize how hungry I was until I sat down. I ordered a hamburger with French fries, a root beer, a bowl of cream of mushroom soup and a slice of cherry pie.

I took gulps of my drink until it was nearly gone and then stared at my hamburger sizzling on the grill. Off in the corner two guys in a booth had started to arm wrestle. The match was dead even and it wasn't just for show. Near as I could tell it was for the affections of a little brunette who wasn't half bad to look at although her voice was piercing and nasal as she begged them to stop. Both guys were locked in and pulling for their lives, faces red and sweating. The one with his back to me had the bigger arm, but the other guy was holding his own. That girl must have really been something when her mouth was shut.

A counter girl set a bowl of soup in front of me and while I ate, the match was won. Both men let out a huge groan on the final push like they were delivering babies right there in the diner. I looked back but couldn't tell who had won, they were both spent and rubbing their forearms.

The brunette threw them for a loop when she raised her voice to an even higher pitch and said, "You two are both animals and I don't want nothing to do with either one of you," and she stormed out.

Without the girl around apparently the guys had nothing more to fight about because they stayed in the same booth together the whole time it took me to eat my lunch and drink a second root beer.

I ordered a coffee and a newspaper, sipping while I turned pages. Buried on page four was a two paragraph story about a local fighter found dead in his apartment. The police, it said, were looking into foul play. What the reporter left out was that they were looking in my direction.

When the shadows outside started to get long I knew it was time to start pounding the pavement . . . that, and when the counter girl started sighing loudly and stopped giving me refills on my coffee. She began mopping the counter closer and closer to me and even got the sports section, which I had discarded, wet with her rag. I threw down two quarters as a tip when I left.

Out on the street I had to think where to possibly find a fight. There were no fight halls in this neighborhood. There were bars and cheap restaurants. There was a pool hall and a liquor store blazing with lights to lure the drunks like moths to a front porch lamp.

People started to drift out to the sidewalks. Tomorrow the workweek started again, but for now the evening was soft and the air was cool. People moved quickly to their destinations. The volume of the Kansas City night increased too. In the late afternoon the neighborhood was relatively quiet. There were sounds of the occasional car horn, kids squabbling with their moms, a dog pent up in an apartment but now, at dusk, the jukeboxes filled with nickels and the squabbles switched to bickering couples. The newsstand man was hawking the late edition and a pushcart owner clamored along, dinging his tiny bell to the point of irritation calling out, "Ices! Watermelon, cherry, pineapple from Hawaii! Ices here!" like he was Puccini at the opera.

I looked at the faces of young men passing by, searching for one who looked like maybe he was a few dollars down to a bum like Baxter. Two-bit gamblers and guys who'd rather make bets on a basement brawl than a real sanctioned fight were easy to make. I was looking for sweat on the upper lip. A guy with holes in his shoes. A guy who was constantly jingling the seventy-five cents in his pocket to reassure himself that he wasn't completely busted.

I didn't see any.

I went back to the newsstand. JOHNNY'S was written over the top of the crude wooden structure. This guy Johnny probably saw all the comings and goings from his place on the corner. I figured he might know where to find Baxter.

"Hey Johnny, you know a guy named Baxter? Runs a fight game around here."

"I don't even know a Johnny. My name's Mario," he said in a heavy Italian accent.

"Well what's with the . . . ." I pointed up to the sign but it really didn't matter. I was in for a long night.

I went from bar to bar, pissing off bartenders and waitresses by not ordering drinks. All I wanted was an answer to my question. I tried the pool hall, a hot dog stand and a guy playing a banjo for pennies. Nothing.

I passed by a drug store that was closing up shop and I could read the clock inside. It was straight up midnight.

The pharmacist stepped outside. The bells on the door tinkled, their sound growing muffled as the man closed and locked the door. He tucked the key in his pocket and was just setting his hat on his head when a skinny fellow trotted up to him.

"Aw geez Bill, you closin' already?"

"It's twelve o'clock. Get lost."

"But I need those pep pills you give me last week. I'm all out. They work real good, Bill. Real good."

"Will you buzz off?" Bill tried to push his way past but the skinny guy was persistent. He looked like he'd just come from a coffee drinking contest. His hair was wild, blond and pasted down with pomade except for one rooster tail standing up right in the middle of it all. It bobbed up and down as he pleaded with Bill.

"C'mon, Bill. I got a big one on the hook tonight. I need to stay alert. These boys will take you for all you got if you lose focus. I got 'em this time though, Bill. I got 'em."

Bill stopped and squared off against the skinny guy.

"Listen to me you bum. Brother-in-law or not, I ain't gonna do you no more favors. Go home and get some rest, that's what you need. And lay off the bets, Wyatt. I told Faye she wasn't allowed to give you no more money."

"I'm not asking for money, Bill. I'm all set after tonight. All I need are those pills. They're doctor prescribed pills, Bill, you said so yourself. You—"

"Shut up and leave me alone! Forever! Don't come around here no more! You hear me? No more!"

Bill shoved past Wyatt and kept right on going. Wyatt stayed and it looked like the thought flashed through his head to smash the window on the drug store but he stayed put. This was my man.

# 24

*Fokoli*

Ray Ward left and I couldn't do anything but watch him go. I knew he was our guy. I also knew I was going down as soon as Tolene got his balls blown up to man size. Felt like I knew a lot of things right then. The worst thing I knew was that Laura was going to die. I knew it before the phone call came . . . the one that went to Bob White's desk instead of mine.

We'd followed Ward around for a few hours. He wandered around downtown. Ate. Read a paper. My gut told me he was waiting around for something, but Tolene called and told us to finish the Carlisle report. That meant leaving Ray out there on his own, which was probably the point—make me look incompetent when another stiff showed up, killed by the guy I was tailing.

I screwed a piece of paper into my typewriter and thought about how it might not be so bad if I didn't have to do this kind of work anymore. That's when Bob's phone rang.

He answered and listened for a minute then passed it to me. "Hospital for you."

There wasn't much fanfare about it. I don't know what I expected; maybe for the world to stop spinning for a minute or so out of respect for me and mine. "I'm sorry, she's gone. We couldn't stop the seizures." The doctor sounded younger than me and that made me feel old and tired and useless. I hung up and waited for that stillness I expected. My world had just ended . . . why was everyone else still moving? Laura was gone and I was sure the whole world could feel her absence. But the homicide room kept buzzing and the phones kept ringing like no one cared that my wife was dead. My ears started to ring after I hung up and I wanted to shoot everyone within five feet because maybe that would make the ringing stop.

Bob watched me. "Everything okay?"

He knew I was married. But he didn't know much else.

"My wife has been sick," I said now. "She just passed."

"I'm sorry," he said. "Sorry for your loss."

But I didn't know if *I* was sorry. Maybe I was relieved. She'd hated me for so long I didn't know what it felt like to love anymore. Or to be loved. Right then, something scooped out my insides and left me hollow. I nodded at Bob and said thanks for the condolences. I'd let the hospital work on getting her body prepared and when I had Ray in custody again and entrenched in the legal system that would land him on Death Row, I'd bury Laura and I'd start over someplace other than here.

I felt like maybe I should cry about her, but I couldn't bring myself to feel that much. Dried up. That's what I was.

"I'm going out to get that guy," I said.

"He didn't kill your wife," Bob said, not understanding what I meant. "Getting him won't bring her back."

"It'll keep me busy," I said, not really wanting to talk to Bob. Didn't really seem like we needed to talk about that just then.

"You can stay here if you want," I told him. "Maybe keep working on the Chicago thing. It's going to get messy soon and they'll want us on it."

"The captain will want us both on it." Bob was fidgeting, playing with a rubber band and then a paper clip while he sat there at his desk. He fidgeted a lot. Especially when he was nervous.

"Stop fidgeting," I said. "It gives the perp the edge."

Bob put the paperclip in his drawer but picked up the rubber band again. "I don't think it's a good idea."

"It's the only one I got."

There were plenty of things Bob could have said to that. He could have told the captain and had me suspended. He could have threatened to get another partner. But I guess he knew I needed to be on my own just then, although I could tell he thought it was because Laura was dead.

Maybe I just didn't want him to see that I was relieved to have her gone.

I fished the lighter out of my desk drawer, pushed my hat onto my head and gave Bob a wave, figuring it was only a matter of hours now before we weren't partners anymore.

Negrotown was more rundown than I remembered. A white man wandering around this neighborhood in the middle of the day made the blacks nervous. A white cop passing through in the evening could damn near start a riot. "You gone run us in, Cracker?" a man shouted at me from his porch where he sat sharing a bottle with his three friends.

I kept driving until I reached the house where the sheriff's car was still parked in the packed dirt of the front yard. I stopped beside the cruiser and cut my engine. Sheriff Frederick T. Michaels himself stepped out onto the front porch, hands on hips.

"Well, well, well," he said as I rested a foot on the bottom step and met his stare. "What brings the fifth precinct out here?"

"Gut instinct," I said.

He laughed a little and rubbed his head. "Well, now."

"I'm working the boxing killings," I said, watching for a light to turn on inside his bland face. It didn't take long.

"You don't say."

"Kid killed in the ring."

"Yep, yep," he said, nodding. "Then Hobbes and then Delancey and now . . ." he gestured toward the door, "this."

"Yeah," I said.

"Well, now." He thought for a minute. "Now I know Mr. Dane here used to be a fighter. But I can't say as I agree the cases are related. Maybe if you filled me in . . ."

"Sorry," I said. "It would take too much time. How'd you like me to take over this case?"

Michaels rubbed his chin a little bit, letting his eyes wander across the litter-strewn street to the angry crowd on the other side. "I tell you, son," he said after a minute, "folks here don't much care for the city police. Your department has a tendency to overlook things that happen down around these parts."

I knew that was true but it was one of those things I pretended wasn't a problem. I'd gotten real good at pretending over the last couple of years. "I'm sorry," was all I could think to say. I took off my hat and held it in my hands like a kid who's sorry for all the bad things he's done. And right then, I was sorry. I was sorry for everything. If I were a crying man I'd have broken down and begged for the case so I could make everything in the world an ice cream cone.

Michaels watched me for a minute while he took a couple of cigarettes from his pocket, passed one to me. We both lit up. I stood with my foot on the bottom step and leaned my hip against the porch railing while I smoked and looked across the street at the crowd.

"Any of them know the folks that lived here?" I asked.

"Probably."

He didn't say anymore for awhile. We finished our smokes in silence.

"Well now," he said, blowing out the last great puff of smoke when he was done. "I suppose I could let you at least take a look in here, but I don't know that I'm comfortable giving up the case." He motioned me up the porch steps as he looked over his shoulder at the crowd. "People here depend on me."

I kept my hat off as I moved into the house. It was heavy with quiet . . . the kind of quiet a place takes on when something bad has happened inside. It's at all the places where people are killed; like the place has a life of its own as long as its people are living and breathing; like the walls vibrate with that life. But kill someone there and the vibration stops. That's just how that house felt when I moved inside ahead of the sheriff. And I figured it was how my house would feel when I decided to go home again—like now that Laura was dead, so was the building and everything inside it. I stopped the thought before I lost control.

"Smell of blood is a little heavy back by the bathroom,"

he said. "That's where it happened."

I stepped through the small hallway off the kitchen, hating the way my shoes echoed in the silence of the house.

"Yessir, this is where Mrs. Dane fed Clark a shell," Michaels said. "He was a real bastard, I'm told."

I held my hat in my hand and looked at the spill of blood covering the bathroom floor and drying into a black sludge that was already drawing flies.

"She was laying here on the floor," Michaels said, and I could see the handprints belonging to a small woman smeared on the wall and on the floor by the toilet where she most likely tried to push herself up.

"Near as I can tell," he continued, pointing into the room. "Dane fell over here and she had the shotgun and pulled the trigger and just blew him apart."

"He ate the gun?"

Michaels nodded. "Near as we can tell that muzzle was in his mouth."

I stepped into the room and knelt by where the woman had lain. I imagined the gun in her hand, the muzzle in his mouth. I studied the wall where the blast knocked the plaster into the next room along with half of Dane's head.

"What kind of shape was she in when you picked her up?" I asked.

"Well now," Michaels shook his head, "not good. Not good a' tall. Medic said he didn't know if she'd even live 'til they got her to the hospital."

"How do you suppose she got the muzzle in his mouth?" I asked, watching the corners of his mouth turn down.

"What?" he said after a minute.

"How," I said, slower this time, "do you suppose Mrs. Dane got her husband to sit with the gun in his mouth long enough for her to pull the trigger?"

"Well now," Michaels said. "I reckon he was knocked out."

I pointed to the wall. "Look where the blast hit. He was sitting. And even if he was knocked out, how did she do it?" I made a show of looking around for a weapon. There was none. "What did she hit him with?"

Michaels shuffled his feet a little.

"And how would she have overpowered him in the first place?"

Michaels thought about that some. "I don't rightly know," he said. "I just don't rightly know."

I had no right to tell him he was doing a lousy job with the investigation. He was right with what he said earlier; the fifth precinct ignored Negrotown. We counted on the county to clean up what messes were made down here.

I left the house and moved out onto the porch to have a look at the crowd. I counted heads. Fourteen. Fourteen people and a twenty would get me forty that none of 'em knew a thing. I stepped off the porch anyway, settling my hat down over my eyes so I looked like I meant business. I wasn't used to being the one in the minority and I didn't like the feeling.

A few of the people on the sidewalk across from Dane's house were women. They had small kids with them. The kids were all different ages and they all had runny noses. I checked my watch and wondered if it was past suppertime for these families. Three of the women stepped forward, chests thrust out like they were daring me to start something. I felt a smile tug at the corners of my mouth, but then a memory of Laura acting tough in an argument we had over linen napkins came to mind and I didn't feel like smiling anymore.

"You gone arrest us?" one lady asked. She held a sleeping baby in her arms.

I touched the brim of my hat. "No ma'am," I said. "I just want some information about the man that lived in that house there." I pointed to Clark's place. Michaels was standing on the porch with his thumbs hitched in his pants.

"He beat Roberta somethin' fierce," she said. "Deserved what he got, you ask me."

"No one's asking you," a man said. He staggered out of the crowd, holding a bottle of rye. He bumped into the woman and the baby in her arms started to cry.

"Watch it there," she said, patting the baby on the back. Then she pointed at me. "And he's asking me."

I flashed my badge at the drunken man, like maybe that would send him on his way. He smiled like maybe the badge was just a joke to him and staggered off across the street in the direction of Dane's house. He paused next to Michael's car and took a deep drink off the bottle, then tossed it toward the porch. Michaels didn't do a thing, just stood there on the porch with his thumbs hitched in his pants.

"Lousy drunk," the woman said.

"Roberta is Dane's wife?" I asked her.

She nodded. "She and Velvy shoulda done him in a long time ago, you ask me."

"Velvy?" I asked. No one answered.

Another woman, holding the hand of a little girl about five years old stepped forward. "That's enough, Letty. Time to get the children home." She wouldn't look my direction, even though I was standing right in front of her and towering a foot or more above her.

"Letty," I said to the woman who'd been talking. "That your name?"

She looked at me, her eyes huge and brown and full of fear, like maybe it was a real bad thing for a cop to know her name. I could see the pulse in her throat, beating wildly as the crowd started to back away. A cop had said her name and God help her now. She stood frozen to the spot and the baby in her arms, sensing the change in her heartbeat, started to fuss a little bit. She stared at me for a minute like she was trying to decide what to do—turn and leave with the others, or stand and talk. She patted the baby on the back, softly, and he calmed a little bit. The touch calmed her too and the pulse in her neck slowed a little.

"Yeah," she said. "I'm Letty. What of it?"

I shook my head. "Dane's dead," I told her. "I'd like to find out if there was anyone besides Roberta involved."

She thought about that for a long time. People had gone back to their porches, standing and staring at me and Letty talking on the street. I could tell they were feeling like she was turning on them and I could tell Letty was feeling that way too. "Dane got what he deserved," she said. Then she pulled the baby closer to her and moved along down the sidewalk.

I blew out the breath I'd been holding, feeling Ray slip further away from me, smelling his part in all of this, but helpless to prove it. Michaels gave me a little wave from across the street and I trotted over to meet him.

"They won't talk to you around here," he said.

"Who's Velvy?" I asked.

"Dane's kid. Doesn't live here anymore."

"Why don't you let me have this case?" I asked. "I'll work it for you."

He shook his head. "They'll never let me back in here if I turn this over to you, Fokoli. It's hard enough to get anything done in this neighborhood. It's just getting to where folks don't run when they see my car anymore." His eyes narrowed. "No, sir, you don't want this case and I don't want you to have it. You just run along now before you get yourself into trouble."

Michaels had a way of making me feel like I was back in school, getting my knuckles smacked with a ruler. I climbed in my car and tried not to rub my hands so he could see.

I drove away, seeing the sad faces looking at me like I was the enemy and felt small and bad and guilty. I turned south and drove two blocks, passing a rundown pawn shop and a pool hall. The guy who spoke to Letty and threw the bottle was staggering along down the street and he had two friends with him now. I pulled over to the curb and turned the car off.

The three stopped and looked at me like they wanted to chew me up a little. They wouldn't. I had a gun.

"What you want?" The guy in the middle stepped forward. He had a dirty beard and smelled like yesterday's garbage. "We didn't do nothin'."

"I want to know about Dane."

The guy on the left started to laugh. "Why you wanna know about him? He's dead."

They all three laughed like that was funny, but then the guy with the beard stopped laughing and his eyes got big like he'd just thought of something important. "That fucker died owing me five bucks. Goddamn." He shook his head like now maybe it wasn't such a good thing after all that Dane ate lead.

"You can get it from Velvy. The kid's always good for his old man's bills."

I scratched my chin and acted like I knew exactly what they were all talking about. "I could probably help you get your five," I said.

"Oh yeah?"

"Yeah."

"And how's that?"

"Tell me where Velvy is and I'll give you five bucks right now." I pulled out my wallet and counted out five ones.

"Could buy a bottle with that," one guy said.

The guy with the beard met my eyes, trying to tell if I was going to snatch the money away once he told me. He wiped his lips once, then again.

"Take it," I said, pressing the money into his palm. "I won't take it back. But if you try to run before you tell me what I want to know, understand I'll shoot you in the leg. And then I'll shoot your good looking friends here too."

"Shee-it," he said, crushing the money in his hands. "I'll tell you."

# 25

*Ray*

I stepped up to my new friend Wyatt and spoke to him like we were old pals.

"Got a hot one tonight, huh? Laying down a few bets?"

Wyatt looked me up and down but his energy got the best of him and he just started spewing with the talk. He never stopped moving either. Shifting from one foot to the other, hands in and out of his pockets, in and out, in and out. He ran a hand across his hair and put the strays back in place more or less.

"Yeah I got no stake though. I can buy in to a poker game for a hundred bucks. I got 'em this time, Mac. I got 'em beat at their own game this time for sure."

I whistled. "A hundred bucks? That's pretty steep. I was looking to maybe lay down a five spot on a good fight. I hear Baxter puts on a good one around here."

"The fights?" Wyatt looked one way up the street, then the other. "Fights? Yeah. I know of a fight tonight. Baxter, yeah, that's his name. He's the one takes my money at the end of the night. Hell yeah I know him."

"Can you take me there? I'll spot you a fiver. I hate to gamble alone."

That was all it took. If I had a pocket full of pep pills he might have moved a little faster to help me, but I doubt it. Wyatt tugged on my arm and we were off down the street to find a fight.

Wyatt seemed to have forgotten all about his card game and the fight with his brother-in-law. I doubt he could have kept much straight inside that head of his. Listening to him talk was like listening to someone turn the dial on a radio as fast as they could. Bits and pieces came through but most of the time his voice was just static.

We came to an alley. I thought to myself, Here we go.

He knows I've got money so he's going to try to roll me for it.

He had energy to spare but it was chemical, not natural. Lack of judgment and vision will lose every time to the clearer-headed of the two opponents. I clenched a fist and waited.

He led me around to a set of stairs leading into a basement. I could hear the yells of bloodthirsty fight fans coming from below and the stench of cigarettes, blood, and some other almost animal smell. With the sounds of yelling and the glow of yellow light catching the smoke rising out of the hole it felt like we were at the stairwell to Hell.

"Down here, bud. You got that five spot? You don't want to be flashing a bankroll down with this crowd. That's advice for free there, Mac. No siree, Bob."

I handed Wyatt a five dollar bill from the wad I had taken off Delancey. Blood money. And I was about to lay it down on another fixed fight.

Wyatt led the way down into the basement. The cinderblock room was crowded and hot and choked with thick smoke from cigars and cigarettes in the mouths of nearly every man there. This wasn't what I was used to with a fight. No one had brought their girl in a mink coat to be trotted out for show. This was the kind of place that wives never knew existed. That extra cash for the week that was supposed to buy Junior's new shoes never even made it home. It stopped here and here it would stay.

I was so overwhelmed by all the sights and smells I didn't put it all together right away. It was when the sounds of snarling and yapping pierced the chatter and shouting and Wyatt's running mouth that I realized just what I had wandered in to.

The crowd surrounded a low pit where two dogs were tearing each other to pieces. The men cheered each time one dog got a good grip on the other. When a dog clamped its jaws down on his opponent and the teeth sank into the muscle the men went wild. The dog who had been bitten, a tan brute with a whip tail and a wide head, bucked and turned but the other dog, its black and white body one thick tensed muscle, would not loosen his grip. Blood ran down out of the mouth of the black and white. When he panted, spit mixed with the blood until a dark red soup flowed down the tan dog's leg.

I had seen my fair share of violence standing ringside, but this was vicious beyond anything I could imagine. I used to think that nothing could be more violent that what a man could do to another man but this proved me wrong.

As I watched, black and white pinned the tan dog to the floor and then released his grip and dove for the tan dog's mouth. The attack caught the tan dog in the jowls. Black and white whipped back and forth with his massive square head. Bits of the tan dog began to rip off and with each wild flailing of black and white's head, powered by a neck as thick and muscled as the best fighter's thigh, tiny droplets of blood spattered the front row and they loved it.

The cramped, low-ceilinged room was almost too loud for me to take but at the conclusion of the match it subsided and men began exchanging cash between them, and handing new markers to the three goons patrolling the ring.

A man came out of the back carrying a long pole with a loop on the end of it and he managed to snap it around black and white's neck to lead him out of the fight pit. The dog was still so fired up after the fight that it lunged and snarled at everything and everyone, flinging bloody drool as it did.

Another man came and dragged the body of the tan dog out of the ring, leaving a smear of blood to mark the path of his exit.

Wyatt had disappeared into the crowd and had undoubtedly already lost the five bucks I gave him. I hoped to get the attention of one of the goons so I could ask about Baxter but I didn't need to. I spotted him in the same green suit jacket and same crooked tie that he wore the night of Rex's fight.

He stood high in the corner on a small riser so he could look down on his dominion. His cigar was lit. Either the temptation of all the other smoke in the room broke his will or he was making enough money that he knew he could afford a new one tomorrow. I pushed my way through the crowd to him.

"Baxter! I need to talk to you."

He looked at me like he was trying to place the face.

"Place your bets with any of my associates. No refunds."

"I need to talk to you about Delancey and Hobbes."

He played it cool. His cigar pointed down and that was his only tell that he might be nervous.

"This way." He jerked a thumb over his shoulder and I followed him through a door into the adjacent basement unit. The smoke wasn't as thick here, and it was cooler, but it wasn't any place I wanted to stay. Baxter had a small desk wedged in the corner of a room filled with dog kennels. Six dogs stood like bulls in the chute inside their tiny pens. They barked and snarled. Four of the kennels were conspicuously empty.

Baxter walked past and kicked the front of one kennel as he scooped up a pile of papers on the desk and slid them into the top drawer.

"Shut up!" He barked almost as loud as the dogs. The flimsy wooden crates didn't seem sturdy enough to contain the slobbering rage inside.

When he sat down and grew still the dogs calmed also. I remained motionless for fear of setting them off again. The noise from the other room was muted and droning but still dangerous like the buzz of a bee hive.

"You're the brother, right?" Baxter put his feet up on the desk, intentionally showing disrespect to his guest. I knew how these types worked. Always gaining the upper hand in any tiny way possible. He couldn't have thought less of me than I did of him so I let him think his tactics were working.

"Rex was my brother, yes."

"Yeah, I saw that fight." He blew a cloud of putrid smoke that hung around his head for awhile. It dulled his sweat-greased forehead from my view. "He didn't do so good, your brother."

"If you saw it, you know."

"So why see me? You, I mean."

"I need to find out who wanted Rex taken out."

He took his feet down from the desk, bristling at the accusation.

"Hey, hey, hey. Nobody wanted that kid killed. That was an unfortunate byproduct. Some people may have wanted him to take a few months off from the ring but that Delancey doesn't know when to stop punching, dumb kid."

"He's not punching any more."

"No?"

"You know what I'm talking about."

The next fight started up outside the room and the crowd was screaming for blood. One of Baxter's goons stepped in with us now that all bets had been taken. He wore a black suit jacket over a black shirt and his chest was as wide as the front grille of a Studebaker. The dogs didn't make a sound. He must have been even tougher than he looked to intimidate all those fighting dogs. He took up a position like a doorman with his hands crossed in front of him just staring ahead, pretending not to hear what we were talking about. I looked down and saw dog blood on his shoes.

"Let me get this straight, Rex's brother. Are you coming in here and accusing me of bumping off your brother? You were right there at ringside. You know I wasn't wearing no gloves."

"I just want to know who ordered it done. I know you're small change in this town and couldn't make a call like that."

Baxter bit down on his cigar and coughed smoke as he yelled at me. "I'm a bigger man in this town than you and ten of your brothers put together! Don't you forget it! I want something done and it gets done, real done. So don't come in here telling me how big my dick is. You ask anyone on the street, they'll tell you." Baxter's yelling made the dogs start barking again. Baxter paused, puffing smoke like a steam train stuck at the station. He let loose another, "Shut up!" to the dogs but kept his eyes fixed on mine.

"So it was you who made Delancey bash Rex's head in with weighted gloves?" I said.

"I told you I didn't do no such thing."

"Well, either you did or you didn't. Small change or not. Which is it?"

I kept the corner of my eye on the goon but he hadn't moved a muscle. I sized up the room for a weapon. There was an ashtray on the desk and a bamboo cane that looked out of place leaning on the desk but that was about it. The bare bulb hanging from a cord in the ceiling was no use. The best thing in this room was the brick walls. If the goon made a move I'd have to back him up into the corner and knock his head back against the brick . . . and hope those damn dogs didn't bust through the walls of the kennels.

Baxter spoke calmly and with a crooked grin. He was overemphasizing the niceties to make himself sound more intimidating, but he came off sounding like Bela Lugosi trying to frighten a school girl.

"Vincent, could you go get Otto and bring him in here. I think mister Rex's brother would be of interest to him."

I doubted this was good news and I started to wonder how I'd let myself get in this position. Small space, one exit, unfriendly soil and now it was about to be three against one. At this rate I was having better luck down at the police station.

The goon stepped back outside and the piercing yelps of a dog losing the fight cut through the open door. The men shouted back their approval of the mauling. I was glad I could no longer see the fight pit and glad when the goon shut the door behind him.

Baxter smiled at me with his cigar jutting out of the side of his mouth like a cartoon rat. "I'll let you know something about life. There's always someone higher up than you. Am I the top dog? No, I ain't. I know this. But am I the top dog to these guys who work for me here and at the fight halls? You better believe it. I'd rather be the top dog in a small yard than the big dog that everyone is always trying to take down. You seen the fight out there. When two top dogs try to take each other out it ain't pretty. So did I call for your brother to be taken out? No, I didn't. I may have made a suggestion or two because I knew that he was gonna screw up my guys if he kept on winning. I may have let some bigger dogs know that he was ruining our plans for the summer fight season. Got it all scripted out like a Hollywood serial. Come back next week and see how it ends, only I know how it ends. But with a guy like Rex, now I don't know how it ends any more."

"I could tell you. Rex wins."

"That's what I was afraid of. So I make an observation to a bigger dog than me. He says he already had his eye on Rex. Says he knows Rex could beat any of our guys. Says he knows it for sure and the only way to stick to the script is to make sure Rex sits out a few months. Put him in the kennel so to speak."

Baxter turned and tipped his cigar ash on the dog in the pen closest to him. The hot ash burned the dog and it yelped before retreating to the far end of the crate.

"Your beef is really with Delancey. He got overexcited. But I gather you already had a little talk with him."

Baxter picked up the bamboo cane and I realized what it was for. He poked one end of the cane through the wire of a dog kennel and jabbed at the dog, a mostly white dog about the size and shape of a fire plug. The dog growled and snapped at the cane and almost managed to rip it out of Baxter's hand before he pulled it back, laughing. Keep them mean. That's how some managers like to keep their boys. Rile them up so they want to tear anything they see limb from limb. It never works. They might win a few, but the man with technique will always win in the end.

The door opened and the goon came back in, this time with Otto. I backed up.

Otto was an all-black mass of quivering muscle that pulled at the end of a leather strap the goon held. He leapt up at me and his snapping jaws flung spit in every direction. His pink nose was scarred and both ears had either been cropped or torn off nearly down to his skull. His chest was wide, his head a square and his jaws took up the whole lower half of his face. Otto was pure intimidation on a leash.

Baxter stood as the goon struggled to keep Otto from tearing my throat out.

"So, like I said, your beef is with Delancey but someone," he winked at me, "already took care of him, so we have nothing more to discuss."

"You never answered my question."

"About who? The King? Oh you'll never get to see him. No, no, no. Much too big of a dog for you to see. Stay in your own yard. I guess you need a reminder."

Baxter nodded and wedged the cigar in the corner of his mouth as he sat on the edge of the desk for the show to begin. The goon let the leather strap go and Otto was free to lunge at me. I ducked and brought my hands up to my face by instinct and, acting on instincts more prehistoric than mine, Otto clamped down his jaws on my arm. He gripped my right bicep and as he fell to the ground he took me with him. I curled up into a ball as best I could but he didn't care. He had a grip and he wasn't going to lose it. If I had managed to get him off all he would have done was to dig in and bite me somewhere else so I just stayed balled up as he thrashed his neck from side to side, ripping my jacket and shirt and starting a flow of blood down my arm.

The power in the animal was unbelievable. Otto stood only to my knees but when he jerked that head of his he dragged all 150 pounds of my weight along with him. I thought about trying to get a punch in with my left and maybe go for his eyes, but the pain in my right was starting to make any planning difficult. Floating above the sound of Otto's snarling in my ear, I heard Baxter's laugh. He watched from his perch on the desk. The other dogs were barking too. The sight of the brawl and the smell of blood drove them into a frenzy.

Otto tugged and one of his canine teeth dragged along my arm cutting a trench in the muscle as it went. The ground in front of me was wet with blood. My own.

Just as I started to think that I had to do something or I was going to die Baxter called out, "Enough!"

The goon took the bamboo cane and started to hit Otto

on the head with it as hard as he could. The whip and crack of it hurt my ears. It took ten sharp hits to get Otto to release. Once he did the goon jammed the leather loop around his neck and violently tugged at Otto to make sure he couldn't get another mouthful of me.

I stayed on the floor.

The goon dragged Otto out and handed the leather strap off to someone else just outside the door and then returned. I watched all this from my position on the floor so I just saw the goon's feet and Otto's paws exit and then the goon's feet return, dragging something. He dropped it right in front of my face . . . the carcass of the latest loser from the dog pit. The dog's tongue hung out and was split down the middle like a snake's with a quarter-sized piece missing from it. Both of the dog's eyes were open, but only one socket held an eyeball. I was powerless to move just yet.

I forced my eyes away from the dead dog and watched as the goon's feet exited the room again now that I was no longer a threat to the boss.

After a minute of Baxter screaming "Shut up!" and kicking at the cages the other dogs quieted down.

I was breathing hard and my arm hurt so much it was starting to go numb. My new borrowed clothes were bloodstained and smudged with dirt from the concrete floor. So much for staying inconspicuous in public.

"So you see," Baxter said, "there's nothing more for you and I to discuss. But I hope you will remember this little chat if you ever think of trying to find me again." He sat back in his chair and laughed again. He struck a match and relit his cigar. He tossed the still-lit match into the kennel with the white dog and it yelped and jumped back from the flame.

I pushed myself up on my knees and away from eye-level with the dead dog. To my side a dog lunged to the front of his kennel and snapped, banging against the wire and wood. I tumbled out of the way and let out a little yelp of my own.

"You can let yourself out," said Baxter.

I forced myself up again, maneuvered into a crouch, and

finally willed myself to stand. It was like lifting myself off the canvas at the seven-eight-nine count. I cradled my arm against my body, feeling drops of blood roll off my fingers and splash to the floor. Baxter was purposely ignoring me as he got his stack of papers back out and began thumbing through them. I could tell he wasn't even reading them but just putting on a show of pretending I wasn't there.

I bent my right arm. A fireball of pain shot through but I could still move it and that was a good sign. I looked down just in time to see the match stick burn out inside the white dog's crate. I looked back to Baxter. The best weapons in the room had been right in front of me.

I stepped forward and kicked down, hard, on the corner of the white dog's crate. The wood splintered and the wire screen popped free. The dog was agitated by the violent jostling of the crate and also eager to see if this hole in the wire was big enough. He pushed through with his snout and then used his tightly wound body to burst the crate apart.

I stepped back. The dog ignored me and went right for Baxter, as if he had been waiting for this moment for a long, long time. I spun and kicked at the next crate, which held a brown dog with one good ear and one missing. That crate split as well and the brown dog followed the trail set by the white dog.

Baxter couldn't ignore me any more. The white dog got to him first and leapt through the air landing right in his lap and pushing the chair over backwards as it bit into his cheek. Baxter howled like a dog in the pit just as the crowd outside surged louder, celebrating the death of another fighter.

I destroyed a third crate with three swift kicks. A black and tan dog leapt to join the others in tearing at Baxter. He was behind his desk now on the ground so I couldn't see much but the sounds were enough. I turned to go but then stopped myself. Carefully, I stepped back over to the desk and grabbed the stack of papers that Baxter had been fiddling with. When I leaned forward to get them I caught a glimpse of the three dogs on him.

The white dog had torn off a chunk of his cheek and

Baxter's molars peered through the gap. The dog's muzzle was stained red now, as it ripped at Baxter's throat. The black and tan dog clamped powerful jaws down on Baxter's right leg, thrashing it about, bending the knee in ways it wasn't meant to go. The brown dog alternately sank his teeth into Baxter's side and snapped at the white dog's flank, but the white dog was too blood crazy to notice.

I took the files and ran.

Once through the door I could no longer hear the carnage I was leaving behind with all the yelling in the big room, some of it happy and some of it angry. Off to the side a fight had broken out between two men over a bad bet but it could never match the intensity of the dogs.

The carcass of another losing dog was being dragged out of the pit and I caught a glimpse of Otto, the victor, getting poled back to the holding room. Looked like my arm was just his appetizer.

# 26

*Fokoli*

County Hospital was as deep in the center of town and as close to the tracks as a place could get. It was the kind of place that served the poor, the unwed mothers, and any other folks that crawled in off the streets. No one from my side of the tracks had ever been treated at County. Laura died at Lady of Lourdes and I wondered why that mattered to me just then. Did it make me any better, having a wife that died uptown? In the end, dead was dead.

I flashed my badge at the desk, feeling its weight all of a sudden and tired of that feeling. My feet were heavy too and I began to think that maybe this is what grief felt like . . . like you had to carry around what you'd be missing for the rest of your life. Right then, Laura's absence was a heavy load. "You okay, officer?" the girl behind the desk asked.

"Detective," I corrected her.

"What?"

"I'm a detective, not an officer."

"Oh." She stared at me, waiting for me to say something and I stared back, not knowing why I was there. I was thinking about Laura in the other hospital. "Was there someone you needed to see?" she said after a minute.

"Roberta Dane."

She looked at a list she kept back behind her desk and gave me a room number on the third floor. I climbed the steps with feet that felt too heavy to be mine and found Mrs. Dane's room.

A thin black kid sat beside the bed watching her. The way worry lines creased his brow I figured he was family . . . probably Velvy, the kid Letty mentioned. I stood in the doorway and waited for him to see me. When he did, he jumped up like he was scared. "Who are you?" he said. He kept his hand close to his mother, like he was trying to let her know it was all going to be fine, even though she was sleeping under that white sheet.

I showed him my badge.

"She did it in self-defense," he said before I said anything.

"Sure, kid," I said, walking around toward the other side of the bed and pulling up another chair. I sat down and gestured for him to sit down again too. We sat there, staring over the bed at one another with his mother there in between us. "You Velvy?" I asked.

He didn't seem inclined to answer for a minute, so I let my eyes wander down to his mother. She was thin enough to show bones, even through the blankets. Her lips were swollen and dry and crusted with blood. Her eyes were swollen so much it wouldn't have mattered if she was awake because she wouldn't have been able to see anything. Her left ear was cauliflowered, like a boxer's.

But her hands were beautiful. Soft and brown and perfect. I wanted to pick one up and hold it, like I never could for Laura.

"Don't you touch her," Velvy said, like he was reading my thoughts.

I pulled my eyes away from the broken woman on the bed. "You Velvy?" I asked again.

His nod was so slight I barely saw it. "I'm looking for Ray," I said and watched his eyes narrow.

"Don't know him."

"Come on, Velvy," I said, inching my hand toward his mother's.

"Don't touch her," he said again. His voice was low, but there was danger in the tone. I suspected Velvy could take care of himself if need be.

"How'd she do it?" I asked him. "How did your mother get him to sit still long enough to pull the trigger?" He stared at me and I wondered if we would sit here all night like this, while Ray slipped out of reach. "They're going to be cleaning your dad out of that house for a long time yet."

Velvy smiled a little at that and swiped a hand over his

eyes. He kept his other hand on his mother, as if afraid to lose the feel of her.

I reached out and took hold of her hand . . . the one closest to me. So now we each had a hold on her. And Velvy didn't like it. At all. He grew still and all I could hear was his breathing, deep and hard above the whisper of air blowing in and out of his mother.

"Take your filthy hand off her," he said. His teeth were clenched now and I hated pushing him, hated using the broken woman to get what I needed.

I stroked her hand a little. "I bet when she's all healed up she'll be a right pretty woman. She'll be real popular with the guards."

Velvy tensed and rose a little bit from his chair. He didn't want to come across the bed at me, but I could tell he would if I pushed much harder.

I squeezed her hand. "How about you and me step outside for a smoke?" I said, letting go of her hand and stepping away from the bed.

Velvy rose and adjusted her blankets, smoothing her forehead a little bit. I felt a pang for Laura right then. Did anyone smooth her forehead while she lay in the hospital? My feet felt heavy again, but they got me out of the room and down the hall to the waiting room with Velvy right behind me.

I sat. He stood, shoving his hands deep into the pockets of his pants. He was clean and pressed and had good shoes. "Where can I find Ray?" I said, leaning back and lighting a cigarette.

Velvy didn't say anything and I felt seconds ticking away underneath his silence.

I smoked awhile, thinking of how far I'd really go to get Velvy to sing about Ray. It would have to be all the way. I'd have to put her in jail if Velvy didn't cooperate. I weighed a thousand pounds right then, feeling it in my neck and shoulders, pressing me into the hard chair. It took all my strength to crush out the cigarette and as I watched the smoke I blew out curl upwards into the air, I wondered what it would be like to feel so light.

"I'm going to get coffee for us," I said. "When I get back, you'll be here and you'll talk or your mother will go to jail." I stood and walked, my legs trembling with the weight of it. It wasn't Roberta so much as Laura, I knew. But she was sick and hurt and I was bullying her. It felt bad, like I was hurting Laura all over again.

My eyes stung.

There was coffee on a hot plate behind the information desk. An old woman sat at the desk and looked suspicious when I asked for two cups with cream and sugar. I showed her my badge and then she smiled and asked if there was anything else I needed. I told her just the coffee.

Velvy's hands were shaking when he took the cup. "When was the last time you slept?" he asked. "Your eyes are red."

"Long day." I almost smiled as I said it. Velvy was smooth, like the kind of kid I'd have fun ribbing if we weren't both mired in shit up to our eyeballs.

He sat and rested an ankle on his knee. "What are you going to do with Ray?"

I shrugged. "Same thing we do with all murderers," I said and I could tell he didn't like hearing that.

"Ray saved my mother," he said.

I thought hard about what to say to that. "Ray made it possible for your mother to murder your father," I said. "Your mother pulled the trigger."

Velvy tried to laugh about that, but it came out as more of a sob. "What do you want?"

"I want to know where he is."

"I don't know anything about that."

"Then tell me where you think he is."

Velvy drank his coffee for awhile. I drank mine and if anyone passed by they would think we were just two fellas passing time in a waiting room. One black, one white.

"I don't know, man."

"Me and my partner followed him around some today. Until we got called back to deal with other problems that needed our attention." There was no sense in telling him a cop's life is half paperwork. "He was downtown here. A few blocks over. Any idea why?"

Velvy shrugged. "Window shopping?"

"Come on, Velvy."

He met my eyes. "Swear to God I don't know. Swear on my mother I don't know."

He looked rough . . . wrung out and pulled tight and it was a look that said he wasn't lying. So I said, "Thanks for your time," and I stood up, holding out my hand for him to shake. He handed me his empty cup and walked away.

My breath made angry bursts of mist as I made my way through the dim parking lot to my car. I was back to thinking about Ray Ward and murder and Laura and what I really wanted was to sit on my couch with a bottle. But what I needed was to find Ray before someone else died.

I started the car and pulled into traffic, hit one stoplight, then another. By the third I was sure about the tail. Looked like a department car, the driver careful to stay two to three car lengths behind me. I didn't bother to lose him. I was heading back downtown to pick up Ray's trail where I left it three hours earlier.

# 27

*Ray*

I got a few blocks away from Baxter's place and pulled into a side alley to check my wounds. Not as bad as I thought. From the sound of the dog in my ear and the pain I felt I thought for sure my arm would be hanging by nothing more than a cracked bone and a loose tendon, but it was really just three puncture wounds and one deep cut where Otto's tooth had traveled a good inch through my muscle. It was sore as hell and starting to stiffen up and I really needed to get it cleaned out. All that bullshit they tell you about a dog's mouth being cleaner than a person's is, well, just bullshit. No better way to say it.

The list of places I could go was shrinking. I felt suspicious about making it back to my house. It was a long journey and chances were that Fokoli had the place covered by cops. Velvy was also a good bit away, and I had already broken in on him once, but even after wracking my brain, he seemed like the only friendly face left in the city.

I spotted a pay phone inside a Rexall across the street and made my way over. I tried not to make eye contact with anyone inside as I hurried to duck into the phone booth. Christ, I must have looked like the guiltiest man in Kansas City.

A middle-aged pharmacist in a white coat stood behind the drug counter, training a younger kid who soaked in the wisdom through inch-thick glasses. A woman stood flipping through a rack of magazines and as I sat down inside the booth I came more eye level with her purse and I saw that she was slipping tubes of lipstick into it with her other hand. I smiled and felt a slight comfort at not being the only guilty person in sight.

I dropped a dime in and heard the ting of the bell. I dialed Velvy's number. After six rings a woman answered. It was a common phone in the hallway of his building so I figured on getting anyone but him.

"Can I talk to Velvy?"

"He ain't here."

"What? Did he say when he's coming back?"

"I don't know. He's up at county with his momma. She got beat up real bad. Might not make it I heard."

Yeah, and I saw.

"Thanks," I said and hung up. I lifted up the phone book with my good arm and thumbed through to find a number for County Hospital. The woman shoplifting had moved on to compacts and mascara. She was really loading up while the kid in the glasses got his lessons.

I fished in my pocket and realized I didn't have another dime. Shit. Time to get creative. Getting change from the two at the counter seemed dangerous since they were obviously going to see my ruined arm through the ripped shirt and all the blood. And being the types who think of themselves as real doctors, surely they would try to force help on me. Besides, the girl was closer.

I opened the phone booth door and lifted myself up with my left arm and was quickly behind her before she could do anything about it. I knew she wouldn't scream. I was at her back so she couldn't see my damaged arm and I'm sure the smell of the blood and the dog made me seem more intimidating than I really was.

"Listen lady, I see what you're doing and unless you want me to blow the whistle to the old man and Specs there, all I want is one thin dime to make a phone call."

She kept calm, eyes forward on the two behind the counter.

"All right, Bub. Ten cents is a fair trade," she whispered between clenched teeth.

She reached into the purse and somehow under the pile of stolen makeup she brought out a few coins. She held out her hand behind her, never looking at me.

"Here, take it all. There's a dime in there somewhere." I picked through the coins and took only the one dime.

"This is all I need. Thanks." I backed away and sat back down in the phone booth. She moved slowly and calmly to the door and walked outside. I had a fleeting notion that she might go get a partner to come back and beat my head in, but I convinced myself she worked alone because I needed to make that call.

The dime dropped. The bell dinged. A nurse answered.

"County," was all she said.

"I need the room of a Mrs. Roberta Dane."

"Hold."

A few seconds of static passed by then Velvy answered the phone. I explained my situation to him without trying to sound too crazy, but I'm sure it did anyway.

"Ray, you know I'd do anything for you but this is my momma here. I don't know if she's gonna make it. I don't wanna not be here if she passes. I should have been there for her before this. This is a shit way to make up for it but it's all I got right now."

I felt guilty for even asking. Some friend I was.

"Of course Velvy. I don't know why I even called. You stay there. It's where you should be."

"I'll ask the doctor next time he comes by and maybe—"

"No. You stay. I'll be fine. I shouldn't have called."

"Yes, you shoulda. You in trouble, you call me. Only reason she's alive even this much is 'cause of you."

"I'll be fine. You stay. Thanks."

I hung up and didn't give him time to be a hero to me. I sat quietly for a full minute trying to come up with a plan B. That's when I thought of Glenda.

Glenda was Rex's girl. I doubt she had even heard the news. She lived close to here. I never met her, but I'd picked Rex up from out in front of her place a few times. Dropping in for a meet and greet at this hour and in my condition wasn't putting my best foot forward but I was exhausted, weak, and a little anemic from losing a good dose of blood, and I was starting to feel woozy. If she turned me away then so be it, but at the very least I could tell her face to face about Rex.

I tucked Baxter's papers up under my bad arm and stumbled back out onto the street. It took a minute to orient myself with my memory of where her apartment was. I shuffled off in that direction keeping my left hand firmly gripping my rights biceps to stop the bleeding.

I arrived at Glenda's at one fifteen in the a.m. according to a clock outside of a bank a block back. Rex had been seeing her on and off for a year or more. He didn't want to settle down until he quit fighting, but he saw her once a week or every two depending on when we were on the road. He would tell me they had went out dancing or to dinner and not much else. Rex was shy like that.

I rang the bell to her apartment and the door buzzed open without her even asking me to identify myself over the intercom. Trusting gal. I had a fleeting thought that maybe Rex had scheduled a date with her that night. She would be mad as hell about the hour, but she would be even more upset when I spilled that Rex was dead.

I got to the landing outside of her second floor apartment and tried to pull myself together so at least I wouldn't scare the poor girl when she answered the door.

The door swung open and it was obvious I wasn't the person she thought she had buzzed in. She stood in the door and spread out her hands to cover over the thin pink robe with ruffled edges that she wore over some other pink and ruffled things that you might get from a store in Paris. This girl knew how to dress for bed.

She was beautiful. Long brown hair that turned big corkscrews down below her shoulders like Shirley Temple all grown up. She was tall, maybe an inch more than Rex was and about the same as me. Her lips were full and shiny and the way her face was slightly worried as she looked at me made her very sexy. No time to admire her though. Time to explain my presence.

"Glenda, hi, I'm so sorry to barge in like this. My name is Ray. You knew my brother, Rex. I wouldn't have come by if I wasn't in trouble."

I peeled my hand away from my arm to show the

damage. She gasped slightly but then reached out a hand to me.

"Come in."

She ushered me inside and shut the door. The room was girly and soft. Pinks and whites and pillows everywhere like a little girl's fantasy bedroom. She escorted me to a small sofa and brushed a few pillows off onto the floor to make room for me to sit down. I tried my best not to get blood on anything. I must have looked more out of place than a pig in a perfume store.

"Is Rex with you? Let's get a look at that arm."

She was in full Florence Nightingale mode. I sat back and let her peek at my wounds as I set Baxter's papers on the side table. She didn't shy away. Tougher than her frilly pink getup would suggest. I could see what Rex liked about her. Most women are afraid of fighters because it's too brutish and violent. I never saw Glenda at a fight but I figured she could handle seeing Rex after he came off a twelve-rounder. Even the best fighters ended up with puffy eyes and patches on the cheek bone where the skin got rubbed off by the glove leather.

Time to drop the bomb on her.

"Thanks Glenda."

"No problem. I guess we'd better become officially introduced. How do you do?"

She reached out and shook my left hand with a polite and proper smile.

"Not so good," I replied. "How do you do?"

"Well, now that that's out of the way you need to take that jacket and shirt off and I'll get some whiskey. Don't think I'm a square but it ain't for drinkin'. We need to clean you up and put you back together, Humpty Dumpty. You look like you're about to come apart like a two-bit suitcase."

Her way of talking was no-nonsense. It didn't jive with the girly-girl surroundings. It was obvious Glenda wasn't raised in a country club. I figured she hadn't been raised in Kansas City at all. She spoke fast like a radio actress and threw in all kinds of jazz talk like you read about in stories about New York City.

She went into the kitchen as I struggled to remove my jacket. I was only about halfway done when she came back holding a bottle of whiskey but no glasses.

"Here, let me help you."

She eased me out of my jacket and then helped strip off my shirt. I felt self-conscious about being shirtless in a strange girl's apartment but she didn't flinch and went back to examining my wounds. The news about Rex was stuck in my throat. I closed my eyes and hoped I wouldn't hit her too hard.

"Glenda, I need to tell you something."

"Sometimes, Ray, when you get in a jam, the thing you need most is someone who doesn't ask questions. I'll just mind my own and you spill only what you can't keep in. Rex has told me so much about you so I know you must be in a real jam and you only came here because you needed to. Rex really looks up to you, y'know."

"It's about Rex."

She lifted her eyes from her work. They held a hint of fear.

"Is he in a jam too?"

I kept her in suspense while the words fought their way out. "He's dead."

She dropped the bloody jacket and shirt on the pink and white rug and it looked like a scab on a brand new baby's flesh. She didn't swoon or tear up; she just stood there looking past me for a moment.

"What happened?" she said low and somber.

"Fixed fight. Died in the ring."

"Is this part of it?" she said indicating my arm which was oozing blood slowly again.

"In a way. I'm trying to find the guy who put in the fix."

She waited, thinking, the muscles on the side of her jaw clenching and unclenching. Then she said, "Well, isn't that a poke in the eye? I'll get you some bandages." She exited toward what I figured was the washroom. Not a single tear ever fell, but I think she was the most upset of anyone I had told about Rex. I could see it in her eyes.

When Glenda came back she refocused on her task of patching me up.

"Come here, over the sink." She led me to the kitchen and dabbed at my punctures with some gauze.

"Mind if I ask what happened here? I keep digging, am I gonna find bullets? You don't have to tell me."

"Dog bite."

"For real?"

"Yep."

She shrugged as if to say, "That's a new one."

"No way around it, we're gonna have to douse it with the booze. You ready?"

"I guess so."

I turned away and Glenda poured the whiskey over my arm. The alcohol stung so bad it felt like Otto returned for a second taste. I stifled a scream but Glenda heard it squeak out. She didn't laugh which I appreciated.

Without warning she doused me again. I tensed and the four wounds burned the way I assume a hot poker would. Give me a fist to the face any day over that.

The front door bell rang.

"Excuse me." Glenda left me at the sink to go answer it. The alcohol seeped into the wounds and down into the torn muscle like tiny drills under my skin. I heard her speaking into the intercom and I used the distraction as something to take my mind off the pain. She didn't even ask who it was.

"Not tonight, Mannie."

The crackly speaker couldn't hide the drunken slurs of the man downstairs.

"But baby, I need to see ya."

"I said not tonight. Make it a rain check."

"But baby . . ."

She got stern with him. "Quit bleating your trap. Your credit is good. Now blow. Drift."

"But baby, it's been more than a week. Just let me come up for a little while . . ."

"Mannie, are you gonna beat the bricks or do I need to

call out the bulls?"

"Why Glenda you wouldn't—"

She cut off the intercom and came back into the kitchen. My head was fuzzy but not too fuzzy to add two plus two. The nightgown, the pink lace, the callers at one thirty in the morning: Glenda was a prostitute. I never would have thought it of Rex.

She returned and examined my wounds, now clean. I watched her carefully. If she knew that I knew she didn't let on. Maybe she figured Rex had told me what she did for a living, so there was no secret to be kept. I stood there, speechless, feeling sorry for her even if it was obvious she didn't need my pity.

She wrapped my arm in the gauze, pulled the silk sash from her robe and used it to make me a sling. She led me back to the couch and then went to the bedroom to change. When she emerged again the costumed frills and lace were gone. She wore a collared button-down shirt and tan slacks like a grocery clerk. Her hair was pulled back in a ponytail and her lips were a more normal shade of reddish pink now that the lipstick was wiped away. Anyone else would have looked like just another Midwestern girl but her beauty didn't need all that help. If anything, she was better looking once she dropped all the hardware.

"Anything else you can tell me about Rex?" she asked as she sat down on the couch next to me.

"I can tell you a lot, but I don't think you want to hear any of it."

She sat in silence for a beat, then she snapped to. "I'm so sorry I didn't even offer you a belt of libation for yourself, even after I poured it all over your arm."

"No thanks."

"You don't mind if I do?" I shook my head no. "You make sure I stop at one. Hearing this news I'm feeling like I'd like to get good and gone."

"I'll watch you." She went to the kitchen and poured herself a drink. When she came back it looked to be more of a triple than a double. She saw me look at the glass.

"I know," she said. "Looks like I'm doing next week's drinking early, huh?"

She smiled. It was easy to see what Rex liked in her. I just couldn't believe that so many other men had seen the same thing, if you get my drift. She took a long sip and then set the glass down on a small table and lifted the lid to a cigarette case.

"You want one? I still have Rex's favorite brand."

"Rex smoked with you?" That was against training. Seemed like Rex had a lot of secrets.

"Oh not much," she said, defending him even in death. "Just mostly after . . . after our dates. Only one. My fault. I'm a bad habit."

She struck a match and lit her smoke. She exhaled through her nose. Somehow, I didn't mind the smoke when it came from her.

"So Glenda, I hate to ask but . . ."

"Can you spend the night?"

"Yeah." It was a question I'm sure she got a lot but in my case it was strictly platonic.

"Of course you can. Don't even sweat it." She took a sip of her drink. "My God, Rex's brother. I feel like I know you already."

"Then you have me at the advantage because I don't know anything really about you. Rex never talked about any girl he was dating."

She blushed slightly; I think appreciating the fact that I was still dancing around the idea that Rex was paying her to date him. She seemed to relish the chance to keep off the topic of Rex's death. So was I.

"Well, let's see. I grew up knee high to a piano leg most of my life. My daddy played for a living. Jazz. Played with some of the greats too when they would come through town. Even met Fats Waller one time and Fats told my dad that he had the stuff."

"You're from here?"

"Oh sure. I grew up right here in Kansas City. I was a little mop head runnin' around the jazz clubs. My dad used to bang the eighty-eights four or five nights a week and he'd tow me from gig to gig. I never did have a bedtime. Mom died giving birth to me. He was a mess, my dad, but I loved him. He was a real every-which-way drunk but he took good care of me and he raised me in show biz. Dad would stand me up in the corner and make me wait until he was done with the set. Pretty soon I started dancing because the music was just too hot to handle. People loved that. Dad would see them watching me polishing the leather and he'd call me out on stage and the crowd went wild. Little twelve-year-old girl tearing it up. Tips went through the roof so Dad was a convert. We ran that trick for a few years. I loved it. The music, the people. I met some real swell cats.

"Then Dad had to go and have a heart attack right on stage one night. Right after he hooked up with a real hot band too. Things were looking okey-doke for me and him and then, poof, it was all gone to dust. That's when I went into business for myself. Three years ago. I'm nineteen now and when I get twenty-one I'm going to Hollywood. They could use a hoofer like me out there. I can pound the boards like no one else. I'm sure to get in the pictures."

"I'm sure you will Glenda. I'm sure you will." My eyes were getting heavy. I had hoped to go through Baxter's papers tonight but that seemed less and less likely.

"I want you to know, Ray, that I really cared for Rex." Her eyes were sincere and she seemed younger, more vulnerable. She looked nineteen for the first time. "He wasn't just a fella I saw from time to time. He was special. I know you thought so too, don't get me wrong. You and Rex had blood and now, well, for you to go after his killer and get the blast put on you like you did tonight . . . well that shows real brotherly love. Rex would want it that way."

"That's what I keep telling myself. It's the only way I've made it this far."

She saw how tired I was and stood to make a gesture of ending our evening together. She stubbed out her cigarette in a crystal ashtray.

"You're welcome to the couch, Ray. I can get you a

blanket. Afraid I don't have any pajamas for you to wear. I think all of mine are a little on the girly side for you."

"That's okay. I appreciate everything you've done for me tonight."

"You know, if you wanted . . ." She paused and looked down. ". . . we could share the bed."

I was the one now who looked away. "No, it's okay. I wouldn't want to take advantage."

"Sorry. Force of habit. Goes with the biz. Still, it would be a hell of an improvement over Mannie." We both smiled.

"Thanks just the same." I slid my shoes off and put my feet up and could feel sleep coming on the way you hear a train coming down the tracks. It was close and it wasn't stopping for nothing.

Glenda took a blanket off a side chair and draped it over me. I must have been quite a sight. Beaten up, arm in a sling, two-day-old clothes on with a pink tasseled blanket over me. Glenda leaned down and kissed my cheek and whispered good night. I've never slept more soundly.

## 28

*Fokoli*

Carter McWilliams or some other asshole from I.A. was still tailing me, no doubt feeling like a big shot for being the guy who would bring me down. What he didn't know was that I was thinking seriously about taking *myself* down. You can't beat a guy who's taken himself out of the race.

The crowd thickened as I got nearer to the south slum. Streets lined with rundown apartment buildings on one side, pawn shops and bars on the other saw plenty of foot traffic as a rule, but I could barely get my car through the mass of people, some moving deeper into the district, some moving away from it. And everywhere there was the feeling of urgency; of needing to get somewhere else fast. Or maybe it was just me.

I was stuck there in my car, boxed in by the crowd on all sides. I fished around in my pocket and came out with my pack of cigarettes. I lit up, blew out a breath and tried to think about where Ray would be now. Was he in this crowd? There was no way to get deeper into the district and there was no way to pull over to the side of the street to park, so I crawled out and climbed onto the back bumper to see what I could see. McWilliams was half a block back, standing on the back of his own car. Our eyes met and I could tell he was as pissed as I was about the crowd, about being held up, about wanting to be anywhere but here. He scowled and I thought maybe he was actually more pissed. He looked like maybe he'd draw his gun and shoot at me if there wasn't a crowd around us.

I hopped down and started moving along the street, against the current of impatient pedestrians.

"Dogs are loose," a man said, grabbing my arm. His lip was bleeding and he got a little on my suit jacket. I shoved him away and he bumped into another man who started swinging at him. They had each other in headlocks before long and I started pushing my way through the crowd again. There were four hundred thousand people in Kansas City and it felt like everyone was here in this street, getting in my way. I made it another half block and climbed onto the base of a lamppost. McWilliams wasn't on his car anymore, so I figured he must be behind me somewhere, fighting the rush. I wondered what he was thinking. This was a hot spot for bet-making. Did he think I was coming down here to lay odds? For a deal?

I dropped onto the sidewalk and shoved my way through the mass of people, strong-arming anybody who got too close to me . . . which was everybody. After a half block or so the crowd thinned out and anyone who had the balls to look me in the eye moved aside and kept walking.

I'd never been this deep in the district before. I'd taken protection money from businesses a few blocks over, but I hadn't been there since I decided to go straight.

The crowd thinned, but there were enough people left for me to see that they were coming from an alley across the street. I moved in that direction, following the remnants of the crowd and the noise of snarling dogs.

The alley was dark and smelled of trash and blood. Two small but muscular dogs worked on tearing each other to pieces at the end of the alley. There was a group of men standing around watching. "Shoot him, dammit," one of them said.

"Fuck you. I ain't shooting that dog. He's a fighter. Look at him."

"If he gets out of here . . ." The guy didn't finish the thought. He aimed the .38 he was holding and pulled the trigger.

There was the loud crack of gunfire, then another, and both dogs lay still. The men stood with their hands in their pockets, sleeves rolled up, staring at the ground. "Shit," one of them said.

There was a stairway in front of me, heading to the basement beneath the brownstone. Drops of blood, dark and shiny, led the way. A door at the bottom stood open and I moved inside, almost choking on the smell of sweat and blood and dog shit. "Jesus," I said.

A big man, obviously the muscle for the boss, slumped in a chair just inside the door, trying to wrap a piece of torn cloth around a gash in his leg. He looked up at me. "They shoot them?" he asked. When I didn't answer right away, he jerked his head in the direction of the alley up the stairs. "The dogs? They shoot 'em?"

"Yeah."

He blew out a breath and I couldn't tell if he was relieved or upset about the news. "This is a pisser," he said as he finished tying off the bandage and reached for the bottle of rye on the table. He took a deep pull and let out a sigh.

"You should have somebody look at that," I said, not really caring about his leg and not wanting to tell him who I was either.

He shrugged.

I pulled out my badge. "Christ," he said when I showed it. "This is all I need."

"Oh, so you're in charge here?" I said.

He shook his head and took another pull from the bottle. "No."

"Who is?"

The man jerked his head toward a narrow doorway. "Baxter. In there with the dogs."

I moved through the doorway. The room was sprayed in red. Four men stood, hands on hips, assessing what had happened there.

"What's this?" I asked.

The men turned around. I recognized two of them. And they recognized me.

"Fokoli." Frank Polanski and Roger Reid said my name at the same time. There was relief in their voices.

"It's okay, boys," Polanski said, moving forward and slapping me on the shoulder. Polanski ran a pawn shop and always wore lots of gold rings. "Detective Fokoli is here to help us clean things up."

I let them think that was true. "Where's Baxter?" I asked, stepping deeper into the room. Beyond the four men was a desk and I could see that someone had been sitting behind it when the chaos started. Whoever it was had been tipped over and only his feet were visible, peeking up at us over the desktop. "Who is this?" I pointed to the feet.

Polanski made a face. "Used to be Baxter. Some crazy man busted in here and kicked in the cages." He backed out of the way so I could see the low row of kennels against the back wall, latches broken, doors hanging open.

"You sure this guy's okay?" one of the four asked. His hand floated around the waist of his pants like he was going for his gun.

"I wouldn't do that if I were you," I told him. His hand moved back to hang limp at his side. I stepped to the desk and looked at Baxter's shoes. Fancy. A cigar, never lit but a little chewed, was tossed carelessly on the desk, like maybe ol' Baxter set it down, thinking he'd just light it later when he had more time.

I looked over the desk and I gave a low whistle. "Well," was all I could think to say.

"We didn't do that, Fokoli," Polanski was quick to point out.

"Shut up, Frank," one of the two I didn't know said. "He knows we didn't do it."

I turned around and looked at the dogs on the floor. "They fight to death or did you shoot them?" I asked.

Roger Reid gave a sharp laugh. "Little of both, to tell you the truth."

I put my hand on my hip, holding my jacket out of the way with my forearm, so they could see my holstered gun. "So who kicked in the kennels?" I already knew.

"Skinny guy," one of them said. "Was in here talking to Baxter and all hell broke loose."

"He wasn't that skinny," Polanski said. "He was dangerous looking though."

I didn't want to listen to these idiots. Baxter was dead.

Killed by Ray Ward with the help of the dogs. My hands started to itch with the need to wrap them around Ray's throat. I wrote down a number.

"Call this guy," I said, handing the note to Polanski. "His name is Bob White. He'll come and check this out."

Polanski started to shake his head because the other three were looking at him like they'd kill him if he called anybody.

"I'll know if you don't call," I said.

The garbage-filled alleyway smelled fresh compared to the bloodbath in the basement and I gulped in the air, wanting a shower and a drink and to be anywhere but here. The men who shot the dogs were long gone. So were the dogs. There was nothing left but a big dark spot that no one would care about come morning. I stood and looked at the blood and lit a cigarette, wondering what in the hell I'd do now.

The guy with the cut leg and the bottle of rye had managed to get himself outside and he leaned against the building watching the blood seep through the bandage and trickle down his pant leg onto the ground. I hadn't seen him at first. He had started to sweat and I could tell the pain was getting pretty bad for him.

"Let me take you to the hospital," I said.

His eyes weren't quite focused but he nodded. We started to walk to my car.

"Not County," he said, stopping and looking worried. The sheriff liked to check in at County Hospital and pick up anyone with unusual injuries.

I smiled a little. "No," I said. "Not County."

The crowd had disappeared and downtown K.C. was eerily silent. Sirens whined in the distance. Bob White and friends, probably. McWilliams's car was nowhere in sight. My car had a broken rear window, but nothing worse than that. The man needed help getting in. I handed him his bottle and lit a cigarette for him and put the butt in his mouth before walking around and climbing in myself.

"He was hurt when he left," he said after a few blocks.

"Who?"

"The guy who let the dogs go. He was hurt in the arm. Looked bad."

"You didn't stop him."

He shrugged and shifted in his seat, wincing with the pain. "Guys get hurt all the time in Baxter's office. Guys who owe him money or who don't do what they're supposed to. I figured he was one of those." He worked on smoking the cigarette. It seemed to help him relax a little. He closed his eyes. I decided I'd take the long way to the hospital.

"Did you see where he went?"

The guy laughed. "Hell no."

"Ray Ward, where are you now?" I said it under my breath, my hands clenched on the steering wheel.

"Ray Ward," the guy laughed as he said the name, his eyes fluttering open and closed. "Was that him? He ruined the dogs?"

My heart beat a little faster. "That's my best guess," I said. "You ever see him before?"

The guy was bleeding all over himself and all over the seat. His eyes were closed and his face was pale. I didn't want a stiff in my car, but even more than that, I wanted to keep this guy conscious and answering questions about Ray. I reached over and took his bottle. There was about an inch or so left in it. I looked at the wound on his leg. Deep and long and oozing.

I turned west and drove until I found a liquor store. We were still a few miles from the hospital and I still needed to question this guy. I fished around in his pockets and found his wallet. His name was Richard Cooper. And Richard Cooper had cash. I took a couple of twenties. I bought three bottles and a pack of cigarettes and carried it all back out to the car. There, I opened the bottle and poured more than half onto his leg. He screamed and moaned, and the clerk looked out the window at us.

"Jesus. Fuck. Fucking shit," Richard Cooper said.

I pulled off my necktie and tied it above the wound. "Do

you know the guy who busted up the kennels?" I asked.

He was sweating a lot and the cigarette I lit for him earlier had burned to the butt and dropped onto the floor of the car. I lit another one and put it between his lips. "Shit," he said again, his eyes were too bright. "What?"

"The guy who caused the trouble back there."

"Who?"

"Ray Ward. Do you know Ray?"

Cooper rested his head against the window. "No. I don't know Ray."

"You sounded like you knew him."

"No. I didn't."

I wanted to punch this guy. Instead, I started the car and drove away. "You were surprised about Ray beating in the kennels." I stopped at a red light and looked at Cooper. Gray skin. The light changed and I pressed the accelerator. "What about his brother?" I asked. "You know him?"

"Rex," he smiled a little. "I saw Rex sometimes." He took a drag of the cigarette. His hair was wet now, sweat dripping into his eyes. The car reeked of body odor and blood.

I studied Richard Cooper. Unshaven, probably a boozehound, probably a small-time crook for that matter. Most of the guys downtown had at least one hand under the table. I thought about earlier in the day when we tailed Ray. He didn't act like a guy who knew he was being tailed. He acted like a guy waiting around for something . . . maybe looking for something. If Ray knew about dog fighting, he'd have stayed out of sight until fight time.

No. Ray didn't know about the dogs. Ray was waiting around to find a stoolie who'd tell him about the dogs. Or Baxter. How did he know about Baxter?

"Did Rex know Baxter?"

Cooper laughed a little again. "Don't know. Don't care."

"But he was a good guy, though, right?"

"Who? Rex?"

"Yeah. Rex."

He laughed again, harder this time. "Rex wasn't always

good."

"How's that?"

His head rolled to the side a little and he pulled the cigarette out of his mouth. Blood was soaking through the necktie on his leg. "Rex came to the dog fights sometimes."

He drifted to sleep again and the cigarette was going to fall on his shirt. I pulled it from between his lips and tossed it out the window. Then I opened another bottle of rye and poured some over his cut. He screamed and opened his eyes.

"Did Rex come to the fights alone?" I asked.

"What? Who?"

I poured more rye. "Did Rex come to the fights alone?"

Cooper shook his head and his eyes fluttered shut again. "He came alone. He'd never bring her to a fight."

"Who?"

His eyes fluttered a little more and I wanted to punch him. But if I did, I wouldn't stop. So I asked again. Louder. "Who?"

"What?" His lips were turning gray.

"Who didn't Rex bring to the fights? Who's the dame?"

"Glenda," he said. "Glenda the Good."

I pulled into the hospital parking lot and blew out a breath. Glenda. I knew her. Not in the Biblical sense, but I'd run into her at the station before. And she lived somewhere around here. She wouldn't be hard to find.

# 29

*Ray*

I thought I was still dreaming. The softness of the pillows, the pink on every surface, including the curtains that filtered a rose-colored haze over the room from the morning sun, and the sweet smell of all things feminine was disorienting when I first woke up. It felt more like the waiting room to heaven than a prostitute's apartment. I had been so blissfully unconscious that it was a crushing disappointment when it all came rushing back to me.

Glenda was up and making coffee. This must be what it's like to have a wife, I thought. She saw me stirring.

"Morning," she said with a smile.

"G'morning," I managed. She looked simple and sweet again. Her hair was in its ponytail and her robe was thick cotton instead of the wispy chiffon she wore the night before. I moved to sit up but unwittingly used my right arm to brace myself. I winced at the pain and crumpled back down. Glenda set down her coffee cup and came to my side.

"Let's see how that arm is doing." She helped me sit up and started to unwrap the gauze which was rusty brown from the blood that had seeped out while I slept. I caught a clock on her side table and it read quarter to ten.

"Sheesh. It's late," I said.

"I know. When I first came out here you were as still as a grave and I thought you'd gone for a dirt nap during the night but then you snorted and scratched yourself so I knew I didn't have a stiff on my hands."

"I was tired."

She studied the wounds on my arm and clicked her tongue.

"Gonna have to do something about that. I need some iodine. This is one job that whiskey just can't lick. It would be the first one that I've found." She smiled and rewrapped my arm in a temporary fashion. "I'll just run down to the drugstore. Anything you need?"

"A toothbrush and a razor would be nice."

"I keep men's supplies under the sink. You're welcome to anything you find." She went down the hallway and called out to me to continue our conversation. "Any thoughts on what's next?"

"I have some ideas. I don't want to mix you up in anything though. Best to leave you out of it."

Sitting there on a soft couch, being tended to by a beautiful girl, it was tempting to just drop the whole thing. Rex wasn't coming back. Even if I found the man responsible for killing my brother, what then? Just kill him and hope that I felt better? Or worry that if I didn't finish the job Rex's ghost would haunt me forever?

Glenda reemerged dressed for the drugstore.

"I have money," I said and I reached awkwardly into my back pocket for my bankroll.

"Don't worry about it. Iodine don't cost much."

"I'd feel better if I paid my way."

"Why is it men don't ever want a woman to pay for anything? I guess I shouldn't complain about that. One time Rex owed me some money," she didn't say what for, "and I took it out in his fists. I made him take a few swipes at a guy I didn't care for. He did it too. Guy was big enough to lay a beating on a steam shovel and Rex popped him twice in the kisser and once in the breadbasket then twice more in the kisser and the guy went down like a sack of potatoes. I won't make you do that or anything. Not with your busted wing."

"Thanks." I handed her a five.

"You stay off that arm. We'll have you playing the violin again in no time."

She was in a good mood, cutting jokes. It put me in a good mood too. "Thanks again. And say hi to your brothers Chico and Harpo, will you?"

She smiled as she left the room. I heard the door lock behind her. I reached behind me and lifted the stack of papers I swiped from Baxter. I wanted to see if I could find a clue in there, but I had no real idea what I was looking for.

Mostly it was tally sheets from the dog fights and straight fights. I saw an address I didn't recognize until I realized it had to be down near the train tracks, and that probably meant a hobo fight. Baxter was into everything. One page detailed the purchase of some fighting dogs and written in the margin was the name of a new fighter who I'd heard of. Next to his name was a phone number and $500 indicating his price for a fix. There was enough here to blow the lid off the K.C. fight world, if I was so inclined.

Page after page of nonsense and I figured it was a dead end. Then on a sheet of yellow legal paper, the first I'd found in the pile, were some cryptic notes that featured the initials RW. Rex Ward maybe? They also had bigger numbers than I had seen in the other pages. A 2,000 and a 3,000. I flipped the page over and there was a name—Clement Voight—written in different handwriting along with the word RECEIVED. Could be something.

There was a knock on the door. I was startled but didn't make a sound. I knew Glenda had her key with her, I heard her lock the door when she left. Whoever it was knocked again, harder. I got up and tiptoed to the door. I stood off to the side and pressed my ear to the doorframe. I could hear voices in the hall.

"Well, did you see her leave or didn't you?" asked one slightly annoyed man.

"How should I know?" whined another in response. His accent was Swedish and his voice sounded old.

I slid over to the peephole and looked out.

Fokoli.

He didn't have any other cops with him but a man of about eighty was with him and rearing back to knock again.

"Did you see her leave this morning?" Fokoli asked.

"No, no, but then I wasn't looking. I was feeding the kitties."

He rapped the door again and the sound filled my ears with panic.

If he found me here he'd have cause to run me in again,

if only for the dog bites and those would link me to Baxter's death. Damn, this was getting complicated. Well, it was already complicated but now it was getting more complicated than Chinese algebra.

I started gathering my things up and trying to clear any evidence of my presence here, figuring I could hide in a closet or something and hope Fokoli didn't sniff me out. What the hell was he doing here anyway? How did he know Glenda? I tabled that thought and its obvious answer for a moment.

I had everything cleared from the room and I went back to check the peephole again since I hadn't heard a sound for awhile. I saw the Swede trudging back toward the stairs, his old lungs working hard to put forth the effort. He offered Fokoli coffee. Great. They were getting chummy.

Then I caught a break.

Glenda crested the stairs and passed the Swede. I couldn't believe it. She didn't seem to recognize Fokoli.

"Hiya, Felix," she said to the Swede as she passed.

"Ah, Glenda. This man is needing to be seeing you."

Fokoli stood straight and tipped his hat. "Glenda," he smiled.

I needed to get lost.

I thought about going out the window, but who knew how many cops Fokoli had staked out below and besides, I wouldn't make it far with my arm the way it was. I went into Glenda's bedroom, not worrying about courtesy or a woman's right to privacy.

I found more pink, more pillows and more perfume. I slid into the closet and that put me with an ear to the back wall of the living room. I tried to listen but all I could hear was my heart pounding away on my ribcage like a heavyweight.

# 30

*Fokoli*

Cooper would be fine. The nurses promised me that. Then they said I looked kind of sick and asked if I wanted to see a doctor too. I started to laugh a little. Then I started to laugh really hard and couldn't stop. I thought about telling them my wife was dead here someplace, waiting for the funeral parlor to come and get her. But I couldn't get the words out. I just laughed. When the nurses finally started to look frightened, I turned and left, doubled over with laughter all the way out to my car. I climbed inside and started to cry.

The sun was up to mark the beginning of the second day without Laura. I started the car, laughing and crying at the same time and figured I'd better go home to take a shower and change clothes.

I knew I was close to catching Ray Ward, but I also knew I was close to coming apart at the seams. And taking Ray in my condition right then would have been stupid. McWilliams hadn't caught up with me again and I figured he was staked out at my place, waiting for me to come home. That was fine by me. I just wanted to see someplace familiar.

Still no sign of McWilliams. Must have been back at the station filling out my pink slip. I unlocked my front door and smelled Laura's soap. The water from her bath was still in the tub, cold a long time now. After it drained, I ran a new bath and got undressed. I climbed in and sat with my knees pulled up to my chest and smoked a cigarette while I watched the water level rise. My hands shook with fatigue and I knew I wouldn't be able to shave even though I needed it pretty bad. When the tub was full, I leaned back in the water and thought about the case.

Rex died in the ring. I'd bet money on Delancey pulling a fast one, but it didn't take a genius to figure out the fight had been fixed beyond anything usual. A good half of the fights in town were fixed. It was a given. And just because a boxer took it the head didn't mean it warranted a full investigation. Besides, the guys responsible for the job, Hobbes and Delancey, were dead. Ray had seen to that.

That's what gnawed at me. Ray killed the guys responsible. But he didn't stop there. Why'd he let Roberta kill Clark? Why go after Baxter? If Baxter was pulling the strings for Hobbes it would make sense that Ray would whack him. But did that mean he was going higher? If Ray was climbing a ladder he'd be going after whoever owned Baxter and on and on until . . . when? How far up did this thing go? What happened when Ray started to whack guys I'd never even heard of?

My cigarette was done, so I dunked the tip in the water and tossed the butt into the toilet.

My head was going in circles and the water was getting cold. I climbed out of the tub and dried off. There was no food in the house, so after I got dressed I stopped at Rosie's, a coffee joint across the street and picked up a coffee and Danish. I ate in the car on my way back to the slum, wondering if I had a better understanding of Ray, and wondering how far I'd go to get revenge on someone who wronged me.

Like it or not, I was developing a healthy respect for Ray Ward and I wondered what, exactly, that meant.

Glenda, if that was her real name, lived in a nice enough brownstone on the edge of the slum. I pegged it for the kind of place fellows liked to go after a night at the dog fights. I buzzed the super.

I flashed my badge. "I'm here to see Glenda," I said.

He folded his hands in front of him and smiled. "Such a nice girl," he said with a Swedish accent. I hadn't noticed many Swedes in the neighborhood. "So many of you police officers come to pay your respects to her since the accident."

"The accident?"

He nodded. "Yes, yes," he said. "Her husband was killed four years ago in a bank robbery on the other side of town.

She had to move over here because she couldn't afford to stay in her home after that. The force has looked in on her almost daily since then, bringing flowers and . . ." his eyes grew confused for a minute, "well, just flowers I guess." He looked at me. "But then, I suppose you know all that," he said, "or you wouldn't be here, right?" His voice let me know he'd take no trouble from me.

"I'm new," I said, not sure I was lying because he expected it or because he really believed Glenda was a widow down on her luck. "The captain told me to come and check on Glenda this morning to make sure she was keeping a stiff upper lip . . . er I mean to see if there was anything she needed."

The man smiled again and told me to follow him. He led me to his apartment, which was furnished in reds and browns and smelled like a hundred cats.

"Let me just take the coffee pot off the burner and then I'll show you up," he said. "Sometimes the kitties like to tip it over and burn their tails."

"I'll just wait right here," I told him, repelled by the smell.

He led me up the stairs, moving slowly, even for a man who looked so close to eighty. "You all right?" I asked him.

"Yes, yes, of course," he said, arriving at the top of the steps. "Here we are. This is her door." He caressed the knob for a few seconds then he pressed the bell.

I closed my eyes and tried to imagine Ray on the other side of the door and I wondered if he knew I was this close. I wondered if he'd kill me if he got the chance. He seemed to use crooked men as target practice. I'd fall onto the crooked side of the fence any day. My palms started to sweat a little.

"Did you see her leave this morning?" I asked.

The old man shook his head. "No, no, but then I wasn't looking. I was feeding the kitties."

I blew out a breath.

"But I'm sure she's here. I would have heard her leave. I always hear it if she leaves."

I doubted that.

The old man patted my arm. "Let's just wait in my place," he said. "I'll fix you some coffee. I know how all you police officers like coffee."

I tried not to laugh. What better cover was there for a prostitute than to tell her landlord that every john was a cop? The old man must have thought there were thousands of cops in Kansas City. I started to ask him about that, but he was already tottering down the hallway again and then there she was, on the stairs. And seeing her again, I could understand why the old man would believe anything she said . . . but then she spoke and the spell was broken.

"Hiya, Felix," she said.

"Ah, Glenda. This man is needing to be seeing you."

I tipped my hat. "Glenda," I said, feeling like maybe she was a lady underneath it all anyway. Nothing was what it seemed right then.

She looked at Felix and then at me. "Another visit from a concerned law enforcement officer. Should I be flattered?" Her voice was a little louder than necessary and I figured if Felix was there and I was there then the only reason she could be asking about the "law enforcement" business was if Ray was inside.

I smiled at her in a way that let her know I knew what was up. "I need to talk to you. It's not about your place of business or anything."

Felix paled at that. "What's he mean, Glenda?" he asked.

I pulled her out of his earshot and pressed her up against the door. Her breath was soft and sweet on my face and I was aware of how much of a woman she was right then. I watched her lips for a second, then got my bearings and looked at her eyes, which weren't all that friendly.

"Glenda," I said, "We need to talk."

She kept her voice low and wore a tight smile so Felix would think everything was hunky dory. "Yeah," she whispered, that tight smile looking almost friendly. "So, are you a copper? As if I have to ask."

I kept my voice low too. "Detective Dean Fokoli. I need to speak with you."

"I don't talk to bulls."

"Is that right?"

"Yeah. They have a history of breaking my china."

Felix was starting to fidget. I leaned in close to Glenda. "I can find something serious to charge you with real easy, here. I don't care what goes on in your bedroom but if you refuse to tell me what I want to know I'll make sure ten beat cops are here every night knocking on your door and every time we search the place we'll turn up a bag of dope and I'll make it my mission to see you spend the next twenty-five years in stir and let me tell you, your looks will be long gone by the time you get out, honey. So just let me ask you a few questions about a mutual friend and we can part ways and never see each other again, like two ships in the night."

"Fine," she said. "Let me get my keys."

Felix was still fidgeting, looking worried. Glenda walked to him and patted his arm. "It's fine," she said.

"I explained to him that I'm new with the force," I added to make it all more plausible.

Felix's face relaxed a little, like he wasn't sure if his bubble of ignorance was preferable to having a prostitute live above him. Glenda and I watched him make his decision. In the end, he settled for ignorance, smiled, and disappeared down the stairwell.

Glenda glared at me. "Damn bulls," she said. "You give me a pain in my craw."

"Sure," I said. "We live for that sort of thing."

She pushed open her door and told me to come inside. "But don't even think about looking through my stuff. I got rights," she said.

"You going to offer me coffee?" I asked. "Your landlord did."

She pointed a finger at me. "You leave that sweet old man out of this."

"Out of what?" I asked her then. "You act like you know why I'm here."

She blew out a breath, like she'd been through this a million times. "Course I know why you're here. You're hot in the zipper like every other Joe who comes through that door."

She lit a cigarette and sank onto her sofa. There was a blanket there, like someone had been sleeping. I nodded at the blanket. "Late night?"

She looked at the blanket and then at me. "I get cold sometimes when I sit out here and read." To make her point, she pulled the blanket over her shoulders. It was warm in the apartment and I watched her for a minute, waiting for her to get uncomfortable. She was tough; I had to hand it to her. She sat for a good few minutes with that blanket over her shoulders.

I sank into the chair across from her and put my feet on the coffee table. "Nice place you have here," I said.

"Yeah," she said. "That and a nickel . . ."

"What."

"What?"

"You said 'that and a nickel.' What did you mean?"

"That and a nickel will buy me a cup of coffee. Don't you know anything?"

She was nervous. And she was getting warm.

"Take the blanket off, Glenda. I know he was here."

She stared at me, but let the blanket slide from her shoulders. "Beat it, Copper."

I laughed, but got control of it before it slipped away and I got crazy again. "Sorry, doll," I said. "Tell me where he went."

She didn't say anything.

I leaned forward and rested my hands on my knees. "You know he's killed four men." It wasn't a question.

"Spare me the hot air."

"It's not hot air, sister. It's the truth, plain and simple."

"Oh yeah? Well, put that in writing and I'll paste it in my scrapbook."

I stood up then and ran a hand through my hair. I was tired and frustrated and I was getting nowhere with Glenda. "They call you Glenda the Good?"

She arched an eyebrow like she didn't know what I

meant.

"You know, like in the *Wizard of Oz*?" I asked. "Is that because you're so good at what you do?"

She stood up and turned away like maybe I'd hurt her feelings. I felt rotten in my gut; the kind of rotten that goes with being *no* good. I thought I'd moved past that feeling when I tried to go straight, but it was back now . . . and all because I'd insulted a hooker.

I figured then that Ray must not have been in the joint because a crack like that would have brought him running. But then I also figured Glenda was the kind of girl that could take care of herself and Ray probably knew that too.

I touched the brim of my hat. "Thanks for your time, ma'am."

She didn't look at me again, just kept her back turned like I was a pig not worth looking at, let alone smelling. I closed the door softly behind me and thought about standing there to listen, but then I figured I'd just head out front and wait for Ray to hoof it away from her place. If he was there, he'd have to leave sometime. I had a feeling he'd want to tackle the next link in the chain. And he'd want to do it soon.

I settled into my car and watched the apartment building door.

# 31

*Ray*

I stepped slowly out of the bedroom, trying to be quiet so I wouldn't startle Glenda, but it backfired. She saw me out of the corner of her eye and jumped and shrieked a little at the same time.

"Jumpin' Jesus you scared me," she said.

I couldn't believe she had kept it together. Glenda was an all right gal and there was no need to add "for a whore" to that thought. Anyone who'd stand up for me after knowing me less than twenty-four hours is okay in my book . . . and I needed the names in that book now more than ever.

"Sorry to scare you."

"I wasn't sure if you were still here. If you want my advice, you shouldn't be for long. That detective has a real hard-on for you. The way he talked without saying nothing makes me think he knows a lot too. He didn't need me to fill in any gaps for him, just where you were. If I were you I'd pull a Houdini and disappear right out of this town."

"I wish I could. Believe me I've thought about it. Then I keep seeing Rex's face all smashed to hamburger meat on that slab in the locker room and I know I can't go until I find the man responsible."

"Ray," Glenda sounded soft and gentle like she wanted to ease the blow of some bad news. "Are you in some real trouble here? I know I said you didn't have to tell me but if I'm gonna get you out of this hole I should know how deep I'm digging."

"It's complicated. I just need to find the guy who ordered Rex taken out."

"And then what?"

God, I wished I had an answer for that myself. I stayed silent.

"Ray, that bull was homicide. Have you . . . ?" The rest

didn't need to be said out loud.

"Self-defense," I lied. Well, it was a lie about Hobbes anyway. With Hobbes I let myself slip. My anger took control for a few minutes. I guess that was enough. Once the genie was out of the bottle death followed me around like a cloud. I didn't want to get Glenda caught under it too. I needed to get out of this girl's life—but fast.

"So you find the guy who put the fix in for Rex and then what? You put him to bed with a shovel? Then you got the cops on you twice as hard."

"What's one more body to them?" It was true. I couldn't be any more wanted for murder. They can only throw the switch on you once, or if they decided to fry me twice then that's their business. I'll be beyond caring at that point.

"I just don't know how I feel about getting involved in all this. I don't normally associate with killers. At least not that I know of."

"And I don't normally kill people. Look, Glenda, I'm grateful for your help, your medical attention, the place to stay, all of it. I should go now before you get more than you bargained for. I've already had the cops at your place."

"Oh please, this joint is like another precinct."

"Still," I said, "Thank you. I need to go find some guy named Voight and hope he can lead me to the King, whoever that is. If I'm lucky it's the same guy and I'll be done with all this."

"Clem Voight?"

She knew him? Maybe I wasn't through with her after all.

"Yeah, Clement Voight. You've heard of him?"

"He's got a stake in the club where I work. He's into about a half dozen clubs across town. A manager type but never does any real work. He's a real big barracuda. Wears flashy suits, spats on his shoes, a carnation in his lapel. All in hopes that none of the girls notice the scars on his face. Looks like he got in a fight with a chef the way he's carved up. He sure does have lots of scratch to throw around though."

"Can you show me this club?"

"I could but you can't get in. It's members only. I don't just go for any old Tom, Dick or Harry off the street you know."

"Was Rex a member?"

"Yeah. That's where we met."

I told myself it was normal for there to be secrets between brothers. If Glenda could get me into Voight's place, it would save me precious time. But she'd have to be open to one more favor.

"Do you think . . . ?"

"I'm way ahead of ya." She reached into the cigarette case on the side table and lit one. She blew smoke up to the ceiling, in deep thought.

"And?" I asked. She held the key to my next step and I was anxious to get it.

"I get the set up." She dragged deep and blew out more smoke. She did it like an amateur smoker, sucking hard and getting it over with fast instead of savoring it like long time inhalers do. "I get it, but I don't want it. I let you in and you find Clem and then you cancel his Christmas. No, I don't like it a bit. I'm out of a job and no one will hire me. Discretion is the name of the game in my field. No one wants a girl who sells out her boss for a song."

"No one has to know you let me in. I just need you to get inside and point him out to me. I can get to him from there. And listen, Glenda, he's no good to me dead. I swear I just want to talk to him. Where it goes from there is up to him. And how cooperative he wants to be."

She laughed at that. "Oh I can tell you right now Clem won't want to help you at all. He's a direct line to Chicago and if he poisons that, well then he might as well pour his own cement for a new pair of shoes."

She crossed her arms and stared at me dead-eyed, daring me to keep going. Smoke curled around her face and made her look tougher than I'd seen her before.

"You leave it to me. All I need from him is a name."

"And if I don't help you? Do I get deep-sixed?"

"Glenda, come on. It's not like that. I'm just trying to do right by my brother. Your name will never even come up. I'll be gone from your life forever. I'm not even asking for me. I'm asking for Rex."

"I knew it would come around to that. Do I have a target on my back or something? Guys like you are always aiming for my soft spot." She ground out her cigarette and sat down in an armchair. "Okay, give me the stack up."

I sat on the sofa and talked fast, not wanting to lose the momentum for fear she would falter.

"All you need to do is get me in the front door and pretend you don't know me. We just need to make one stop before we go."

"Where's that?"

I knew this would sound bad but I had to protect myself first and my reputation with Glenda second.

"I need to you to contact a friend of mine, Velvy. He's a Negro. Hope you don't have a problem with that."

"Of course not." She looked a little offended.

"I can't call him in case the cops are watching him. If Fokoli found you I'm sure he's been to see Velvy already. Tell him to pick us up tonight at eight o'clock. They might be looking for my car so we'll have to use his. And tell him to bring his gun."

Glenda looked stricken, like I'd just asked her to toss a bag of kittens in the river.

"What do you need a cannon for?"

"Just in case. People tend to answer questions more quickly with one in the room and since my fists are out of order," I indicated my arm in its silk sling, "I figure I can use a little help with this one."

Glenda contemplated my logic.

"I can't say I like it but I'll go with it. For now."

"Thanks."

I gave her the address at County Hospital and she went into the bedroom to change clothes. I took the chance to shave and run a hot towel over my face. It felt glorious. I was getting close to the end and I could feel it. My arm was even starting to feel better, as long as I kept it in the sling. I wasn't ready to start working the speed bag or anything.

My elevated mood fell again when I saw myself in the mirror. Water dripped from my chin. I stared deep into my eyes and I saw Pop. I saw in the mirror someone I used to love and respect but who turned out to be a son-of-a-bitch. It was the same feeling I had when I couldn't hide any more from the truth of what Pop was. Now I was confronting the truth of what I had become. I could keep telling myself that what I'd done was all justified and was all for Rex, and I do believe that, but that wouldn't change the fact that looking into mirrors would be unpleasant for the rest of my life. I ran a dry towel over my face and scrubbed until my skin felt raw, but there was no cleaning away that feeling.

When I came out of the bathroom Glenda was all business. She had dressed in a tight-fitting skirt and blouse in black with bright white pearls around her neck, in her ears, and one big one on her right ring finger. Her hair was flat and smooth on top of her head and tucked under in the back making it short, but ripe for the reveal of cascading locks when she was entertaining clients in the bedroom. I bet they liked that.

"First thing we need to do is get you a new set of clothes. You can't set one foot inside the Matchbox Club in that get up."

I looked down at myself. My dirty, blood-stained shirt awkwardly buttoned over my impromptu sling, the sleeve with tooth holes in it. Pants speckled with blood and soiled with dirt from a dog fighting pit. I was a sight.

"I know a place where you can get a suit on the cheap. Velvy can take us there on the way. If he doesn't laugh in my face when I ask him, that is."

I reassured her. "Velvy is the one person I can trust right now." I rethought that statement. "Well, one of two." Glenda and I shared a smile across the silence.

She pulled a black sequined handbag over her forearm and waited for me to open the door for her.

"Thanks again for all of this," I said.

"Would you stop saying that? You sound like a scratched record."

I opened the door.

"I'll be back before too long. Wish me luck," she said with an exhale that betrayed her nervousness.

"Good luck. This will all be over real soon and your life can get back to normal. Just keep thinking about Hollywood."

"You can sing two choruses of that, brother."

She leaned in and kissed my cheek. I was glad I had shaved. We shared a look and I could see doubt behind her eyes but so far she trusted me. I only hoped I would live up to it.

# 32

*Fokoli*

A car can get to smelling real stale during a stakeout. And a guy can give himself away by dropping all his cigarette butts out the driver's side window. I worked with a cop named Neuhouse once. We sat outside a thug's apartment for two days, smoking pack after pack of cigarettes. I crushed mine under my shoe and put the butts in a paper sack inside the car. Neuhouse just dropped 'em all right outside his window.

When the gang shot Neuhouse with a .22 from the third floor of the apartment building, it was because of those cigarette butts. Neuhouse slumped over on me, his blood pooling in the front seat and soaking into my pants. We never caught those guys. And I've always been extra careful with my cigarettes after that.

I pretended to read the paper while I waited for Ray to slink out of the apartment. I waited for Glenda to come out and check if the coast was clear. I waited for something to happen and while I waited, I wondered if Tolene had men out looking for me again. The I.A. guy hadn't been around all day. Maybe he was too busy pumping Bob White for information. Bad thoughts. I needed to shake them off.

Glenda walked out the front door awhile later, like she owned the street. I sat up a little straighter inside the car, torn between following her and sitting on the street waiting for Ray. It was possible she had Ray holed up someplace else, but my gut was telling me to stay put.

There was a phone booth on the corner and I thought about maybe putting in a call to Bob White, but I didn't think I should trust him anymore.

Glenda headed off up the street, her hips swaying like she was open for business. She didn't seem to mind the stares and the whistles. As for me, I watched and enjoyed, but I stayed put. She didn't have any luggage with her, and a dame like that probably had three closets full of frilly lady things. So she wasn't skipping town. She'd be back. And I'd be waiting.

After two more hours, and a couple of cups of coffee, I really needed a bathroom break. Plus, I was hungry. There was a drug store a couple doors down and if I hurried, I could make it there and back before too long.

I climbed out of the car and looked up toward Glenda's window. Still no movement there. I took note of all the cars lining the street, feeling like the air was getting heavy. A pain behind my eyes told me it would rain before the night was over. A spring storm would make following anyone difficult. It figured something like this would come up. I shook my head and headed for the drug store.

I cleaned up a little in the bathroom while the soda jerk made me a turkey on white and a chocolate shake. I tried sitting at the counter to eat, but that didn't give me a clear enough shot of the street in front of Glenda's, so I had the kid wrap up my sandwich and I headed back to the car.

Four cars that had been parked along Glenda's side of the street had left. And only one had driven in and taken a spot a few spaces down from her front door.

The air started to feel heavy again and I chewed on my sandwich, feeling the people passing me on the passenger side of my car, seeing the people moving in front of Glenda's door and hoping they all knew enough to get out of the way if Ray wouldn't come along quietly.

The front door to her apartment building opened and the black kid stepped out first. Velvy. He tried to look like he belonged there, like he scoped out the street for cops every day of the week. But the truth was he was nervous. I could see the sweat on his forehead from all the way across the street. He walked to that single car, parked a little too far away to be inconspicuous and climbed in the driver's seat.

I put my sandwich and my shake down on the floor of the car and pulled my gun from its holster. The world slowed to a crawl. I slid across the seat and climbed out on the passenger side door so I could put the car between me and Ray. He hadn't used a gun on anyone yet, but hell, the guy was so creative with how he killed people I figured it was best to stay as far out of his way as I could.

A couple of ladies wearing too large hats looked at me as I crouched near the front wheel. "Crazies," one of them said. "This neighborhood is overrun with crazies."

"I know. It didn't used to be like that, you know," the other said.

"I remember when I was a girl . . ."

I stopped listening to their prattling and concentrated on Glenda's door. Velvy had started his car and was backing it up across the empty spaces, positioning himself by the front doors.

When Glenda opened the door, Ray was beside her. She pushed the door open with one hand and had the other tucked in the crook of his elbow. He'd cleaned up some since the last time I saw him; but his arm was in a sling and he moved like a man tired beyond his years.

I stood. "Ray Ward," I called.

He and Glenda stopped and looked at me and I could see the recognition creep into his face. There was no surprise there, only exhaustion. But beneath that, there was hard determination. He kept his eyes on me, never flinching, not even when I held up my badge and aimed my gun and started walking across the street. He opened the back door of the car and helped Glenda climb inside. His eyes never left my face.

Velvy's window was rolled down, and he watched me, that sweat from his forehead running into his eyes a little bit now.

I ignored Velvy and focused on Ray. "Don't move," I yelled.

His eyes were dark and determined and more than a little bewildered as he stared at me. "Don't you move," I said again. My voice was softer, but even with the street noise, I knew he heard me.

"They fixed the fight," he said.

I squared my jaw. "They fix every fight."

"But this was my brother."

He inched toward the passenger door a little, his eyes on mine. I felt the Colt in my hand and pulled the hammer back. There was the crack of a small caliber gun and I saw the puff of gray smoke blow out of Velvy's window before I felt the sting in my shoulder.

I think Ray swore a little, but I can't be sure and, if he did, even that was controlled. He looked like maybe he wanted to see if I was all right, but I was aiming and firing, hoping to hit someone, even as Ray dove into the car and Velvy drove away, tires squealing.

I raced back to my own car, feeling the sting of the wound, but knowing it was just a graze. I'd be fine. I started the engine, did a u-turn, cursing and honking and flashing my badge so everyone would get the hell out of my way. The shake spilled on my sandwich and a forty-five cent lunch was gone just like that.

Velvy was a good driver. I aimed my gun out the window a couple of times, thinking I'd shoot out his tires, but that sort of thing never works in real life. It was a Hollywood lie, just like true love and big money. All of it, lies.

He led me through the warehouse district, and back over toward Negrotown, and folks standing on the streets there cheered like we were a parade. It would rain soon. And I needed to think about getting Laura into the ground. Those little thoughts plagued me and I lost sight of Velvy for a minute. His car was a long, green Buick, but he handled it with ease and he had the advantage of knowing the neighborhood.

He took a hard left, through a residential district and I almost missed the turn, riding my car up onto the curb where it swallowed a child's tricycle and spit it out again as a twisted mess.

A hubcap flew off and rolled past me, but I didn't know if it was from Velvy's car or from mine. He made another sharp left and by then people realized one of their neighbors was being chased by a white cop and they all started throwing things at my passing car.

Velvy made a hard right and we found ourselves on a long straightaway. And there were no people. I was beyond caring about Hollywood by then, so I leaned out my window and aimed for the left rear tire and squeezed off two rounds. Velvy jerked his car to the left side of the road and for a moment I thought I hit him. But he corrected and moved ahead, faster now. My own car struggled to keep up. He moved toward warehouses and I followed, hurrying down one blind roadway after another.

In the end, it was a pushcart that made me lose him.

We'd managed to get close to the river and Velvy drove along the cement barricade that separated the water from the warehouses. The barricade ensured that a middle man had a job. Ships weren't allowed to unload directly into warehouses; they had to go to special docks to be unloaded and from there, cargo was reloaded onto trucks and trailers that carried it the three or four blocks to the proper warehouses. Talk of removing the barricade inflamed the dock workers and talk of union came about. The working man loves a union.

And it was that kind of thinking that made me lose my focus. Velvy veered hard to the right and I wondered if he'd finally crash, but he swerved to miss a pushcart carrying hotdogs and popcorn. I swerved too, but clipped the cart on its side. I slowed then, not much, but enough for Velvy to escape.

The vendor was fine. His cart wasn't. And neither was I.

My arm was throbbing and I'd lost Ray Ward. Again.

The vendor swore at me in Polish. I didn't say anything, just waited for the cops to come. Damn, I thought. Goddamn.

# 33

*Ray*

What a ride. Velvy did a great job of driving despite my shouting almost the whole time. I yelled at him for firing the gun, for shooting a detective. I was yelling at him to slow down and not get us killed by running into a lamppost or a street car. Now the ride was over and the roar of the engine had calmed and my hollering had quieted.

Glenda stayed silent for the whole chase, wide-eyed and white knuckled the whole way. This had already gone beyond what I had promised and I felt terrible.

"Is everyone okay?" I asked. Glenda nodded and Velvy wiped sweat from his upper lip.

"Why'd you have to shoot at him?" I asked Velvy again, much calmer this time.

"He was aiming to shoot you and I was in between you and him. What was I supposed to do?" His voice was high strung and trembly.

"I think we should drop off Glenda back at her place. She's been through enough." I wanted to keep from dragging her through the mud even though I was in it up to my neck. I wasn't thinking that I had no backup plan. Luckily, she was.

She finally spoke up. "You can't get in to the Matchbox without me."

"I'll find another way."

"How? With that pop gun? You won't get two steps onto the carpet." She didn't wait for a rebuttal. She was coming in with me and that was that. She turned away from me and started giving Velvy directions. "You know where the Spinning Wheel is?"

"Yeah," he said nervously.

"Head for that and turn off Thirteenth Street. We need to get Ray a new suit. You could stand a little sprucing up yourself."

Velvy obliged, but I could tell he wasn't used to taking orders from a woman. I rode passenger in the front and Glenda in the back so I feared that he felt like a chauffeur.

I really wished he hadn't shot Fokoli. But the way he kept coming at us and the way he drove made me think he wasn't hurt any too badly. That, or he was as vicious as one of Baxter's dogs.

Pop always said a good fighter knows when to pour it on and a great fighter knows when to quit. "That towel ain't just for sweatin' on," he would say. I'll be damned though if I ever met a fighter, Pop included, who knew when to throw in the towel. You might as well fight your next bout wearing a dress. No one respects a quitter and there are a lot of guys who got punched out of their wits or ended up dead like Rex and died with nothing left but respect.

I should have thrown in the towel for him. I should have been doing it right then and there. Stop the car. Call it off. Ring the bell. Over and done.

But I didn't. Stupid. I only spent enough time in the ring as a fighter to cut my baby teeth, but I got all the bad habits down pat. At least now I had a new suit.

Glenda tried to pay but I refused. An old Italian man fitted me for a suit, then picked out a jacket for Velvy, who he made wait in the car. Velvy didn't make a stink over it. The man even took away my old bloodstained clothes.

It was getting late and we all got in Velvy's Buick to head over to the Matchbox club. Velvy had trouble getting comfortable with his new suit jacket and more specifically the gun he tucked into it. Glenda stopped meeting my eye and she didn't say much except for giving directions to Velvy.

We pulled up across the street from the club, a nice place that seemed classy despite the transactions going on inside. At least Glenda would attract a higher level of clientele here than at some places. A purple awning fluttered in the wind outside the joint. It had MATCHBOX CLUB scrawled across the canvas in fancy script, and a picture of an open matchbox on it with the words TOO HOT curling out, written in lines of smoke. A bouncer stood just outside the door next to a short podium. He was a heavyweight. More of a wrestler build than a boxer but built for a fight in either case.

"Okay," I said, "here's the plan. Velvy, you stay here. Glenda and I will get inside and see Voight. Hopefully it will all go well. If I'm not out in a half hour, come in after me."

"Why do I got to wait outside?" Velvy asked.

"I don't want to come in with a posse. It might intimidate him."

"Aren't you trying to intimidate him?" he asked.

"No. I'm trying to talk to him. If he gave the order himself then I know where he is and I can come back another time when we're more prepared, and when I can use both fists."

Glenda spoke up but she was pessimistic, not encouraging. "With that cop on your tail I don't think you can wait very long while you convalesce."

"I'm counting on things going right." Believe it or not, I didn't laugh after I said that. Why the hell did I expect this little unannounced visit to go right when all the others had gone so wrong?

Velvy took the gun from his coat and handed it to me. "You need this more than me. If I need to come in then it's too late."

"No, I don't want to walk in with a gun. I don't want to invite trouble."

"Then take this." He pushed the handle of a knife into my hand. It was big like a hunting knife or something. I practically threw it back at him.

"I don't want that!"

"Jesus Christ, Ray." Glenda was officially out of the precious patience I had earned with her.

Velvy implored me. He spoke low and serious. "Ray, you go in there with nothing and they'll give you a lot worse than a dog bite on your ass. You got to at least have a fighting chance. You wouldn't go into the ring with your hands tied behind your back, would you?"

He was right. If I hadn't had my razor with Delancey I'd be dead or in jail. I walked into Baxter unarmed and look where it got me. Reluctantly, I took the knife. I could feel Glenda's stare of disapproval burning through the back of my neck.

"Let's go," I said. I just wanted to get it over with.

"I's gon jess wait here for youse, Massa Ray," Velvy joked. Trying to calm my nerves or his? I wasn't sure.

"Keep the engine warm."

Glenda didn't let me take her arm as we crossed the street. The air smelled of impending rain and I thought I heard a low rumble of thunder in the distance across the plains.

Glenda didn't make any big deal of playacting for the bouncer.

"Hey, Reese. He's with me." She jerked a thumb over her shoulder to me. My new suit made me presentable enough. He stepped aside and held the door for us both.

The door opened to a stairwell leading up to the second floor where slow jazz tunes tumbled down the steps like a waterfall. The club was dark with deep red paint on the walls and black carpet lining the steps. Dim lighting oozed from overhead fixtures. The top of the steps opened up to a decent sized room. The small four-piece band played on a stage wedged into the far corner and a few couples lazily danced, draped over each other like dirty laundry. The conversations were hushed and the room smelled like a hundred perfumes all swirling together in a pot. Candles lit the place and red sheer curtains hung in between each booth along both sides of the joint making little private coves where couples could noodle around or make a deal to do so. The bar was lined with women—Glenda's coworkers—and men would step up and ask them to dance or ask them to retreat to one of the private booths. The deals that were being made were all very out in the open. This wasn't a dim street corner with a five dollar whore open for business, this was high-class coupling—with a price tag to match.

Glenda nodded a hello to the bartender and leaned in to

speak to me in the low hushed tones that seemed to be a house rule.

"Voight's office is behind the band." I looked to see a door just off stage left. "Last chance to turn tail and run or do you really want to jaw with him?"

"I'm close, Glenda. I know it. Either he's the guy or he knows the guy who called for Rex to be taken out. I have to find out."

"Well then, come on." She started out toward the dance floor. I grabbed her arm to stop her. Another thick-necked bouncer leaned forward out of the shadows. Glenda waved him off.

"Change your mind?" she asked.

"I want you to stay here. No need for you to go any further."

"Honey, you couldn't get in the front door without me and you sure as hell can't get in to see Voight without me on your arm. I'm your free pass."

I gave in and let her lead the way. We sidestepped the dance floor and walked along the row of private booths. Candles made each enclosure glow red and I could hear snippets of laughter from girls who were being paid to laugh. I glanced over at one silent booth and saw a girl with her hand down the front of a pudgy guy's pants. His head was thrown back and his eyes closed in bliss but she looked like she was waiting for a bus. The way she was going at it he was lucky she didn't tear it off before she was through. Or before he was.

We reached Voight's door. Another solid bodyguard lurked in the shadows.

"Hiya Mooch, you big side of beef you. He in?" Glenda had saved her acting for this moment. She might make it in Hollywood yet.

"Who's dis?" His voice was as low as the baritone sax blowing on stage.

"Friend of mine. Got business with the man inside. You gonna open the gate or do I need to scream for help?"

Mooch frowned but opened the door. He eyed me up and

down as I passed. I kept my focus on Glenda and followed her into the dimly lit hallway just inside Voight's office.

The office door had thick velvet on it wrapped around layers of padding so the jazz band faded into the background once we were inside. The hallway was more of a tiny vestibule and the office was around a corner to the right. Smart. No one could burst in and start shooting without him knowing it and having a second or two to react.

Glenda went first and I followed into the room dominated by Voight's large oak desk sitting like a docked battleship. Voight himself was seated behind it. She wasn't kidding about his scars. They were deep and long and crisscrossed his face like tire ruts on a muddy road. Whatever he had been through was quite an ordeal.

"Glenda," he spoke like a rusty radiator. One of the scars cut across his neck and it was obvious his vocal cords had been damaged somehow. "How can I help you and your uncle?" He smiled but his joke was more to make it known that I was a stranger. His top two front teeth were capped in gold.

"This is Ray. He wanted to see you. He's a friend of a friend." Already she was distancing herself from me.

"Well, any friend of Glenda's . . ." He didn't stand, didn't try to shake my hand.

"Mr. Voight—" I started. Glenda cut me off.

"Hey man, my tonsils are dry."

"Oh, pardon my rudeness." Voight rose and I discovered he walked with a limp. This guy was the full package. I doubt Glenda really wanted a drink but she did want me to see this and I thanked her silently. He didn't ask what Glenda wanted and he didn't offer me a drink.

"Mr. Voight," I started over. "My brother was Rex Ward."

He clinked a cube of ice into a glass. He didn't turn around or act overly surprised so I kept going.

"He was killed a few nights ago in a boxing match. I thought you might know something about it."

He poured two fingers of liquor from a crystal decanter

into the glass and limped over to give it to Glenda. He waved a hand for her to sit on a small sofa. I stayed standing. He limped all the way back to his desk before answering.

"If it happens inside the ring in this town, I sure as hell do know about it."

It wasn't really an answer to my question but it was a start. I continued. "I'd like to know who put in the fix."

"Who said it was fixed?" He was swaggering even as he sat. Here was a guy used to winning.

"Were you there?"

He stared at me but didn't answer. For a guy who had been chewed up worse than my arm he still gave off an intimidating vibe.

"My brother was killed with weighted gloves. Buckshot. The kid, Delancey, who did it, went a little over the top. I know it wasn't supposed to be a hit . . ."

"You don't know nothing."

I had no response to that so I kept on going. "I just want to know who gave the order to have Rex taken out."

Voight put a finger to his chin like he was thinking. "Now let me tell you what I know. I know Delancey is dead. So is Hobbes, his manager. So is Baxter from what I hear, and I'm thinking I know who did them all. I'm looking at him right now."

"I'm just here to talk. Give me a name and I'll be on my way."

We stared at each other for a long time. The ice clinked in Glenda's glass as she drained the cocktail.

"I think you should go now. Glenda, dear, you wait at the bar. I'll have a talk with you later."

"When I go she comes with me and I'm not going until I get what I came here for." Stand strong. Don't let him push you back into the ropes, Pop's voice echoed in my head. The toughest acting ones are the ones who can't back it up. If you can really do some damage you don't need to go around acting like you can. Beware of the quiet ones. Rex was always quiet. I used to be quiet but I found myself getting louder every day.

The scars on Voight's face began to turn red, a darker red than the non-rutted parts. Anger boiled in him and seeing him start to lose his cool sent a wave of calm over me. I knew I had the advantage.

"Who the *fuck* do you think you are coming into *my* joint and threatening me?!" When he raised the volume his voice sputtered and struggled to get out like he was swallowing a rattlesnake at the same time as he shouted. "Huh? Who the fuck are you?" He slammed both hands down on the desk so hard that his inkwell upended and spilled. He ignored it.

I just stood and stared. There is a time to keep your feet dancing, but this was a time to keep them firmly planted.

"You think I give a fuck about your kid brother? I didn't even know the kid except to hear that he might screw up the bets coming down from Chicago this summer. I got my job to do. I don't care who it is, if the word comes down to knock a guy out for a few months, I do it. What the fuck difference does it make if someone gets killed or not? All that says to me is that he wasn't that fucking good in the first place. Maybe we had nothing to worry about with the pansy."

I felt a flush come to my face. I stood firm though.

"Use one of my own whores to bust in here and see me? Pal, you think back to what that buckshot did to your brother and it ain't nothing compared to what Mooch and a pair of brass knuckles is going to do to your little piece of pussy here."

I turned to Glenda. Tears welled in her eyes and she clung, white knuckled, to her empty glass.

"Leave her out of it."

Voight went into another rage. He stood. "Don't you fucking tell me what to do!" His voice was like a pile driver breaking rocks.

The door burst open and I thought for sure Mooch was coming in after me like Otto had at Baxter's, but instead I saw Velvy. Mooch was close behind. Velvy was out of breath and struggling to keep out of Mooch's clutches. He was soaked. The rain had started.

"Boss, boss, I need to see you boss." It was more of his servant routine. This time it wasn't for a joke.

Voight was caught off guard. "What the fuck is this?" he roared.

Mooch tried to explain while at the same time trying to restrain Velvy.

"This nigger just come up in here hollerin' about he had to see this guy."

"Boss, I'm glad I found you, boss." Velvy was convincing in the part.

"Well, get him the fuck out and take this other piece of shit with you. Get Marvin and take him out to the river. See if he can swim."

Velvy swung around with a right cross to Mooch's chest, just below his heart and Mooch sucked air. This gave Velvy time to reach into his brand new jacket and draw his gun. So far this had all gone about as well as any other meeting I'd had. A gun escalated the debate pretty quickly though.

He aimed at Mooch who threw his hands up in the air while still struggling to fill his lungs.

"Reach!" Velvy said a little late and then looked at me like I knew what was supposed to come next.

Voight was frozen, but he managed to say, "Well, this is a fucking pip."

I tried to speak calmly but my eyes darted from Voight to Velvy and back again. "You said the order came in. Who from? Just tell me who wanted Rex out of the way."

"You want The King? You really think you can get in to talk to The King?" A tumbled gravel laugh escaped Voight's damaged throat. "Fuck, I only met him once. He never comes out of that house. You try kid. Go ahead. You go see him and start sobbing for your little brother and see how far it gets you. If it could make him an extra two bits on the book he'd put his own mother in the ring on the losing end of a fix."

He spoke with a smile behind his voice and I didn't doubt his story, but I also knew his words were designed to distract me. His hand crept toward his top drawer.

"Yeah, you go see The King. Ask him why he wanted your brother gone. I'll save you the trip, kid. Money. That's all The King cares about. Money is more valuable than your brother or anybody's brother you dumb sack of shit."

He jerked the drawer open but I was ready. I drew the knife and leapt across the gunboat of a desk. I didn't have my right arm to punch with so I had to lead with my left shoulder and use my whole body to knock Voight back into his big leather chair. With that extra few inches of reach I could have gotten to him before he fired the gun he pulled from the drawer but I made contact just as he squeezed the trigger. The gun retorted as we both hit the chair and I drove the knife down into his thigh. He screamed out in pain and it mixed with Glenda's scream of terror. The smoking gun thudded to the floor.

I spun my head around to see her curl up in the chair and drop her glass. It was Velvy that was hit. He was holding his ear and gritting his teeth, but he kept his own gun trained on Mooch who wasn't sure if he had the advantage or not so he stayed put rather than get a bullet in the gut.

"You okay?" I asked.

"Think so," he said through grinding teeth. I turned back to Voight who was starting to sweat as he huffed and puffed. I straightened up, straddling him in the chair.

"Where do I find The King?"

"I told you I don't know! I only met the guy once."

I twisted the knife in his leg and he cried out again. Lucky for me I could barely hear the band outside so I knew that no one out there could hear us. Blood started to pool on his seat and ran down his legs to the carpet. I guess he would have two limps now.

"Don't make me finish the job that someone already started on your face."

I heard Glenda's panicked voice. "Ray, for God's sake stop it!"

I had to ignore her. I was so close to Voight's face I could see the deep trench of each scar across his cheeks and jaw where a blade had cut him down to the bone. My knife was surely giving him some nasty flashbacks.

I hated this part. When you've got a guy on the ropes and you know you've got him beat you still get in those couple extra shots to make sure he won't come back from an eight count—but you stop before it gets too ugly. That point had passed awhile ago. This was no gentleman's game.

Glenda was sobbing. Velvy kept cursing under his breath. I stole glances over to him and saw that he was losing focus and that Mooch wasn't going to stand still for much longer. I yanked up on the knife and it sliced up and out of Voight's thigh which had quite a grip on it. He howled and leaned forward to grab his leg in a futile attempt to stop the bleeding.

I crossed over to Velvy and relieved him of his Mooch-watching duties. I held the knife up close to Mooch's throat.

"Do you know where The King is?"

"Hell yeah, I make deliveries there all the time. I'll take you. Jesus Christ just put the knife down."

Well, shit, that was easier than I had thought. I reached into his belt and took out a blackjack he had stashed there.

"You make any move I think is trying to fuck me and I'll kill you." I tried to sound as deadly as I could.

"You don't got to worry about me. I don't owe nothing to these creeps. That guy?" He pointed at Voight writhing in his chair and spat in his direction. "And the King? You do what you want to him. The guy's a dirt bag. Weirdo. He ain't been out of the house in years. Good riddance."

I didn't trust him as far as I could throw him. It all sounded swell, but too good to be true.

"You're coming with me," I said. I went to Velvy's side and swapped the knife for the gun. He was bent over and still sucking air through his teeth, trying to contain the pain. I stood him up straight and saw the hole. It was a tiny red circle oozing blood right behind his ear. It looked bad. I turned to Glenda.

"Can you get him to the hospital?"

"Fuck you."

"You're right. It all went wrong, but he needs help. Can

you do it?"

She nodded through tears. She still had a little compassion left, just not for me. I knew there was a good chance she'd run as fast as she could the minute I was gone and not help Velvy at all, but I was counting on her better side to come through. I hoped the fact that I didn't kill Voight was a sign of good faith.

"All right Mooch. Let's walk real slow. You drive." I held the gun in my right hand, tucked up into the sling. I might not have been able to punch, but I could use one finger to pull a trigger if I needed.

It crossed my mind that trusting Mooch was a huge mistake, but I was too close to stop now. And after all the mistakes I'd made already, what was one more?

# 34

*Fokoli*

I knew Ray was on his way up the ladder to the man at the top but I didn't know who was on the next rung and I didn't know how to find out. I'd had one of Baxter's men phone Bob White and I could only hope he'd done what I told him. I also hoped Bob found out something useful while he worked the scene.

But first I needed to find Tolene and see if there was anything he wanted to tell me—like, "You're fired," for instance.

Bob sat at his desk filling out papers. Lots and lots of papers. "Tolene's not in."

I smiled a little, surprised at being happy to see him. "Those from the dog fight, Bob?"

Bob looked at me like I wasn't his favorite person anymore. "Yeah," he said. "Forty-two dead dogs. Vice squad went in and shot them all. Said they were too vicious for animal control to transport." Bob looked a little sad about that.

I picked up a file. "Need help with these?"

Bob took it away from me. "No, thank you."

He looked at the blood on my shoulder. "Ray take a shot at you?"

"No." I didn't say anything else and he didn't ask any more questions. I took off my jacket, fished a first-aid kit out of my desk, and patched myself up. The shirt was ruined, but the wound was just a scratch, like I thought.

I poured myself a cup of coffee, thinking about how to get Bob to talk to me when he was so sore. I poured him a cup too and I carried them back to his desk. "What did you find out at the kennels?"

Bob blew on his coffee. I lit a couple of cigarettes and handed one to him. He shook his head while he stared at me.

"I.A. showed up there," he said. "They were looking for you."

I nodded. This wasn't news to me. "Tell me something good."

Bob shook his head. "You should leave," he said, looking over his shoulder. "Tolene is going to rake you over the coals. You disobeyed orders, went looking for Ray when you were told not to."

I shrugged, but Bob looked scared. Like maybe he didn't trust me anymore. "They say you're crooked," he said.

"I was."

"But not anymore."

"We can talk about this after I get Ray. I promise. I'm not crooked anymore, but things are catching up with me. I don't want to say any more about it. I want to catch Ray Ward." And it was all true. Except the part about catching Ray Ward. I didn't know how I felt about that any more. Ray was just a guy trying to do right by his brother, trying to do what I should have been doing for the last fifteen years—make the world a better place. It sounded like the poetry Laura used to read, but there it was, the truth. And the truth was anything but black and white.

"Baxter didn't run the show," Bob said.

"No?"

"No. He ran that kennel, but there's more out there higher up."

"How high?"

Bob shrugged. "No one knows."

"Who ran Baxter?"

"Don't know."

"I wonder how to find out."

Bob blew out a breath. "That's the million dollar question."

I told Bob I had to leave again. He nodded and I knew he'd tell Tolene as soon as I was gone. Fuck them if they followed. I didn't care anymore. I stumbled back outside, toward my car. My sleeve was sticky from the blood drying there. So fuck Velvy for shooting me too.

It was dusk now and lightning lit up the sky every few seconds, followed by heavy, rolling thunder.

I drove to the pool hall, thinking that DeLuca had stirred up a lot of trouble with his talk of union in the first place. Maybe he had an ax to grind with Baxter's boss and would give up the name. Then again, if he knew Ray was after Baxter, DeLuca might keep quiet just to give Ray enough time to finish the job.

A thick-necked man who looked like some sort of bodyguard was standing at the door of the pool hall when I got there.

"Mr. DeLuca ain't seein' no one tonight," he said.

I kneed him in the groin and punched him in the gut. Then I stepped over his moaning body and made my way to the back.

DeLuca was chalking up a pool cue. A woman in a dark blue dress was propped up on the edge of the pool table. She gave me a sideways smile. "Tony won't be happy when stands up again."

I ignored her. I wasn't in the mood for a coy dame. DeLuca finished chalking his cue and took his shot, knocking two solids into the left side pocket. I didn't see their numbers. I was watching DeLuca. He ignored me and chalked up the cue again. He lined up the shot, and took it, but this time I picked up the ball before it made its hit.

DeLuca stood slowly, giving me a smile that didn't quite reach his eyes. "Detective Dean Fokoli," he said, looking past me to his man on the floor by the front door. "I trust you'll pay any hospital bills my man requires."

"Who ran Baxter?" I asked.

His eyes flashed and his right arm moved just a fraction, like maybe he was going for his gun out of a gut reaction, but stopped himself just in time.

I let him see my amusement. "Who ran Baxter?" I asked again.

He walked to the bar and signaled for a drink. "You are an interesting man, Detective," he said. "You come into my place of business, render one of my men useless, and have the audacity to question me regarding matters about which I have no knowledge."

"Chicago is your place of business," I told him. "And seeing as how I'm a cop, pretty much this entire city is *my* place of business, which means you are in my territory and I'll ask you anything I damn well please." I stared at him a moment. "And you'll answer."

"What makes you think I know Baxter's boss?"

"You're here exploring the possibility of a union. You've got the whole boxing world keyed up. You lost your fur shipment when Hobbes was killed and you need more men to control since you won't have the money from the fur. I'd say it's in your best interest to know who all the players are."

"Baxter wasn't a very big player."

"I'm guessing his boss is."

"Why so worried about his boss?"

I didn't know what to say to that. If I told him Baxter's boss was in danger of getting whacked, he'd probably just smile and say "Good." In the end I said, "Maybe I want to arrest the bastard."

DeLuca laughed at that. "I don't believe you."

"Tough. I ask the questions. You answer them. That's how this works."

His face reddened and I could tell he was trying to keep his temper in check. The woman in the blue dress strolled over and rested her arms on his shoulder. He shrugged her off and slapped her across the face. She held a hand to her cheek and blinked back the tears that sprang to her eyes.

"You see?" DeLuca said, "I do what I want in my own place."

The big man I'd punched was crawling to his hands and knees. Sweat had drenched the sides of his head. He leaned forward and vomited on the floor. Lightning flashed outside, giving the room the feel of a bad horror movie. The woman staggered over and sat in a booth. I dipped my handkerchief in DeLuca's iced drink and handed it to the woman.

She smiled her thanks and held the cloth to her face.

"Who ran Baxter?" I asked again. "You can answer me here or downtown."

A door in the back of the room opened and a thin man with a pockmarked face entered. He strode to DeLuca and whispered something in his ear.

DeLuca's eyes grew wide and he began to laugh. When he was done, he told the bartender he wanted champagne. "We don't have champagne," she said.

"Then go out and buy some, you fat dike," DeLuca said. "This is a celebration." Then DeLuca's eyes slid in my direction. "Why don't you run back to your police station, Detective," he said. "You'll be hearing news about Baxter's boss soon enough."

# 35

*Ray*

Mooch was a terrible driver, partly because he had a terrible car. It was a Model A past its prime five years ago. It bucked and lurched along on a bad clutch and bald tires and with Mooch wedged in behind the wheel it was a death trap trailing a cloud of burning oil. Certainly the rain didn't help. It came down in a fine mist that made the whole world slick with moisture. Mooch seemed reluctant to use his wipers, or maybe they were busted.

I kept the gun on Mooch because I still didn't trust him any but keeping an eye on him was tough. The ride was so bumpy and jerky that unless I kept my eyes forward on the horizon I risked getting seasick on land.

When I left Glenda and Velvy I knew that was the lowest I had sunk. Leaving behind a friend with a head wound and dismantling a young girl's life in less than twenty-four hours was worse even than beating a lowlife like Hobbes to death. A fine line I know, but I felt guiltier about the two people who had done nothing wrong except knowing me.

Maybe Velvy would get a room at County Hospital next to his mother. Maybe they would get side by side drawers in the morgue. It was anybody's guess.

Glenda had surely lost her job but that wasn't such a bad thing. I hoped for her sake she would take off to Hollywood earlier than her plan. The alternative was to get a job at a smaller, less reputable club or, God forbid, start walking the streets. I didn't have much left from the money I took off of Delancey, but it was hers as far as I was concerned. She'd earned it. I doubted I'd ever see her again though.

Mooch guided the Model A out of the city and toward the suburbs. I tried to pump him for information on The King.

"So, you've been here before, huh?"

"Yeah, bunches of times. Making deliveries. Money drops, that sorta thing."

"Does he keep security there?"

"Nah, not usually. Maybe one guy just so he don't have to talk to no one. Not many people even know where he lives so he don't need to worry about it much. Most guys who get in trouble are jerks like Voight. Low level guys. You 'member that Wizard of Oz movie? The King is kinda like that guy behind the curtain. No one really knows who he is and everyone is scared of him."

I didn't figure Mooch for a guy to go see a kid's movie. I didn't really know what he was talking about, I hadn't seen it, but I nodded anyhow. Next he spoke with a smile like he was telling me a secret.

"You know they call Glenda 'Glenda the Good' like in that movie? But, you know, like sexual."

"Thanks for clarifying," I said. "So don't you think by helping me you're making a bad enemy?"

"Aw, I don't give a crap. I wanted to get back to Boston anyway. I only moved out west because of some, uh, trouble. You know? But that's been seven years now and its all blown over. Time to get back to a real city. This was just what I needed."

"Glad I could help." I still thought it might just be a line to make me drop the gun so I kept my defenses up.

We moved on through residential streets and I watched the houses get bigger and bigger until we finally stopped in front of a large two-story with brick columns and a wide lawn.

"This is it," said Mooch. "You want me to come with you to the door?"

"Yeah." I wanted to keep him in my sights until I got inside. If I stepped out and he hit the horn—if the horn even worked on that pile of junk—I would lose my element of surprise. The house looked quiet. A single porch light was on but none of the windows were illuminated. Just my luck I'd get all the way out here and he'd be gone.

Mooch led the way up to the front door and pounded with the side of his fist like he was trying to wake the dead. I tucked the gun back up into my sling but kept a finger lightly on the trigger.

The door opened slightly and a young man with a beefy heavyweight build answered. I even thought I recognized him from a few undercards.

"Yeah?" He wasn't inviting us in but he didn't seem to want to shoot us dead on the spot either.

I didn't speak immediately so Mooch butted in. "Hey there. We met before, I work for Voight. I'm here to see The King."

"Who's this?"

"A friend."

The heavyweight eyed me up and down then turned back to address Mooch.

"He ain't here."

Mooch grinned. "He's always here. We didn't have time to call for an appointment."

"What's it about?"

"Aw for Christ sake." Mooch shot a hand forward and pounded the door which flew back and smashed into the heavyweight's face. He staggered back and blood burst from his nose. Mooch stepped into the entryway and grabbed the heavyweight by the lapels and smashed his forehead into the already bleeding nose. The heavyweight nodded and went out, slumping in Mooch's grip. Mooch gestured with a jerk of his head on that thick neck for me to come in.

"All yours," he said. I knew then that I didn't need to worry about Mooch any more.

"Thanks," I said as I passed. From here on out it was just me as Mooch stayed with his prey to stash him or be there in case he woke up so he could send him to dreamland again.

I walked through the dimly lit house and my shoes tapped on tile floors. I listened but heard nothing as I looked in room after room as I passed but saw no one. I moved through the kitchen and turned left to the west wing of the house which seemed larger inside than it had from the front.

I stepped carefully and wished there was more light. I had no idea what I was going to say when I finally got to see The King. What do you say to a guy who ordered your brother killed? I tried to calm my nerves and my anger by reminding myself that the order hadn't been to kill Rex, just to rough him up so he couldn't fight for a few weeks. That only made it a little better.

The slow anticipation of my walk through the house didn't help my level of tension. My finger started to twitch so I took it off the trigger. I felt a bead of sweat rise on my upper lip and my new suit suddenly felt like a straight jacket.

A light peered from under a door at the end of the hall. I licked the salty sweat off my lip and walked forward. I hesitated outside the door, debating whether to knock or just burst in. I chose somewhere in between by easing the door open and peering inside.

It was a large office with dark wood bookshelves and a desk. A single desk lamp threw amber light through a stained glass shade and the room smelled musty and dank like a fight hall after a night of bouts.

A man sat behind the desk and seemed enveloped by it like a bird in a nest. Papers were piled high on every corner. A glass coffee pot bubbled away on a shelf behind him. He looked up at me as I stepped in. He wore a beard which was thick and more suited to a mountain man than to an agent of the Chicago mob. It also delayed my recognition of him, but then it hit me.

The King. It was him. My father.

# 36

*Fokoli*

DeLuca was holding his stones and heaving his supper on the floor when I left for the station. I'd racked him hard enough to bruise my knee.

The police radio buzzed with reports of disturbances up and down the docks, in Negrotown, and in the boxing hangouts. Rumors of union were spreading quick. Even the bosses were panicking now. My guess was that the activity at the docks was due in part to visitors from Chicago making their way downriver with their own shipments. Yessir, Ray Ward managed to stir up a real hornet's nest.

Tolene was in his office and had asked to see me by the time I got back to the office. I ignored the request and sought out Bob White. He said, "Somebody stabbed Baxter's boss."

"Dead?"

"Not yet," Bob said.

"Who is he?"

"Guy by the name of Voight. Holed up at the Matchbox Club. Keeps his work there pretty hush-hush. Doesn't go out in public much."

I checked the bullets in my gun and headed for the door. "I'm on my way."

"There's a lady here to see you," he said.

"Lady?"

Bob nodded. "Says she won't talk to anyone but you."

I thought about that for a minute. "Does Tolene know?"

Bob shook his head and rose from behind his desk. His shirt was rumpled, his tie undone, and he looked like hell. "Look, Fokoli," he said, meeting my eye. "You'd better see that woman and do it quick. That guy from I.A. has been with Tolene all night long."

I wondered what Bob had told them. And I guess he figured I was wondering about it because he held his hands up. "I didn't tell them anything, Dean. You've been aces the whole time I've known you. What's done is done. But there are a few rumors floating around and none of them are good."

He looked over his shoulder like maybe he was a little concerned about being seen with me. Not that it mattered anymore. Bob wouldn't have me to deal with after tonight. Things were unraveling . . . both for me and Ray Ward.

Glenda sat in the steel chair, her eyes wide and shining with tears. It didn't take a genius to see the tears weren't because of sadness. She wore the look of a woman terrorized and betrayed. She stayed quiet as I walked into the room, not so much as even sniffing back the leakage coming from her nose. She had her hands wrapped tight around her purse.

I moved slow, knowing she'd spook if I came at her too fast. I pulled the chair out as quiet as I could and sat down across from her. I let her get used to that for a minute, then I lit a couple of cigarettes and passed one to her.

Her hand shook as she took it from me. "Thanks." Her voice sounded hoarse, like she'd been crying for days.

I wanted to push her, to make her tell me everything in a hurry because I knew it wouldn't be long before Tolene found out I was in the building. When he did, he'd ask for my badge. I didn't know that for sure, of course, but it added up. My past was here, caught up with me at last.

I shook off those thoughts and looked Glenda over. She'd been through something. And my gut was telling me it had to do with Ray Ward.

"So tell me about it," I said, hoping she would.

She used that shaking hand to put the cigarette to her lips. After she took a couple of drags, she fiddled with her purse a little and pulled out a handkerchief. She was too much of a lady to blow her nose in front of me, but I could tell she wanted to.

"I saw my boss . . . attacked . . . tonight," she said.

I guessed then that Voight must have been her boss. "Really?" was all I said.

"Mr. Voight hired me to . . . entertain . . . at his club awhile back."

She was just a kid, so she couldn't have been "entertaining" long. But I didn't say that. I just waited.

"When Ray stopped by my apartment for help, I had no idea . . . I just . . ." She covered her face with the handkerchief, but to her credit, she didn't break down.

"Are you telling me Ray attacked Voight?"

She nodded. "He was crazy. Angry."

I needed to get the whole story. I knew that. But I also knew Ray wasn't done and my legs were screaming at me to run from here and find him. I forced myself to take a deep breath. "What happened?"

Glenda met my eyes and I could tell she was trying to decide if she should break the code girls like her lived by—never talk to a cop. She frowned and maybe hated herself a little, but she talked. "Ray got hurt by a dog," she said. "I patched him up. He said he was getting even for what happened to his brother." Her mouth started to quiver a little bit, but she got hold of herself. "Rex was a good guy. I had a soft spot for him, you know?"

There was a water pitcher on the table. I poured her a glass and told her to keep talking.

"He'd heard that Voight was Baxter's boss. He told me he hadn't meant to let things get so out of hand. All he was trying to do was find the guy that ordered the fix on Rex." She shook her head and stared at her hands, like they might have blood on them or something. Then she looked at me and there was pleading in her eyes. For what, I don't know. Understanding, maybe?

"Go on," I said. "What happened after you fixed him up?"

"You showed up."

I laughed a little. "After that."

"I took a message to his friend. Velvy. We picked Ray up," her hands fluttered a little, "Velvy shot at you."

"I'm fine," I assured her.

She gave me a thin smile. "We got him some new

clothes and then I got him into the Matchbox Club."

"Where he jumped Voight."

She buried her face in her hands. "I've never seen anyone bleed so much before." Her eyes were wide, like she was still seeing it all, right there in front of her. She regained her focus and looked at me. "Voight shot Velvy. I took him to the hospital."

"What about Ray?"

She thought hard, like everything was going fuzzy for her. "He was going to see someone they call The King. He's the one who ordered the hit on Rex."

"How do I find The King?"

She shook her head. "I don't know. Mooch took him."

"Mooch?"

"Bouncer at the club. He makes deliveries to The King sometimes." She shrugged. "At least that's what he said."

I thanked her. She had a long night ahead of her. There was no way we were letting her out of the station until a statement had been officially taken and typed and the I's dotted and the T's crossed.

"My partner's going to come in and write down everything you told me," I said. "I'm going to go try to find Ray before he does anything else really stupid."

She gave a feeble smile. "Mooch drives a Model A."

Bob was still behind the desk pushing papers. He scowled when he saw me. "It's a shooting gallery out there tonight," he said. "I'm heading out to the docks. All the other detectives are on other scenes."

"Send a patrol car," I said. "I need you to take Glenda's statement."

Bob didn't say anything. And we sat for a minute, sizing one another up. "Please," I added after awhile.

He shook his head, but he picked up the phone at the same time and I knew he was going to play ball with me. "Thanks, Bob," I said.

He phoned dispatch, told them to send a patrol car to the docks, slammed the receiver down and rose from his chair while he straightened his tie and put on his jacket. "You owe me," he said.

I held out my hand. "I don't think I'll be seeing you after tonight."

He waited a beat, but then put his hand in my own and we shook. "Sorry about all this mess," he said.

I shrugged. "If there's one thing Ray Ward has done for this city, it's get rid of some real lowlifes. Right?"

Bob gave a weak smile and shuffled off toward the interrogation room.

I sat at my desk for a minute, wondering how to find Mooch, wondering how to find a Model A. I phoned dispatch and issued an all points for it. While I waited for the city's finest to call something in, I pulled my badge and headed for Tolene's office.

"Where the hell have you been?" he yelled after he told me to come in.

"Fighting crime."

He wasn't amused. Carter was there too and he looked happy to see me. "Detective Fokoli," he said, smiling, "we've been reviewing your cases over the last two years."

"Yeah?"

"Yes," he said, looking pleased.

I suppose I should have felt frightened, or ashamed, or angry. But mostly I felt relieved. I'd never be whole again until I put this station behind me. "And what did you find?" I asked.

Tolene leaned back in his chair, his mouth a tight line. When he spoke, it was through a clenched jaw and white lips. "Nothing. You covered your tracks well. But you—"

"I disobeyed an order today when I went looking for Ray Ward and that's grounds for termination. Yeah, I know."

"We can't afford a scandal right now," Carter said. "The city is falling apart out there. If you'll agree to go quietly . . ."

Tolene leaned forward in his chair. "We can't trust you to be part of this team anymore."

"I see," was what I said. And I did see. I deserved prison

for my part in what happened to Mark, for what it did to Laura.

"Give me your badge," Tolene said.

I laid it on the table and headed for my desk, a smile on my face and a load off my back.

I made one final call to dispatch before I left the building. They had a hit on the Model A. I walked out into the night, climbed in my car, and went to find Ray Ward.

# 37

*Ray*

"Pop?" I said. I felt like I'd just been hit hard in the short ribs and was gasping for air. It was that feeling you get just before you know you're going down. The world starts to warp and turn sideways but you still think you can hang on and you don't realize you're on the canvas until the ref is standing over you counting out five-six-seven. Somehow I held on.

He looked at me long and hard like he was trying to remember who I was or maybe he was trying to decide how to get rid of me.

"Ray," he said in a voice much older than the man I remembered.

"Are you . . . ?" I didn't want to believe it. The fact that he lied about where he had gone was easy to believe. But how was I supposed to believe that he gave the order to have his own son ravaged in a fixed fight with weighted gloves?

"You've been a busy boy. I just got a call from Voight's office not too long ago."

"Pop, how could you?"

He chuckled. "There's a lot to explain."

He leaned back and his tall chair, decked out in oxblood leather, creaked like a worn-in boot. He didn't seem worried about why I was there, even though it was obvious he knew about the bloody trail that led to finding him. The silence that punctuated our conversation was thick with a kind of static that roared in my ears. I could hear my own heartbeat. The coffee pot sounded like it was hooked up to an amplifier. The noise was excruciating.

"So start explaining," I said, hoping he would to fill the silence as well as to satiate my curiosity.

"How's your arm?" He smiled behind those thick whiskers. He had the beard of a man who had stopped caring. The stale odor in the room was one of someone who didn't bathe regularly any more. Peeking out from his slumped figure he showed a pot belly that would have disgusted the Pop I knew. He looked tired and old and spent like the old-timers who hung around the fight halls some nights—the ones who were all punched out and spoke in rambling non-sequiturs that always came back to hazy memories of a fight from back in the day. Pop had that look of a bare-knuckle brawler who had seen his best days pass by him twenty years before. He was damaged on the outside from the ravages on the inside.

"My arm will heal. You know why I'm here?"

"Yep." He scratched at his beard and I noticed his untrimmed fingernail. "It's Rex."

I nodded. He wasn't going to offer me any more. I saw his strategy from the outset since he taught it to me and I, in turn, taught it to Rex. He was dancing, laying back and taking stock of what I knew and how I was going to come into this round. I expected the rope-a-dope; he'd let me spill it all out, get hopping mad and show all my vulnerabilities and wear myself out so then he could swoop in during the last round and deliver the knock out. I wasn't sure how it might come so I kept my guard up.

"You wanted him knocked out of the ring."

"And then that damn kid." He shook his head and clucked his tongue like it was just one of those crazy things, like a center fielder dropping a fly ball in the series. His own goddamn son.

"Delancey," I added.

"Yup. I wanted Clark. I guess I just went back to the old well that I knew, not really realizing how old we'd gotten. In his day, Clark was the best fixer you could get. He would take a dive for peanuts or if you needed him to, he could punch the daylights out of someone and make it a convincing show. But that was a few years back." He swiveled in his chair. I stood firm, still concealing my gun. I wanted to hear everything he had to say.

"I gather, though, that you took care of Delancey. And

Hobbes. And Clark from what I hear. I know damn well Roberta couldn't do that to the man."

I just stared.

"You done your brother proud, son." The words burned in my ears.

"Don't call me that," I hissed back at him.

"Don't think for a minute I wouldn't have made things right myself. I didn't want that to happen, not one bit. Hobbes had no right to put in some kid who don't know an uppercut from his asshole. No sir."

"Why are you doing this?" I wanted to know too many whys to count. And I knew he wouldn't have an answer for any of them.

"Look, when I left your mother I did it because I knew I had done wrong. I knew I couldn't stay or the next time . . . well, I had enough regrets already. So I took off. But where the hell was I gonna go? I didn't have any money. I left all of it with your mom. I'm guessing by your face right now that she never told you that."

"She didn't say a damn thing for three weeks while she was in the hospital."

"Fair enough. But I left her the house and you boys and I just tried to get lost in the world. But Ray, the fights is all I know. It's all I ever knew. I even tried working an honest living doing construction, I dug roads and I even drove a truck for a week. None of it suited me. So when these boys here needed someone who knew boxing in Kansas City, well, I was their man. I get to do the only thing I know how to."

"Fix fights."

He sighed. I don't know if he thought he could talk himself back into my good graces but he seemed let down that I wasn't giving him an inch.

"I steer things this way and that so the boys in Chicago get paid. That's it. Most fights are still legit. I wanted it that way. If all people see are fixes then they'll stop coming to the fights and then nobody gets paid. That's what I told them. But then they had big plans for this summer to bank a lot of dough with a few guys and they needed to be able to script it out. Rex stood in the way of that and no one knew it better than me. I've been watching you two boys. Been real proud too."

I had to look away from him. A small bulletin board hung in the corner and on it was an eight by ten photograph of Rex and a few yellowing headlines from the fight pages. I couldn't stand to look at that either so I fixed my eyes on the carpet at my feet.

"I knew Rex was ready to make a run for a real title. And I knew you two would never go in for a fix. It was the best I could come up with. Just get him out of the way for the summer and you two could start over in the fall when he was recovered. Hell, I thought sure when your mom died you'd move to New York anyhow. That's where he should have been. That's where he could have been a real contender. But I couldn't exactly phone you up and tell you that."

"If I'd have known you were here in this town you bet your ass I would have gotten as far away from here as I could."

He nodded another "That's fair" nod. He seemed to have justified it all to himself. My emotions were clogged trying to get out. No single feeling could burst through the top so it was all a muddle and it made my head spin.

"I've been looking for the man who gave the order," I said, raising my eyes to his again.

"You found him," he spoke with that same old fighter's bravado. Beneath the time-scarred exterior was the same middleweight heart beating inside. The gun shifted uncomfortably in my hand.

"Ray, you surely owe me a world of hurt. I know that."

I was getting pissed off at how human he sounded. I wanted him to be the pure son-of-a-bitch I knew him to be. I had to remind him again and again why he was so hateful.

"Rex is dead and you're not. That's not right." I felt my teeth starting to clench.

"No, I suppose it isn't. But here we are."

More of the stifling silence enveloped the room. I couldn't keep still any more so I moved toward his desk. My feet shuffled like sandpaper on the rug. He swiveled in his chair, keeping me squared up with his body as I walked. Strategy or old habit? I didn't know. When I got close enough I could see around the corner of a framed photo on his desk. It was Mom. This enraged me. He had surrounded himself with pictures of a family he abused and abandoned. It was a violation.

"You have no right."

He followed my eyes to the picture frame.

"Now, Ray, your mom and I had a lot of good years before you were even around so—"

"You have no right!" I lashed out with my right hand, pulling it from the sling and slapping the picture frame off the desk with the gun. The glass broke when it hit the floor, but I kept my eyes forward and watched him as the sight of the gun registered on his face. He froze and the posture of defeat seemed to overtake him even more.

"Ray . . ." He didn't continue. He was out of words. So was I, but I couldn't seem to get the gun to do any talking for me. I held it tight to my side, aiming at my father. My arm seared white hot with pain but I held firm to the grip of the pistol. I did not fire.

I thought about the knife in the car and about Mooch in the entryway. I could go get him and pay him to kill Pop. I knew he'd do it if I asked. But this was my fight. I'd been sending Rex into the ring for years to fight bouts I didn't have the skill for and I was tired of winning by proxy. I was tired of not feeling the deep satisfaction of a fist connecting with another man's flesh. I was tired of not being close enough to hear a rib bone break or get the warm splatter of an opponent's blood on my face. I had been ringside too long.

I stepped forward and stood over Pop. He looked up at me but didn't stand, didn't raise his arms in defense. He was throwing in the towel. Leaving himself open for whatever I had in mind.

I reared back with the gun and spanked it across his face. His neck jerked to the side and he slowly brought his head around straight again to reveal blood trickling out of his mouth and onto his beard.

I remembered back to one night when I first saw him as the man who was jealous of his son's ability, the night Rex caught him off-guard with a left jab. It was the only other time I'd ever seen him bleed. Blood wound down out of the same corner of his mouth and I saw hate make the whites of his eyes turn red and then he came at Rex like no father ever should against his son. But Rex used Pop's own lessons on footwork—how to draw power for your punches and how to maneuver an opponent's balance to work against him. In three quick exchanges Rex had punched Pop to the ground and their relationship was forever ruined. I often thought that it was in that moment that Pop finally felt his mortality.

Now he looked up at me, a broken and empty man, and was powerless to defend himself any longer. His justifications had run out. He must have felt the same way as he did that night with Rex.

I took the butt of the gun and shifted it to my left hand and began raining down blows.

I couldn't stop.

# 38

*Fokoli*

"You a cop?" The man was big and irritated and he stood over the unconscious body of somebody who was probably supposed to be a bodyguard.

"Not any more," I said. But I drew my gun and gestured for him to move aside. He did. "Are you Mooch?"

He nodded.

"I'm looking for Ray."

Mooch pointed toward a room down the hall. "In there," he said. As I headed in that direction he called after me, "It ain't pretty."

I guess I already knew that.

Ray's suit was dirty. The room was dim, so it was hard to tell for sure, but I'd have bet my own mother's life it was blood. Blood from the corpse behind the desk.

Ray stood above the mess on the floor, looking lost. Maybe all the killing finally caught up with him and his mind just froze. I'd heard of that happening.

"You okay, kid?" I took a couple of steps toward him, wondering how he'd react to me getting close.

He turned and looked at me and I could see the gun hanging at his side. Blood dripped from the grip onto the floor. Blood dripped from his hand too. I took a step forward, keeping my own gun at my side but my finger on the trigger . . . just in case.

"You might want to drop that, fella," I said, nodding at the gun.

Ray looked down at his hand and his eyes widened in surprise, like he wondered what that thing was and how, exactly, it got there. The pistol fell to the floor with a thud. His shoulders slumped a little then, like he was relieved.

"Meet my dad," he said, nodding to the stiff. "Ordered

the hit on his own kid." He snorted in a halfhearted attempt to laugh at the irony of all this, but there was just too much to take in, I suppose, and he couldn't quite get himself to appreciate it just then.

"So he was a bastard, your old man," I said.

He looked puzzled, but nodded and leaned back against the wall like maybe his legs were too weak to hold him up anymore. "You going to arrest me?"

I shrugged. I didn't want to tell him I wasn't a cop anymore. I had no way of knowing just yet if this guy was half-baked or not. And I didn't want to let him know there was no back up for me waiting outside.

"Let's get out of this room," I said, picking up the gun and moving toward the door.

Ray followed. He seemed lighter somehow; like he'd done what he set out to do and whatever happened to him now was somehow okay.

Mooch still stood guard in the front of the house.

"Anybody call the cops yet?" I asked.

He shook his head. "All's quiet out here."

I nodded and me and Ray moved into the living room. Ray's dad had a nice stash of booze and I fixed each of us a drink. "Open your throat and pour it in," I said. "You need it."

His eyes were still suspicious, but he drank. Then he coughed a little and noticed the blood on his hands. "I've always tried to be a good man," he said after awhile.

For a cop, the knee jerk reaction is to laugh yourself silly when a killer says something like that to you. But everything Ray had done was done for his brother. So I didn't laugh right then. I thought about Laura and how little I ever did to help her. Then I thought about Mark. Yeah, it was best right then if I just kept my trap shut.

"Did you see my brother, Detective?" Ray asked after minute. "Did you see what Delancey did to his head?"

"I saw Hobbes. Did Rex look something like that?"

A muscle worked in Ray's jaw. "Yeah," he said. "Something like that."

"Lost your temper, I guess."

He shook his head. "It wasn't like that. Hobbes lied. He lied to everyone. And he let Rex die."

"Like you let Delancey die?"

His eyes narrowed. "That was self-defense. I was trying to leave. He jumped me."

Whatever Ray was, he wasn't a liar. My gut told me that much. I nodded. "And Clark Dane?"

"Got what he had coming. All I did was help Mrs. Dane do what needed to be done." He slid his eyes in my direction. "Is she still alive?"

"Last I heard."

He smiled a little at that news. "Good. She deserves a good life."

I looked at the sling. "How's the arm?"

Ray shrugged. "Hurts. But there's no infection. Glenda did a good job." He chewed on his cheek for a minute while the thought. "Is that how you found me? Glenda?"

I didn't answer that. "Tell me about Baxter."

"What about him?"

"He was half eaten by dogs."

Ray shook his head again but kept quiet.

"Now I suppose one could argue," I said, "that you technically didn't kill Baxter. You merely made it possible for the dogs to do what they'd been itching to do for quite some time. Am I right?"

He shrugged. "Shouldn't we be doing this downtown?"

"I'm just trying to make sense of it all," I said. "So the dogs whacked Baxter, right?"

He stared at me for a moment, his eyes tired and old beyond his years. "Yeah."

"Right. And Voight?"

"Shot my friend. Shot Velvy in the head." He stared at the floor. "Then he tried to shoot me."

"So, self-defense again?"

He shrugged like he didn't really think it mattered what he said anymore. And all I could feel right then was sad. For Ray. For me. For Laura. For Glenda. For Velvy.

I jerked my head toward the den. "So tell me about your pop."

"Made my mom into a scared rabbit," he said. "Beat her senseless. Left us when we were still kids. But he taught us to box. I haven't seen him in years. I never expected . . ." He swallowed once, then again, like it was too hard to let the words out past his chest.

"You never expected your own family to do something so lousy," I finished for him. "You never expected the guy who ordered the hit on your brother to be your own father." My voice was unnaturally loud. I was trying to stamp out thoughts of Laura and the terrible betrayal she felt . . . the betrayal that took her life. That kind of thing can kill a person. But Laura hadn't destroyed the person responsible. She'd destroyed herself.

"Get out of here, Ray," I said after a few minutes. "The cops will be here soon. I'll get rid of your gun. Just go."

He looked at me like I was crazy. But there was hope in his eyes too . . . and I hadn't seen that in him before.

"Go," I said again. "Take that Mooch fellow with you."

He stood, like he was afraid to turn his back on me. Like I'd shoot him or something. I wiped his gun down and wrapped it in a nearby newspaper. I wrapped my own gun in another and handed both weapons to him. "Here," I said. "Just leave them on the front step or on the curb. I'll get them after awhile." When he looked concerned I added, "I'll get rid of yours. Don't worry."

He turned to leave.

"And tell Mooch to get a different car," I called after him. "Every cop in town is looking for that thing."

I heard the Model A drive away. I listened to the sound of the motor fade into the distance as I poured myself another drink. I called the station and let them know they could come get the body of The King and then I walked out the front door.

Ray had left the guns on the curb out front. I unwrapped them and put mine back in its holster. Then I drove to the river and tossed Ray's out into the dark water.

Feeling lighter than I had in awhile, I climbed back into my car and drove away.

# 39

*Ray*

He let me go. Sitting in the rusty bucket that was Mooch's Ford I still couldn't believe it. The rain had let up so I stared out of the open window into a black night that smothered the prairie. I rolled it all around in my head. He gave no reason. He just sounded like he understood somehow.

I didn't envy him his job. Prowling around at night coming face to face with lowlifes and killers, at least Fokoli was getting paid for it. I had nothing but my brother's memory to keep me on the case.

Mooch wasn't thinking about what Fokoli had done. He was too busy cooing over the stash he had found in an open wall safe in the library. While I was in with Dad he had a lot of time to root around and since he knew the layout somewhat he knew there was always cash around.

"Would you look at all this folding money?" he laughed as he drove. The stacks of bills were sitting out on the seat between us. Wind from the open windows made them flutter and they looked like little green birds with rubber bands around the middles and two little wings flapping in the breeze. It made me nervous for them. I thought surely they would come undone and fly away into the darkness of a Kansas night.

I was also nervous because Mooch kept swiveling his head to look down at his treasure and taking his eyes off the road. More than once we slid into a rut at the side of the pavement and he had to jerk the wheel back onto smooth ground.

Mooch drove me to the train tracks and let me out. He stuffed a stack of bills in my pocket and I was too drained to argue with him. I didn't know what I would use it for, but I was sure I needed it so I thanked him.

He said he was going to ditch the car on the Missouri side and then hop right on a train back for Boston. With all that money he could afford to leave his possessions behind and start over. I assume he made it there. I never heard from him again.

A year ago. My God.

I holed up in the house Rex and I used to share and every day expected the cops to come storming in to arrest me. After the first month I started to go outside but only for short periods of time to visit Velvy at County Hospital. He was slow to recover and sometimes he just sort of stopped in the middle of doing something and stared like someone had unplugged him or something. He always came around but those spells scared me, and him. Roberta died about two weeks after Velvy checked in. She went quiet in her sleep and Velvy was by her side. He kept her Bible on her bedside and even though Velvy never read any passages to her he said she knew the good book so well that she was going over the best parts in her head. With all that time to lay and sleep she had plenty of time to prepare for meeting Jesus, he said, so she was good and ready. I used some of the money that Mooch had given me to buy her a plot and a big marble headstone. I never told Velvy it was from me, but I think he knew.

I think about what happened that week every single day, many times a day. I've had trouble sleeping and for awhile would only doze about three hours at night and then again in the afternoons.

I worked out in the basement gym where Rex and I used to train. Punching the heavy bag was one way to block out the thoughts. Just the sound of my own breathing and the slap and echo of leather hitting leather made a comforting noise that kept the dark memories away.

I tried once to look up Glenda but she wasn't at the same address. I've been looking for her name in the movies but haven't seen it yet.

I read in the papers about Detective Fokoli and how he

was dismissed from the force, but it had nothing to do with me. Seems he was caught up in some graft or something and he caught a hunk of blame for some union busters who came down from Chicago and spilled a lot of blood last spring.

The money's all gone now. That's why I'm thinking of picking up a fighter or two to manage. This young Negro kid I saw tonight was definitely a prospect. Not sure if the game is ready for a white manager of a black fighter, but if I hire Velvy and put him in my corner that might soften the blow.

I'm not even sure if I want to be back in the fight game but at some point it's like Pop said: It's all I know. He did give me a lot of good advice early on. Maybe that last bit was just as good. Maybe I'm more like him than I know.

I was born into a life of violence. A spit-bucket life that came out swinging and punched me hard for the first several rounds. It's time to heed the call of the bell and get back out there and start taking a few swings of my own again. Pop always said after you lose there's no looking back. As soon as the final bell rings that bout is in the past.

"Keep your eyes forward 'cause if your eyes ain't forward then your back is turned. And that's when someone will sucker punch you."

That's what Pop said.

# About the Authors

## J.B. Kohl

J.B. is the author of *The Deputy's Widow*, published in 2008 by Arctic Wolf Publishing. In the spring of 2008, she read a short story by Eric Beetner and decided to pester him until he agreed to collaborate on something.

Resistance was futile.

And so, *One Too Many Blows to the Head* was created—to live and thrive in the dark alleys of 1939 Kansas City.

In addition to writing fiction, J.B. works as a technical and fiction editor. She lives in Virginia with her husband and three children.

Visit her at www.jbkohl.com.

## Eric Beetner

Eric is an award-winning short story and screenwriter. He and J.B. connected through his work with the Film Noir Foundation and he wrote to tell her how much he liked *The Deputy's Widow*. From that simple correspondence came a bicoastal collaboration and a quickly finished novel, despite the fact that they have never met in person.

Eric is also a TV and film editor, director and producer who lives in Los Angeles with his wife and two daughters. Learn more about Eric at ericbeetner.blogspot.com.

J.B. and Eric are at work on their next novel. Until then, enjoy these other titles available from www.secondwindpublishing.com

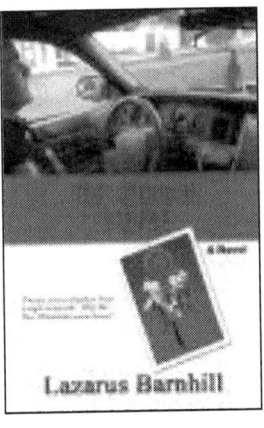

### The Medicine People
### Lazarus Barnhill

After 25 years as a fugitive, triple murder suspect Ben Whitekiller returns to his small eastern Oklahoma hometown. Why has he come back? Why are those who sought him so disturbed at his return? What secrets will Dan Hook, the young officer who tells the story, find out about Ben, and himself?

### Buried in Wolf Lake
### Christine Husom

When a family's Golden Retriever brings home the dismembered leg of a young woman, the Winnebago County Sheriff's Department launches an investigation unlike any other. Who does the leg belong to, and where is the rest of her body? Sergeant Corrine Aleckson and Detective Elton Dawes soon discover they are up against an unidentified psychopath who targets women with specific physical features. Are there other victims, and will they learn the killer's identity in time to prevent another brutal murder?

Made in the USA
Lexington, KY
10 February 2010